CALLIE'S REVOLUTION

The Audacious Adventures of a
Woman on the Run

a novel by

Tony Chiodo

12-25-22

For Colette, Aria, and the people of Mexico

Acknowledgments

Thanks to Carlton Smith, Stephen Allen and Sandhya Maltby for their valuable assistance and encouragement

Chapter 29 image based on a painting by David Hurley

Do you not know that I am a woman? When I think, I must speak.

-Rosalind in *As You Like It*
William Shakespeare

Camerado, I give you my hand!
I give you my love more precious than money,
I give you myself before preaching or law;
Will you give me yourself? will you come travel with me?
Shall we stick by each other as long as we live?

-Song of the Open Road
Walt Whitman

Death whispers in my ear, "Live, I am coming."

Virgil

José Doroteo Arango Arámbula
AKA Pancho Villa
(5 June 1878 – 20 July 1923)

Chapter 1

March 5, 1916

She ran toward the glass enclosed office through a haze of cigarettes and cigars, past desks with sweating men in white shirts bent over typewriters. She clutched a page from the NY Times, convinced it would change her life.

It was a story about Pancho Villa. In the photo he wore a big sombrero, bandoliers crisscrossed his chest, and his teeth clenched a cigarette in a reckless smile. The Revolution was big news.

Callie Masterson meant to make it bigger.

She burst through the door, breathless, and placed the article right under the nose of Mr. Shaughnessy, a tall slender man, with shaggy gray hair and bushy eyebrows, who was putting a match to his pipe. As editor, he called the shots at the *Houston Chronicle.*

"Mr. Shaughnessy, look at this. Pancho Villa is furious at President Wilson for withdrawing his support. They say that he is bound to take revenge by attacking the United States. "

He examined the paper while puffing fragrant clouds of smoke into the air, gazing up at Callie a few times.

"What are you so fired up about, dearie? It's just a matter of time before they get him. It's a ragtag bunch. Why, it says right here they're in dire need of arms, boots, ammunition, and the like."

"Something is going to happen down there. He feels betrayed, and a man like Villa will exact a reprisal. He'll do it in the easiest place he can find-some sleepy, defenseless border town."

"You think so, huh?"

"Yes sir, I do, and I want to be there when it happens." She had both hands on his desk and leaned forward. Agitated, she pushed away a strand of hair that hung limply in her face. The Houston heat made short work of her curls.

"Now, you all alone near the Mexican border might be a very dangerous assignment, young lady. I think-"

"If we could get a scoop on this, be there when he strikes, why our circulation will skyrocket. Don't you see, Mr. Shaughnessy? It's a natural. Get the jump on the *Times* even," she said, shaking the venerable paper in front of him.

She paced around the office, hands behind her back, her head spinning with ideas, articles with sensational headlines already taking form in her head. She always bit her lip when she was fired up. Callie had played Ophelia in a school production of *Hamlet* to favorable reviews and was prone to dramatics.

"He's the Mexican Robin Hood, Mr. Shaughnessy."

"Yes, but he often murders those who don't agree with him," countered Shaughnessy.

"He's a warrior, a desperado, and the odds are against him...he's unpredictable and that makes the government nervous." She paused and tapped her finger on Villa's photograph. "And the people love him! It's pure drama, Mr. Shaughnessy, pure drama."

Callie's dark eyes blazed with the fierce determination that had served her well during labor unrest and racial confrontations in the streets of Houston. The editor ran his fingers through his hair like an exasperated father. "Callie, do you realize what might happen if you were caught in an attack down there? If, God forbid, you were taken prisoner by those Mexicans? A young, attractive American woman of- how old are you now?"

"I'm twenty-four, sir, and I am tough, you know that. Remember, I grew up in Comanche Springs, around cow herders, Indians and drifters. My daddy taught me to shoot a gun and ride a horse as good as any man. I have found that if I am honest and hold my ground and look people square in the eye, things work out. *And*, I can speak passable Spanish. I am the one for this assignment, sir! You know that"

"I would hold myself responsible if anything happened to you. Let me think about it. Let me think."

Callie kept up the pressure. A day didn't go by when she wasn't bringing the latest events of the Revolution to Shaughnessy's attention. Motion picture companies had sent crews down to film actual battles with the *Federales*. She had never felt so strongly about covering a story. It consumed her, for this was a revolution in her own hemisphere and it needed a voice, a woman's voice that would get to the heart of the struggle, in human terms.

Villa was a leader for the young century, reckless and daring. But there was more-she yearned for intensity in her life, away from the city, where she could break out, ride a horse in the big open spaces like she used to, see something of the world, and maybe watch history being made.

A week later *Villistas* attacked a train bearing eighteen American mining employees in Chihuahua. They robbed, stripped, and shot all of them in cold blood, shouting "Viva Villa!" Congress debated whether to invade. President Wilson's policy of "watchful waiting" was being sorely tested. Villa denied he gave any orders to kill.

Callie flew into Shaughnessy's office with the news. "Sir, events are escalating at an alarming pace!"

"It does seem to be getting more serious."

Callie was beside herself. "*Serious?* Why it's blatant. They are attacking Americans with apparent impunity. I tell you, Mr. Shaughnessy, it's only a matter of days before they cross the border. We cannot afford to miss this opportunity. And, it has to be an eyewitness account. How can we *not* do it?"

Callie was on a train for Fort Bliss the next week.

Young Callie plays by the cool clear water of Indian Creek on a hot summer afternoon underneath the generous shade of an ancient cottonwood. Her eyes move to a wavering reflection in the water. She looks up. On the opposite bank a gray-haired Indian sits on his pony, staring at her through narrow wrinkled eyes. He's dressed the old way- fringed buckskin, necklace of bear claws, long braids adorned with bits of cloth, fur, and bone. A well-used Sharps rifle hangs in his scabbard and the knife in his belt catches the sunlight. He eases off the horse and kneels down to fill up his canteen, splashing water on his weathered face and neck. He stands and takes something out of his pocket, looks at it, then tosses it across the creek. The girl follows the object with her eyes as it lands in a bed of leaves. She scurries over to retrieve it. A tiny, luminous blue horse of turquoise, with legs poised in mid-gallop, half the width of her young hand. He nods at her, then remounts and disappears over a rise.

She washes her new gift in the water and places it on a rock to admire it. It shines like a precious stone, a talisman in the guise of a wild horse, her favorite animal.

The sharp wail of the train whistle jolted Callie Masterson out of the dream. She reached into her bag and retrieved a diminutive blue horse. She fondled the smooth stone, as if to absorb some of its magic.

There were four hundred miles yet to go before the Southern Pacific train reached El Paso. She looked out the window and realized the train was approaching the outskirts of San Antonio, not so very from Comanche Springs, the little town where she came into the world, where the old Indian's visit had taken place. She had conflicting feelings about those lean years. An uncertain childhood, strewn with hardships after her mother's early death, left its mark, yet those memories still had a bittersweet draw upon her heart, for her early youth was as carefree and adventurous as any child's.

Images of black land farming country, cut by Indian Creek, where she used to pick up colored pebbles out of the clear water, the sharp scent of mesquite, and waking up to the sad sound of doves cooing in the big oak in the front yard.

Her father moved the family to San Antonio into his mother's cramped house after his wife passed away. Callie never had a bed to herself after that. She invented her own history, kept her poverty a locked secret from classmates in school. And now, ten years later, she couldn't quite believe she had ever lived like that. These things and more came to her as the steady rocking of the train once again lulled her gently to sleep.

Callie opened her eyes to a windswept desert on the outskirts of El Paso, where the sprawling military post of Fort Bliss stood enveloped in clouds of dust. A gust of wind nearly knocked her over as she descended from the train. A young officer hurried to her aid and took her luggage.

"MISS MASTERSON?" he yelled over the howling wind. "I'M LIEUTENANT TROY."

Holding on to her hat and tearing up from dust in her eyes, she nodded, and was driven to the fort in a military truck.

10

Large groups of mounted cavalry moved around like ghosts, appearing then disappearing within the smoky dust. Callie attempted to prettify her cascading black hair, now disheveled from the wind. She was a little embarrassed by the smiling lieutenant and asked about his duties at the fort.

The wind gusts shook the truck as if it were a toy.

"WHAT WAS THAT, MA'AM?" he yelled.

"NEVER MIND!" she yelled back.

They stopped in front of a large brick building and the lieutenant escorted her up a flight of steps, clasping her arm firmly. They entered a large cool vestibule, and once the door closed to the outside the sudden silence startled her.

"This way, ma'am."

He led her down a hallway, where photographs of military parades, expeditions and portraits lined the walls. They stopped at a desk where a very serious looking fellow in spectacles sat. Callie had the feeling that he was not glad to see her.

"Miss Masterson, I am Lieutenant Polanski, press liaison officer for General Pershing. Normally, we house the press in barracks, but as you are the sole female on these premises, General Pershing directed me to assign you to special accommodations. Lt. Troy will show take you there. It's just out back."

"When will I be able to speak with the General?"

"I have scheduled an appointment tomorrow morning at eight am. sharp. His office is upstairs, on the third floor."

"Why thank you. That will be fine."

"Please be punctual."

Before she could respond, he bent his head down and busied himself with papers.

Callie was given her own tiny cottage, complete with a kitchen. A friendly Mexican woman prepared her a plate of beef tamales, *arroz con frijoles*, and flan, a delicious type of custard. She retired early, weary from the twelve hour journey.

She arrived at her appointment a few minutes early and was ushered into the commander's office at precisely eight a.m.

Brigadier General John J. Pershing rose to greet her as she strode in with her notepad. Callie noticed at once that here was a Commander. She appraised his strong, rugged face, square jaw, neatly-trimmed mustache, keen gray eyes, and closely-cropped hair of the same color. The high round collar of his uniform only accentuated his military bearing. She respected this man who had fought in the Apache wars, and on San Juan Hill with Teddy Roosevelt.

"Welcome to Fort Bliss, Miss Masterson," he said, clasping her hand. "Please have a seat. We aren't accustomed to female correspondents here, but you come highly recommended by your editor, Mr. Shaughnessy. However, he never mentioned how pretty his best reporter is. As a matter of fact, when you walked in I said to myself...she looks a little like that actress, in *Birth of a Nation.* Now what's her name?"

"Lillian Gish," said Callie.

"That's it."

"People have told me that I somewhat resemble her, which I consider a fine compliment."

"Well, I agree. Now, what can I do for you?"

"Can you brief me on the latest information concerning the probability of Villa invading the United States?"

Pershing's countenance darkened. "He is very bitter about the President's decision to support his rival, Carranza, and there have been unsubstantiated reports of his plans to carry out a raid, somewhere along the border. We are ever on alert."

"Sir, I have in my files a photo of you and Villa and Obregon taken here at Fort Bliss."

"Yes, as I recall, that was in 1913."

"What sort of impression did he make on you? In terms of his morals and character?" She leaned closer to the desk. "Is he really a Robin Hood?"

Pershing smiled. "To be honest, we didn't talk that long, but I can tell you he is a proud man, somewhat rough in his ways, and the man dearly loves his country. I came away with the impression that he would do anything for Mexico. His men idolize him. He's reckless, possibly dangerous. But, he possesses that special something, oh, you know, like a cinema star."

"You mean charisma."

"Yes exactly. You journalists always have the right word."

"General, you've been on campaigns against the Apache, the Sioux and the war in the Philippines. If you had to fight Villa in Mexico, what would you expect?"

"It's a real mess down there, Miss Masterson. I honestly don't know what to expect-will he have 500 or 5000 men? I just make sure the Eighth Brigade is ready to go when the order comes, if it comes. I'm a soldier."

"Thank you, sir. May I have a look at your facilities? I would love to interview some of the boys."

"Of course, Lieutenant Troy has a little tour planned for you." He leaned across the desk and spoke in a quieter, more earnest tone of voice. "But I want to emphasize this is wild country, Miss Masterson, unpredictable, on both sides of the border. If the Revolution should spill over to our side...well, it would be extremely dangerous for a young woman like yourself. These bandits are desperate men. You know what I'm saying?"

"One can't hide from history, General. It is my calling to report the events, however violent. I can take care of myself, sir."

Pershing considered his audacious visitor, just as he would a new recruit, and couldn't repress a smile. "I've no doubt of that. But let me be honest-my first reaction upon receiving your request was to emphatically deny it. A woman running around interviewing soldiers with live ammunition, and bandits just across the river ready to attack-it goes against all my military instincts."

"Why is that, General?"

"You know perfectly well why. This war business is a man's world. Most, if not all, women are just not equipped to handle it."

"Then why did you agree?"

"To tell you the truth, after the tour I had planned to send you on your way..."

Callie waited.

"In my business I have to be able to assess a man's competence in quick fashion, to determine if he's up to the task, won't crack under pressure."

Callie focused on his words as if her life depended on it.

"Something tells me you have that competence. I see it in your eyes and the way you carry yourself. Let's take it day by day, shall we?"

Callie's posture loosened up a bit and smiled as she rose to go. "I greatly appreciate your confidence in me, sir. I won't disappoint you." She turned to walk toward the door.

"Oh, Miss Masterson?"

"Yes?"

"May I call you Callie at our next meeting?"

"Why of course, General."

"Thank you. It's been a pleasure."

This time he grasped her hand with both of his and then gave her a quick little wink. She had made an important friendship.

Train station in Columbus, NM, 1916

Chapter 2

During the next week, Callie observed maneuvers, gunnery ranges, obstacle courses and some important new innovations, such as transport trucks and machine guns, while also interviewing officers and enlisted men to glean any bits of rumor and opinion on where Villa might strike. Some of them were clearly put off by her female presence.

But soon she grew weary of the military decorum and the numerous tours, briefings and lectures she was invited to. She craved to get out into the desert and explore the border towns, closer to the real action, the revolution.

She studied the map and considered Presidio, south of El Paso, along the Rio Grande. Due west, in New Mexico, was Columbus. She had never been to that state, so she caught a morning train and headed west, out into the middle of nowhere.

Wound up with excitement, Callie pressed her nose against the window for a possible glimpse of whatever she might see in Mexico, which was only a few hundred yards south of the tracks.

She wore a black skirt, and a white blouse to counteract what she assumed would be intense desert sunshine, even though it would be hard to keep clean with all the dust. Instead of her regular buttoned-up shoes, she wore a pair of western boots, which would be more practical and quicker to put on in case she needed to move fast.

The train slowed as they approached the isolated village of Columbus. The red, two-story station seemed gawky to Callie. She stared at the town, a scattered collection of wood and adobe buildings. Hardly a tree or blade of grass relieved the parched look of the forlorn little settlement. Outside of the town stretched a uniformly flat landscape, except for three cone-shaped mountains to the west, the Tres Hermanas. The immensity of the Chihuahuan desert dwarfed everything.

She stepped on to the platform and a shiver went through her. The wild pure space was palpable; a clean dry wind caressed her face, recalling the feel of her childhood home in Texas.

She looked around at the weathered adobes, the rolling tumble weeds, a moaning windmill. She embraced the harshness. The drama of the land moved her.

She did not need directions, for the Commercial Hotel was in plain sight, and she quickly secured a small but tidy room, furnished with a washbasin and pitcher, slop jar, bureau, and bed, with a kerosene lamp nearby.

She came down into the parlor with its curtained windows and oriental rugs. She noted a hand-cranked Victrola and a piano nestled in a corner.

A smiling, well-dressed young man of about sixteen years with black curly hair that needed combing approached her. Callie admired his big innocent brown eyes.

"Miss Masterson, welcome to our hotel. You are the first female reporter to honor us with your presence. Please let me know if you have need of anything."

"Why thank you. And your name, sir?" Callie teased, for she could tell he was a little nervous.

"Oh, of course. I am Arthur Ravel, at your service ma'am," he said, and bowed awkwardly.

"Arthur, aren't you a little young to run a hotel?"

"Oh, it's not mine ma'am, that is, my father, Sam Ravel, owns the building and runs the restaurant. He's having some dental work in El Paso."

"I do hope he comes through it all right."

"Thank you for your concern."

"Could you tell me where the telegraph office is?"

"It's right next to Miller's Drug Store, to your left as you exit the hotel. And we have a telephone switchboard operator, as well. Mrs. Ellie Parker handles that. We're quite up-to-date here Miss Masterson."

"I'm impressed, Arthur. Thank you?"

"Oh, anytime ma'am, anytime," he stammered.

Callie went out on to the dusty street and stopped in front of the Telegraph Office, where she saw a woman in the window with headphones, sitting very erect and apparently engaged in a serious conversation. Callie crossed the street and entered the dry goods store.

A pretty woman with a worried expression sat in a chair making lacework. She looked up and smiled at Callie. "Can I help you find something?"

"Well, I just arrived. I'm Callie Masterson, a correspondent for the *Houston Chronicle*."

"Hello," she said, rising, "I am Susan Moore. My husband John and I run this store. Are you here because of Pancho Villa?" she asked hesitantly.

"Why yes. Have you heard anything?"

She rubbed her hands together, as if they were cold. "I don't know who to believe, Miss Masterson. Some say he's right across the border in Palomas." She paused. It was obvious to Callie that the woman was upset. "Well, yesterday, about four o'clock, a well-dressed man came into the store. I went up to greet him and when I got close I experienced a cold chill that went right through me. He was short, with dark eyes and a mustache. But he had a scar across his cheek that looked quite recent. He wanted some pants, and while I looked for his size I sensed his eyes following me."

She stopped and looked at Callie for some sort of empathy.

"You think he may have some connection with Villa?"

"I don't know. I just know how I felt...that he seemed to be watching me, though I had never seen him before. I just didn't trust him." She gathered her arms about herself and shuddered.

"Perhaps it's all the rumors. You mustn't get so worked up." Callie touched her shoulder. "Are you here all alone?"

"My husband is at the bank." She sat back down. "We've only been here for four months. I'm from St. Louis, and to tell the truth, I just wasn't prepared for all this. I'm not well acquainted with the ways of the border country. Sometimes the wind shrieks for days on end. The store shakes so frightfully, I am afraid to go outside."

She picked up a glass of water from a table and downed it all. "I have such a thirst all the time," she half whispered. "The desert is so hard on one."

Callie started to feel somewhat uncomfortable. This woman was clearly out of her element. She remembered Easterners who had lived near her house in Comanche Springs and were similarly traumatized by the harshness of the southwest. She had always experienced a mixture of sympathy and bewilderment, and wondered why they

18

came west in the first place.

"I must go now, Mrs. Moore. I do hope you feel better soon."

Callie hurried out of the store, without bothering to buy the articles she had come in for.

Heading south, she crossed the railroad tracks and entered Camp Furlong, the headquarters of the US Thirteenth Cavalry.

Callie already knew, thanks to General Pershing, that about 300 soldiers currently occupied the fort, the rest being strung out along the border, including Machine Gun Troops and Rifle Troops. This fact alone practically precluded an attack on sleepy Columbus.

She walked along the row of corrals and stopped to talk to a pretty bay mare, which reminded her of a horse her father had kept back in Comanche Springs. One of her fondest memories was riding along the river with him, on Sundays.

"How are you, missy?" she said, stroking its head. "I bet you hope the bandits stay away, huh?"

"I'll second that motion."

Callie turned around to see a gangly, sandy-haired soldier smiling at her. His brown army uniform had seen better days, and the way he wore his hat high on his head made him look like an adolescent.

"Lieutenant Castleman, at your service."

"I'm Callie Masterson, reporter for the *Houston Chronicle*," she said, extending her hand. "Do you have any idea where Villa might be?"

"There's a lot of rumors going around, but he's somewhere between here and Chihuahua, and that covers a lot of ground. Carranza's troops are keeping him pretty busy, so I don't see him coming up here. After all, Columbus is just a dusty little backwater. What's the point?"

"I see."

"Why ma'am, you almost look disappointed."

"Well Lieutenant, we reporters follow the action. That's why I journeyed seven hundred miles across Texas."

"If you want some action, we're going to do a little machine gun practice. Would you care to watch?"

"Yes sir, lead on!"

They went to an open area away from the stables, where several men had already set up their guns. Targets were set up about 100 yards away.

"These are Benet Mercie machine guns," he explained, "gas-operated and air-cooled, fed by a thirty-round strip magazine. They're mounted on this here bipod, and a loader feeds the strips in while the gunner shoots."

"Sounds very formidable," said Callie, as she took notes.

"Actually, Miss Masterson, between you and me, they're lousy. They jam up if you look at 'em the wrong way. But that's strictly off the record. Well, let's see how they do today."

Callie stepped back and the firing commenced. She had been around guns all her life, but never had she heard such sustained ear-splitting racket. She jammed her fingers in her ears but could still feel the piercing discharge of bullets. Finally, they ceased. Acrid smoke hung in the air and sweat rolled down the young soldiers' faces.

"Goodness, how do you boys not go deaf?"

"Aw, we get used to it, ma'am. It's kinda fun, really."

Callie was hot, dusty and hungry, so she returned to the hotel to freshen up and have some lunch, having left a significant impression on her first encounter with the U.S. Cavalry, as all eyes followed her when she walked away.

Villa on the move

Chapter 3

Callie sat at a corner table below a faded portrait of Kit Carson and sipped a cup of coffee. A smiling, buxom woman in a blue gingham dress approached her.

"Miss Masterson, I'm Lucille Sharpe, a teacher here in Columbus. We don't get too many women traveling alone in these parts, so I thought I would come and see how you are getting along."

"That is so nice of you. Please, sit down."

"Thank you. News travels fast in small towns, you know, so I just thought I'd inquire. Actually, Miss Masterson, I'm awfully curious how such a presentable young woman as yourself decided to come out here to our little town on your own. Is it true you are a reporter?"

"Please call me Callie." She stirred her coffee and chose her words with care. "I am a reporter. The whole idea of the Mexican Revolution fascinates me. I see my role as giving shape to the crazy chaos of the Revolution, so that it makes sense to people. I think it has a lot to teach us. I'm a bit of a rebel myself, so I sort of identify with Mr. Villa. And I want to bring some passion to journalism-the things I have seen are every bit as exciting as what you might read in a novel." She leaned across the table. "I want to communicate the drama that is so often a part of our lives, Lucille. What's going on across that border is the very stuff of drama."

"You would make a fine teacher."

Callie leaned back into the chair. "I tried a little of that in San Antonio, but being a journalist is what excites me. It allows me to walk up to perfect strangers and ask them the most personal questions."

"I never thought about it in that way. That is something. Now, I imagine a pretty girl like you must have a beau back in Houston."

"To tell you the truth, I've been so busy with my career I have rather neglected that aspect of my life." Callie shifted in her chair. "I just talked to Susan Moore, at the dry goods store. She's very anxious about the bandits."

Lucille shook her head. "That poor woman. I believe it's those awful newspaper accounts that upset her so. Oh, dear me, I don't mean to insult your profession."

"You haven't, I assure you."

"Well, poor Mrs. Moore becomes so upset, horrified really, by the lurid accounts of the terrible outrages down in Mexico that her husband tried to keep them from her. I have attempted to befriend her, but she keeps to herself. This isn't an easy place to live for someone like her."

"Tell me something Lucille. I was at the Camp and met a few of the boys there. I hear there are over three hundred of them. What does the army do about...female companionship?"

Lucille looked puzzled for a moment. "Oh that." She leaned a little closer to Callie. "Well you see, Colonel Slocum has girls in the fort to keep things under control, to prevent disease."

Now Callie looked puzzled.

"It's regulated," said Lucille, slightly embarrassed.

"You mean they have regulated prostitution, in an army camp?"

"Yes ma'am, they certainly do. I should correct myself. It was General Pershing's idea. The Colonel just follows his orders."

"General Pershing? Really? "Callie rummaged in her purse for her notepad.

"The reasoning is that is good for morale, whereas, alcohol and drugs create disorder. Still, I think it's shameful."

"Yet, I can see his reasoning. They spend most of their time waiting for something to happen. They have their duties, they clean their weapons, but really they must get very bored out here. It is so isolated; it may as well be Arabia."

"I suppose these things come up at any military outpost," Lucille said, uncertainly.

"And think about it, Lucille-they are all virile young men, far away from home."

Lucille put her finger to her lips, as if to hush Callie. A thin, gangly youth in blue overalls came up to the table and put his arms around Lucille. Callie guessed he might be thirteen. He possessed bright curious eyes and a shock of straight blond hair hanging in his freckled face. "Hello, Ma."

"Hello dear. Callie, this is my son Randy. Miss Masterson is a reporter, out here to write about the army and that dreadful Pancho

Villa."

"Howdy, ma'am. Oh, we're ready for those bandidos all right. They got a bunch of machine guns at the camp, and we got our own weapons, me and my buddies."

"I see. Randy do you suppose you could give me a little tour of Columbus and show me the different roads in and out of town, and such?"

"Why sure, ma'am."

"Have you done your chores, Randy?"

"Just gotta feed the horse, Ma, and then I'm done."

"Well then, meet me in front of the hotel in about ten minutes and we'll be off."

"I'll be there, sure thing."

In ten minutes Callie and her young tour guide were walking along the road that headed south across the border to Palomas, a small Mexican village just on the other side. She noticed piles of windblown sand heaped up against the adobe buildings. The wind buffeted her face, and she licked her lips to counteract the desiccating heat.

Randy stopped and pointed to a cluster of low buildings a short distance beyond the border fence. "That there's Palomas. Ma likes to go over and buy pottery and knick knacks for the house." Callie squinted at the bleak landscape. "It looks exactly the same as here, and yet, it doesn't. It's Mexico."

They turned around and walked north, back toward the tracks.

"This here road leads to Deming, 'bout thirty miles north. If you ever need to hide just drop into that ditch. It's full of brush and it runs along the road outta town."

"I would imagine there's a few snakes down there."

"They usually hear you coming and skedaddle."

They crossed back over to the business district and passed the bank and some well-kept homes. Randy stopped in front of an attractive white two-story frame home.

"This here is where Colonel Slocum lives. He's in charge of the Thirteenth."

"Somebody is a gardener. Look at the nice lilacs and pots of petunias," said Callie. "It seems to have been built fairly recently."

"Yep. Only a year ago. The soldiers like to live in wooden houses. They think adobe is dirty. You gotta re-mud them every year."

They crossed a field and came to a modest adobe home with a small barn. Tall red and yellow hollyhocks leaned against the sienna-colored wall of the house. The brilliant color of these hardy flowers were as little miracles in a sea of tans and browns.

"This is our place. Hold on and I'll show you something."

He dashed into the house and soon came back out with a rifle. "This here's my Winchester 30.30. She's pretty old but she works. I got me a fine deer last fall with this."

"How old are you, Randy?"

"Twelve."

"Why I thought you were at least thirteen or fourteen."

He blushed slightly. "Yeah, I'm kinda big for my age. Well, I better tend to the horses."

"Thanks for showing me around."

She walked back and stopped in Miller's Drugstore, for her throat was parched by the arid country and she craved some fruit lozenges.

A woman, who was clearly pregnant, smiled sweetly from behind the counter.

"You must be Miss Masterson. Small town, you know."

"Small town," said Callie grinning.

"Actually, Lucille said she talked to you. I'm Loretta James. My husband, Milton, works for the railroad. How long will you be staying? Nothing ever happens in Columbus I'm afraid."

"I haven't decided. Maybe another day or two. When is your baby due, Loretta?

"Sometime in early June, so the doctor says. I am most excited."

"I can see that. May I ask how old you are?"

"Just turned nineteen. This is only a part-time job. I'm studying to be a telegraph operator."

"That is wonderful. Well, you take care of yourself."

"Oh, I will. This baby will be the most important thing in my life."

Callie smiled. *That woman will make a wonderful mother. What if that was me, about to have a child? I cannot imagine. You have an entire world to experience, Callie. No time for that now.*

25

After a quiet dinner she wandered outside. There were no streetlights in Columbus and the clear desert air made for a spectacular night sky. The Milky Way arched overhead like a celestial blizzard and Callie was taken back to Comanche Springs, where she often gazed up at a similar sight most any evening, as she sprawled in the grass, listening to crickets and frogs, wondering about her future.

Back in her hotel room she studied the map, and then looked at her calendar. It was Tuesday, March 7. According to the *El Paso Times* there was no fresh news on the whereabouts of Villa. "I'll stay until Thursday," she decided, "then head back to Fort Bliss. Then what- I don't know. Presidio, maybe."

For the next two days Callie talked to various soldiers, officers, cooks, and even one of the prostitutes. She interviewed Arthur, who recalled Villa coming in to her father's hardware store, which was next door to the hotel, and buying a considerable amount of ammunition. Arthur described Villa's swaggering demeanor and his wide sombrero, a big holstered revolver, but more than anything he remembered his beaming smile. This was when the U.S. still favored Villa as a liberator.

She also learned from Lieutenant Castleman that the First Aero Squadron, comprised of a dozen Jenny aircraft from Fort Sam Houston in San Antonio, might deploy to Columbus.

She finally got to see the Camp commander, Colonel Slocum. He told her that people in the little village of Palomas just across the border were all terrified, but the latest information placed Villa sixty-five or seventy miles south of the border. And, besides, Villa wouldn't have the nerve to attack a town with so many heavily-armed soldiers.

Thursday evening, on the eve of her departure, she looked at her face in the mirror. It had already acquired a healthy golden tan and she was pleased how nicely her white blouse set it off. She wondered if a suntan would ever become a popular look for women.

She also looked a bit thinner, having lost a few pounds from the rigors of the trip. Yet, she had never felt better, not just physically, but more alert and clear-headed. She thrived in this clean, sharp environment and knew she would accomplish important work. And somehow she would tell this story to the American people, if not the world, that would startle and amaze them and teach them something important about themselves.

She packed her things to catch the seven a.m. train and crawled into bed with her map. Uncertain about her next move, she threw the map on the floor, read a few of Shakespeare's sonnets, and blew out the lamp.

Callie awakened and sat up. She thought she had heard something-horses, men talking. The clock read 4:01a.m. Had she been asleep that long? She lay back down, closed her eyes, took some deep breaths to relax.

She dreamed someone was playing a bugle, a strange and lovely melody. Silly soldiers, she thought.

Three gunshots ripped through the night. Callie bolted out of the bed and dressed in seconds. She slipped on her boots and was glad she had brought them. She was perspiring, taking short little breaths as she stood in the dark room straining to hear what might come next. Some men yelling in the distance. She collected her things.

More shots followed the yells, closer now. Her mind raced to devise a plan of action.

Grab the suitcase, but get the gun out first. Try and watch what happens…remember everything….calm down….calm down.

She found the Colt pistol, put it in her purse which was slung across her shoulder, then quickly looked out the window and saw murky figures moving about, some mounted, some not, filling up the dark street, shouting in hoarse Spanish.

She rushed into the hallway. Guests in their robes huddled by a window at the end of the hall, unsure of what they should do. "Get downstairs! Get out of the hotel," yelled Callie. "Pancho Villa is attacking the town."

An elderly woman stood at her door and silently entreated Callie to help her.

"Ma'am, where is your suitcase?" asked Callie, rushing up to her. She pointed behind her. Callie grabbed it and closed the woman's hand around it. "Would someone please help this lady downstairs? I saw a back exit through the kitchen yesterday. Don't go out through the front door. Everyone hurry!"

Callie found the fire escape. It descended into a small side alley, but she knew she had to jump the last six feet or so. She leaped off

27

without hesitation, her dress billowing up like a parachute, and landed on her feet. She stashed her suitcase behind some trash cans. She wanted her hands free.

She crept along the wall until she reached the street. Murky shapes moved in the darkness. Callie tried to concentrate on her job, her duty to cover the story, even as a fluttery anxiety began to rise up inside.

The bandits shouted "Viva Villa!" and fired their guns at will. Windows shattered, startled townspeople yelled, and women screamed. Frantic horses thundered past.

The flash of gunfire briefly illuminated sombrero-clad Mexicans, swearing and shouting, shooting, it seemed, at random. Then she noticed flashes of rifle fire from the direction of the railroad tracks.

"Thank god, the boys from the camp are on the attack."

Her eyes grew accustomed to the dark and she saw bandits drag people out of the hotel and dreaded what would come next. Shouts of protest mingled with screams of fear, then gunshots at close range. Moans and pitiful crying as innocent people spent their last moments, bewildered and unprepared for death.

She pressed her body against the cold brick wall and grew queasy at the thought of being taken by the bandits. She embraced the darkness as a hunted animal would.

Someone tried to start his automobile, but he was pulled out and shot.

"Matar a los gringos!" they kept shouting, and Callie crouched down even lower.

"Wait please, I can pay you!" A voice she recognized, he had a room near hers. Someone lit a match so he could write a check, for his life, and the man actually ran off right past her, unharmed.

Remember that one Callie!

Instinct told her she was too close, they might soon discover her. She took a deep breath and cradled the loaded gun in both hands, then crept along the boardwalk toward the telegraph office. To her amazement Ellie Parker sat at that same window, earphones on, as if this were just another day, except that the window glass was completely shattered.

She wanted to say something, but an explosion sent her reeling. Flames consumed the hardware store and in seconds the fire spread to the hotel next door. A man covered in flames ran into the street, shrieking.

Dynamite. Are they going to level the entire town?

An eerie orange glow spread out of the darkness and revealed the entire grim scene. Callie saw at least six people dead in the street in front of the hotel. *Villistas* carried food, clothes, even bolts of cloth out of stores, along with ammunition. Suddenly, machine gun fire erupted in full fury from the tracks, for the bandits were now fully visible, silhouetted against the conflagration.

This enraged them and they fired back every which way, even as they fell in great numbers.

Callie had found scant shelter in the entryway of Miller's Drugstore. A bullet shattered the window glass behind her, sending shards raining down upon her. She cowered lower, like a trapped mouse in a corner. It was too dangerous to remain and too dangerous to move.

Someone close by was firing at the bandits, someone not ten feet from her. She strained to see. A blond head caught the light.

"Randy? Randy Sharpe, is that you?"

Her young friend took aim with his sturdy Winchester from behind a barrel, like a proper soldier. He looked at her, astounded, his mouth open.

"Miss Masterson? What are you doing there? C'mon! I'll protect you."

They ran away from the burning chaos, somehow unscathed, into the darkness. They held their guns in front of them, ready for anything. They passed soldiers going the other way toward the action, crossed the road and slid down into the ditch.

For now, they were invisible and safe.

"Randy," she had to catch her breath, "where's your mother?"

"She and the other women took the kids to the school building. I wasn't gonna miss this for nothin'."

"Randy you're…never mind. I'm glad you're here."

"Yes ma'am."

She caressed his dirty face. Little pieces of glass fell from her hair.

"Oh."

"What's wrong, miss?"

"Oh, nothing. A window fell on me."

"The hotel was right where they hit. You coulda been-"

"But I wasn't." Callie started to choke up, but stifled it with a loud cough.

The thunder of hooves shook the ground as horsed passed just above and clods of dirt peppered them, but they couldn't tell whether they were bandits or soldiers.

"Whoo! The boys of the Thirteenth are givin' 'em what for now. Listen to them guns. It's like music!"

Randy's enthusiasm both reassured and upset Callie. He was only twelve! Now she felt duty bound to get him out of harm's way and forgot about her own survival.

"We have to avoid the downtown. They're shooting in all directions. Can you get us to the schoolhouse?"

"Sure thing. Let's go."

"Oh, Randy."

"Yes'm?"

"Those snakes will hear us coming, right?"

"Hope so," he chuckled.

They made their way along the ditch and ended up somewhere north of the battle. The darkness shimmered with an unnatural glow above the town, punctuated by flames that shot up high into the air.

They crossed a large field and a fleeing animal nearly ran into her. She let out a scream and grabbed Randy's arm.

"It was just an ol' jackrabbit, ma'am."

She caught her breath. "I'm fine. Keep going."

They circled back into his neighborhood. "That's it, over there. I'll bet they're in the basement, so the doors'll be locked. But I know a window I can jimmy open."

He managed to climb up on a large ledge and tried to pry open the window. The glow of the fire was so bright there was plenty of light to see by.

Callie knelt by a bush, just below him, and was getting nervous. She could see horsemen only a few hundred yards away, heading out of town.

Then a lone rider swerved, and headed straight for them.

"Randy, jump down!" she screamed.

30

A bullet crashed through the window as the boy threw himself into the bush.

Callie turned around and braced herself, bit her lip, gripped the Colt in both hands and fired. The bandit was screaming obscenities and bearing down fast on her.

The bullet tore through his neck. He fell like a rock with a dull thud, directly in front of her. The horse veered away and barely missed trampling the young reporter, and she went rolling in the dust.

She stood up, dazed, clutching the pistol. "I killed him. I killed a man."

The bandit lay face down, motionless. Callie stared fixedly at the body. Randy limped up to her, eyes wide. "Gosh! Damn nice shot, ma'am."

Callie bent down and hesitantly put her trembling hand upon the man's back. "My God, I have sent this man into eternity."

The shock gave way to a strange feeling of elation. Sweat rolled down her face, her dress was ripped and there was dirt in her mouth, but she was unaccountably calm.

A door opened and Lucille ran out.

"Randy!" She gathered him up in her arms as if he were a small child. "Why did you disappear like that? Why did you leave me? That was the worst hour of my life!"

Callie could see both anger and relief in her flashing eyes.

"It's okay, Ma."

"Lucille, your young man probably saved my life."

"Ma, she *did* save mine! Did you see?"

"Yes I did and I am so-" She broke down and embraced Callie, while she still had an arm around her son. The three of them stood there, huddled together, amidst the screams and gunfire, as the flames hissed and the battle still raged in Columbus.

An army truck rumbled up to the school and a sergeant jumped out. "Is everyone all right here?"

"Yes, we are all alive," said Callie. "Except for him."

He looked down at the unfortunate bandit. "And who did this?"

"Callie, that's who," said Randy. "She sure saved my life."

"Well, I'll be. You're the lady reporter."

"Yes sir, I am. Where does the battle stand, may I ask?"

"I could be wrong, but I think we've whipped them."

A distant bugle sounded. The soldier slapped his leg.

"Ha! I knew it. The Mexicans are blowing recall. We got em' on the run!"

He ran back to his truck, laughing and whooping, and drove off in a crazy zigzag fashion.

Slowly, women and children emerged from the school, hugging each other, some in tears.

"I have to go and see what is going on," said Callie.

"I'll come with you ma'am."

"No, you stay with your mother, Randy. I think the worst is over."

He looked terribly disappointed, for he had become Callie's bodyguard and wasn't ready to relinquish that position, but she had a story to write and off she ran.

Columbus, NM after the Villa raid

Chapter 4

Callie slowly made her way down Main Street. The darkness began to fade, as if the curse of the violent nightmare was broken at last.

Buildings still burned, as volunteer firemen started a bucket brigade. She passed Miller's drugstore where she had taken cover. When she reached the telegraph office, Ellie Parker sat outside, smoking a cigarette.

"Miss Parker," cried Callie. "You're bleeding!"

"Just scratches, honey, just scratches. That was some night wasn't it? My goodness. This here's the best smoke I've had in a long time."

"Were you able to get through to anyone?"

"Oh yes. I contacted the sheriffs in El Paso and Deming, the fire departments, and Fort Bliss too. The operator informed me that General Pershing was most grateful and to tell the folks here that he and the troops would get here as soon as possible and round up those SOB's, if it took him a whole year." She grinned. "He didn't say SOB, I did."

"Miss Parker you are a real trooper. You really held your ground. I am amazed. You're certain that you are all right?"

She nodded, and Callie moved on amid the carnage now visible in the light of dawn. The bodies of Mexicans were everywhere. Horses lay dead or dying, writhing in the dirt.

She needed to write all this down or important details would be forgotten. The hotel still blazed as she ran into the alley to recover her hidden suitcase. Glowing embers floated down and singed her hair and clothes, but she managed to extricate her belongings and ran back to Ellie Parker.

"May I leave this with you for safekeeping?"

"Of course, honey. Don't you worry, I'll keep an eye on it."

Callie ran back to the hotel with her pad She saw Arthur, standing there dazed, in his pajamas. He looked terrible, all banged up and bruised.

She took his arm. "Arthur? "

He stared, but did not recognize her at first. Then, his eyes brightened.

"Miss Masterson. Oh, I am so glad that you are well. I was worried that-"

"Yes, but I got out in time. What happened to you?"

"They grabbed me, Miss, they dragged me out into the street here, started punching and kicking me. They were shooting our guests. God, it was the worst thing...and they were going to shoot me, but both of them got shot themselves, and I ran off and hid in the mesquite."

He stopped, swallowed and rubbed his face.

Callie put her arms around him and could feel him shaking.

"You did just the right thing. You're a survivor, thank God."

"I guess so," he whimpered.

Callie whispered in his ear. "It's okay to cry. No one would fault you for that."

Arthur trembled, but then stiffened and drew away from her.

"No ma'am. There's work to be done and people to help."

"But where will you stay?"

"I have an aunt nearby. And my father should be returning soon. Thank you."

He went off to join the water brigade the soldiers had formed.

She slowly walked among the bodies, all male, some of whom she recognized. The amount of dead from Villa's army was staggering. She estimated at least fifty or sixty scattered along the street.

She looked more closely and tears welled up in her eyes. Some of the "soldiers" were not much older than Randy.

She knelt down by one of them. He had lost his hat, revealing his tousled and dusty hair. He was thin and small, and the straps of bullets across his shirt looked ridiculous on his young body. His eyes were still open and a look of utter surprise had frozen on his face. He still clutched some candy bars he had stolen from the hardware store. Callie wept. "This is so wrong," she said in a hoarse whisper.

She wiped her face on her sleeve and gently closed his eyes. She found a quiet place by a stable and sat down to write for a while in her notepad.

"Miss Masterson." She looked up. Lieutenant Castleman stood there, rifle in hand, holding the reins of his horse. "I am mighty pleased to see you all in one piece."

"Likewise, Lieutenant. Your boys performed wonderfully."

"Well, I don't think Villa realized how many of us there was. It was pretty touch and go there in the dark at first. We were scared of hitting the townspeople, but when they lit up the hotel them boys was sitting ducks. We had four machine guns set up on the tracks. I'll wager we went through twenty thousand rounds. And they hardly jammed at all."

Callie moved her hand across the pad at a furious pace. "No doubt due to the consummate skill of you and your gallant men. Do you have any idea of casualties?"

"Looks like they got eight of us. Private Griffith, Fred, was the sentinel at headquarters, and he must of seen them first. When they fired at him it woke us all up."

"Is he…"

"I'm afraid they shot him dead, but he got three of the bastards before he died. Sorry, ma'am."

"Don't worry about me. I was raised in West Texas and have heard rough language all my life. Did anyone see Villa?"

"Hard to tell. His best men, the *Dorados* they call 'em, all wore sombreros, so he could have been in there, but I kinda think he hung back in the rear guard. But that's strictly-"

"Off the record, I know, Lieutenant," said Callie, smiling. "Will there be any pursuit, or will you wait on reinforcements?"

"Oh yes. Colonel Slocum appointed Major Tompkins to lead a party of about fifty men to give chase, as long as their ammunition holds out. They already left."

"What will happen now?"

"I imagine that General Pershing will be here pretty soon and decide what to do. This is a serious incident. The United states has been invaded."

"Do you realize that Miss Parker was on the telephone during the battle letting the world know what was happening? She alerted General Pershing."

"Well, that is something. She's a fine lady. I'd best get back to my duties. If you need any assistance, you let me know, ma'am."

"I will, and Lieutenant?"

"Yes?"

"Thank you, and all your brave men."

"That's why we're here, Miss." He mounted his horse and trotted away.

"I do believe I embarrassed you Lieutenant," she chuckled and continued to write more notes.

Callie talked to more townspeople and surveyed the damage in the full light of day. The center of town was gutted, but it was miraculous that so few people died. Villa had paid a horrendous price for his audacious raid. Callie wondered what he got out of it, other than the wrath of a powerful nation. He had lost this gamble, badly.

She picked up her suitcase. Tired and still not quite believing what she had just gone through, she trudged over to Lucille's house, hoping that she might put her up for the night.

As she neared the adobe house she noticed a wagon and some people around it. Lucille quickly came up and put an arm around her, which struck Callie as odd. She approached the wagon and beheld the pregnant body of Loretta James, pale and bloodstained, stretched out on the rough wood planks.

Callie cried out, clutching her face with both hands. "Oh God, no! I just talked to her yesterday. She was so happy, Lucille."

"Easy, honey," said Lucille, taking her arm. A man sat atop the wagon, staring at her. He had a strangely stoic expression on his face.

"It's all right, Miss Masterson. She's in heaven now, with our child, with the Lord. She told me about you. She admired you, ma'am."

The shock of his terrible loss and the unswerving faith in his creator brought forth a strangely peaceful demeanor to his face. He took the reins and urged his horse slowly forward and went down the road.

"I think I need to rest for a minute," said Callie.

"Randy dear, go and clear off my bed." Lucille stared out at the incongruous sight of the fresh desert morning and the smoldering wrecked town. "I feel like I should have done something, had you stay here last night. Why, you're all banged up."

"Don't be silly. I just need to rest a few minutes. All of a sudden, I'm so weary."

Once she touched the bed, Callie fell into a stupor that was half sleep half swoon.

First Aero Squadron on the airfield in Columbus, NM

Chapter 5

Callie opened her eyes in a strange bedroom. She struggled to clear her head, as images of Fort Bliss, General Pershing, and the train journeys all mingled together in a hazy collage, and then all the frightening events of the night attack came back in an instant.

She threw off the blanket and staggered to the door. Her body ached all over, but she was upset she had allowed herself to sleep. "Where are they?" she muttered aloud, and shuffled through the empty house to the front door and pushed it open. She put up her hand to shield her eyes from the bright sunlight and leaned against the wall. Lucille was conversing with some neighbors when she noticed Callie at the door.

"Callie dear, how are you feeling?"

I'm fine, Lucille. How long did I sleep?"

"Oh, well let me see, it's nearly two, so just about five hours I would say."

"Oh no," Callie moaned.

"I'm sure you needed to rest, dear. Let's go in the kitchen and I'll get you some coffee and a little breakfast."

Lucille whipped up some scrambled eggs and brewed a pot of coffee. Suddenly, Randy charged through the door, flush with excitement.

"Glad to see you're up and around, Miss Masterson."

"For God sake's, Randy, call me Callie." Lucille's coffee had greatly revived her.

"Sorry, ma'am, I mean, Callie."

"Sit down and have a roll, Randy," said Lucille.

"Okay. Ma, listen, Freddy's dad was in the army kitchen when they attacked and he threw boiling water at 'em as they came through the door...and one trooper killed a bandit with a baseball bat, and the others had an ax and a shotgun-"

Callie stood up. "Wait just a minute, Randy." She limped into the bedroom and came back with her notepad.

"Boiling water, axes and a *baseball bat*?"

"Yes, ma'am, that's what he said. And Mrs. Smyser, her husband's a Captain, she and her two young'uns hid in the outhouse when the bandidos were banging on the door."

Randy took a break and gobbled up the roll.

Lucille added her news. "I heard Mrs. Riggs-why you can see her house from here-almost smothered her five-month old baby with a pillowcase to keep it quiet when she heard those bandits outside."

Callie nodded and scribbled down every detail and incident they could tell her for the next half hour.

"Ten of our town folk, murdered for no good reason." Lucille shook her head and poured Callie some more coffee.

"Not all of 'em, Ma. Some were guests at the hotel." He gave a Callie a somber look. "Where you were staying, Callie."

"And I was a reluctant witness to that terrible violence. I am thankful it was dark, but my memory of it is bad enough. My goodness, those awful screams. How many of Villa's men perished?"

"They counted sixty-seven dead *Villistas* in the streets. Freddy's dad said they're gonna burn them bodies, pretty soon."

Callie put down her pencil. "Villa must be very desperate. Some of them were just boys. I saw them, fourteen, fifteen years old. It was very upsetting."

"Too many people died, and for no good reason," said Lucille.

No one spoke of Loretta James.

Callie finished her coffee and stood up.

"I must get this information back to my paper in Houston, so I'm off to see Ellie and her telephone. Thank you for the breakfast, Lucille."

She was halfway to town when Randy came running up behind.

"I almost forgot! They took three prisoners and are already building a scaffold for a hanging. In the morning I think."

"Thank you Randy. I don't think I'll be a witness to that."

"No?" he said, surprised. "Well then I'll tell you all about it," and he ran off.

Callie managed to get through to Mr. Shaughnessy on a very noisy, static-filled line. She toned down the actual amount of danger she had been in, so as not to alarm him too much, and was greatly heartened to hear his words of praise and encouragement.

"No other paper has these kinds of details. You did good Callie, really good. This is amazing stuff. I'll be darned if you didn't predict the whole scenario. But watch yourself. Do you hear me? Watch yourself!"

She walked past the center of town, still smoking as weary men doused it with water, and nearly gagged from the stench of damp burnt wood.

The image of Loretta's body came out of wherever it was hidden in her subconscious, but a new strength steeled her against the emotion, put a distance between herself and the tragedy. Otherwise, she knew, she could never become the reporter she wanted to be. She chose to focus on something else.

I killed that man. He was coming at us and was going to kill Randy, but I shot him dead. My aim was good, I didn't shake. It was horrible, but I had to do it. I had to do it. I took care of Randy and I took care of me. I survived.

Her hands shook while she replayed the event over and over in her mind.

She walked through small crowds of people, wagons going back and forth, and soldiers that milled about the ruins, gesticulating and recounting the attack as if it were already an infamous legend. Curiosity seekers snapped photos, reporters grilled townspeople for details. Callie looked south, towards Mexico and wondered how far Villa had gone, and then suddenly remembered that Lieutenant Castleman had mentioned a pursuit.

She ran down to the camp and soon learned that the cavalry had engaged in a running gun battle with the *Villistas* for several hours, until they exhausted their bullets and returned to camp, having killed another 40 or 50. The soldiers reported that the bandits left a trail of litter. The desert was strewn with spurs and bridles, shoes and socks and underwear, sheets and pillowcases, and candy.

Callie continued expanding the story of the attack on Columbus, which she eventually discovered was the first invasion of the United States since the British stormed Washington in 1812. She learned from Colonel Slocum at Camp Furlong Headquarters that the Secretary of War had directed the commander of the Army's Southern Division at San Antonio, Texas, to organize a force to pursue the bandits who had attacked Columbus. Brigadier General John J.

Pershing was chosen to lead a Punitive Expedition into Mexico.

From that moment, events began to happen in rapid and sometimes chaotic succession.

Within days, train after train arrived with supplies, personnel, trucks, and more troops. Columbus would soon be overwhelmed, and the sleepy border town of 400 would swell to over a thousand by the fall.

There would be a Western Column of 2,000 men departing from Hachita, New Mexico, and an Eastern Column, 4,000 strong, leaving Columbus as soon as General Pershing arrived.

Callie resolved to somehow smuggle herself into the expedition. On the day of Pershing's arrival Callie packed her things, just in case she was uncommonly lucky. She also put on her best dress, sprayed on some French perfume she had brought for such occasions, and brushed out her wavy black curls.

She learned from Lieutenant Castleman that the general would arrive on the eleven a.m. train, so Callie was on the platform when it pulled into the station. Military men poured out of the cars. Callie scoured the crowd for her important friend, and was so intent that she ran right into an officer exiting the train.

"Oh, excuse me. I'm so sorry," apologized Callie.

She beheld a handsome young officer, tall and blonde, a strong aquiline nose, and striking blue eyes that looked decidedly reckless to Callie. He stood there, as if about to reprimand her for being so absentminded as to run into him.

"Well, I hope so. I might have been injured." He said it with a slight grin while pretending to examine himself, and she let out a giggle. She also noticed the glint of a single silver bar on his shoulder.

"Captain?"

"Captain Wilde." He ended his little skit and regarded her with more interest. "Now, the last time I saw a girl so distracted as you, she was looking for her sweetheart in Grand Central Station."

Another woman might have blushed, but Callie blithely ignored the sassy remark. "I was actually looking for your boss, Captain. General Pershing is supposed to be on this train," she said, still searching the crowded platform, but a little less intently. "But, he doesn't seem to be here."

"No doubt because he isn't on the train, miss. The general is coming by auto. Now, just in case I have to lodge a complaint, may I have your name please?"

"Callie Masterson," she said, extending her hand with a warm smile and glad her prettifying efforts had not gone to waste. "I'm here as a correspondent for the *Houston Chronicle*."

Someone yelled at the far end of the tracks and the captain waved at them. "They are about to unload my airplanes, so I must attend to that. A pleasure meeting you, Callie. Next time, call me Casey."

He flashed his own affable smile and ran down to supervise the unloading of the Curtiss Jenny planes.

Callie stood there, wavering between her profession and her womanhood, caught by surprise and enjoying the feeling.

"Casey," she said softly. "I have a feeling I'm not done with you," as she watched him go off laughing with his fellow pilots.

She walked to Headquarters and was about to inquire about General Pershing, when an army truck pulled up, and the man himself got out, wearing goggles and covered with dust.

"Callie! My God, I was worried about you." He walked up to her and grabbed her shoulders with his big hands and shook her gently as if to insure himself that she was, indeed, in one piece.

"Yes sir, I guess I'm a veteran now."

He let out a hearty laugh and took her arm as they entered the building. "I'm afraid I don't have time to talk. We have an expedition to get under way. "

Callie forgot about being feminine and bit her lip. "General, I want to go with you."

"That's impossible, Callie."

"But sir-"

"Absolutely not! This is no place for a woman. No more discussion on this. I admire your courage, but be sensible. This will be armed combat. You won't have the safety of a fort around you."

The disappointment in her eyes softened him, a little.

"Now listen, I will direct the officer here to provide you with any news that becomes available from the front that will not compromise our security. That's the best I can do, my dear. You stay safe now."

He shook her hand and rushed up stairs. She remained there for a few moments, still biting her lip.

Yes sir, General, it's the sensible thing, but I don't like it. I don't care for the rejection, sir. I don't like being left behind. It's my story. If I wasn't a woman...

She walked back into town and the sorry condition of Columbus further depressed her.

If I have to stay behind here all summer I will go crazy.

She walked to the end of Main Street and entered the saloon. The small number of male customers all looked at her in surprise. She went up to the bar and sat on a stool. The bartender made an attempt at courtesy. "Afternoon ma'am."

"Might a lady get a glass of brandy in this establishment?"

"Right away, miss," he said, relieved that he had a task to busy himself with.

Callie glanced around at the men who were still staring at her and smiled, one might say, sarcastically.

She drank her brandy and felt better. Perhaps she had taken the General's rebuff too personally. Maybe there were other options. An idea was forming in her mind.

The day of departure arrived and 4,000 troops trotted through the streets of Columbus with General Pershing looking on and crossed the border into Palomas at noon. Included were the men of Custer's famous Seventh, the black Buffalo soldiers of the Tenth and the horse soldiers of the Eleventh. Their destination was Nueva Casas Grandes, where they would establish a base of operations, some 140 miles into Chihuahua.

Callie watched the "parade" with Lucille and Randy. She waved, but doubted if the general had noticed. Lieutenant Castleman took off his hat and gave her a big smile as he passed. A small army band played a march, a train blew its whistle, and the citizens cheered them on.

Callie turned to Lucille. "Lieutenant Castleman looks as if he were in a Fourth of July parade."

"God bless those boys. I pray they all come back."

"Amen, Lucille," said Callie, putting an arm around her.

"I wish I was up on one of them chargers!" exclaimed Randy.

44

The men and horses looked spiffy and ready for action. The young troopers displayed a self-assured cockiness atop their prancing animals; their eyes sparkled with genuine excitement to be in on the chase of the notorious Pancho Villa.

Even though it was still March, the temperature hit eighty degrees, a forewarning of what awaited them in the Mexican desert. They kicked up clouds of dust but the gusty winds scattered them to the heavenly blue above.

They would be 10,000 strong by time they reached their destination.

The next morning Callie wandered over to a field east of town where the airplanes were being assembled. Two were already completed and about to undergo test flights. She wore a pair of dungarees and a white blouse, her hair hanging loose and windblown.

All the pilots wore the same tan uniform, high leather boots, and cap and dust goggles, but Casey sported a white scarf flowing from his neck in the brisk wind.

She stopped for a moment and observed him. He didn't so much stand, as take an attitude, a posture of expectation, as if those flimsy flying contraptions were wild stallions to be tamed. He put both hands on his hips, leaned a little and shook his head.

"He acts like a cowboy," she chuckled.

She approached.

"Good morning Casey," smiling her brightest smile.

He whirled around at the sound of her voice and returned the smile. "Callie Masterson, reporter and fearless heroine of Columbus. We've heard all about you." He elbowed his pal and chuckled.

"And just what have you heard?"

"That you narrowly escaped Villa's bandits, *and* that you shot one of them dead and saved a boy's life. I don't know what to think about you? Maybe we should bring you along, how about it, fellas?"

"That's an interesting offer," said Callie. "Can you *really* fly this machine? Why look, it's made of canvas." She fingered the wing cautiously, as if it were some kind of exotic animal.

"Yep, they have to be light to get airborne. We were just going to test one now. Captain Foulois will be flying as observer. You just watch us, Callie. Oh, and get my name right for the paper-that's Wilde, with an 'e'," he said, with the sly grin.

She stepped back as they climbed on the wing and slipped into their respective cockpits.

Casey pulled his goggles over his eyes and turned to Callie. "You better get back a little farther. It's gonna kick up a whole lot of dust."

Callie moved backwards a few yards.

A mechanic gave the prop a vigorous turn and the Curtiss started with a loud backfire and then roared to life as the propeller spun into a silvery blur. The plane moved quickly away, accelerating across the field and lifting off into the cloudless New Mexico sky. Casey immediately banked off to the south into Mexico and came back over the airfield, only a few hundred feet above them.

Callie shivered with excitement at the miraculous flying machine. "Incredible! How is it possible?" she exclaimed, shielding her eyes from the sun.

After some maneuvering and acrobatics the plane landed in a cloud of yellow dust.

Casey hopped down and swaggered over to Callie. He took off the goggles and spit. "Well, how'd it look from down here?"

"It looked absolutely wonderful. I want to fly!"

"What? Are you kidding me? Have you ever been up in an airplane?"

Callie ran over to the machine and brushed her hand over the wing, this time with obvious relish. "I've never even seen one fly, until today. But it's remarkable just how easily it floats off the ground, something this heavy. It must feel glorious to be up there, Casey."

"Yeah, it's pretty darn glorious, all right."

"Well?"

"You're not the least bit scared?"

"Yes, but I don't care. How can I write about it, if I don't try it?"

He looked around. His buddy had already left. "This is against every rule in the book, but who's gonna see us? Come on, my brave little reporter."

He slipped an aviator's jacket on Callie, then cap and goggles. He stepped back, and laughed.

Callie gave him a push. "Oh, all right, don't make fun of me."

46

"Well, it's not a perfect fit, but it'll do."

He helped her up on the wing and she sat in the cockpit, with the look of a kid on Christmas morning.

"Now don't touch *anything,* except these hand holds," he said emphatically, as he strapped her in.

"Yes sir, Captain."

"If you get sick-"

"I will *not* get sick."

Casey nodded and smiled. "Right. Well, here we go."

A mechanic gave the propeller a turn and it fired up in a flash. Casey taxied it forward. Callie held on with both hands as they picked up speed. She had ridden in a convertible at 40 mph once, but they were already past that when the plane lifted off and she let out a scream that Casey heard over the engine noise, as she absorbed the thrill of leaving *terra firma* and being supported entirely by air for the very first time.

The plane rose unsteadily, buffeted by the wind. Callie felt cut loose from the earth and everything that happened from second to second was brand new. She floated and rolled and pitched right along with the airplane, too astounded to be scared.

They flew over Tres Hermanas, across an empty wilderness that went on forever. He banked to the right and pointed down. Callie leaned over and watched a herd of wild mustangs tear across the land.

Suddenly, there was another, larger town below, Deming, with its tiny buildings and network of roads. To Callie it looked utterly insignificant from the air, surrounded as it was by the empty sprawl of the Chihuahuan desert.

Casey pulled back on the throttle. The Jenny responded by accelerating up at a sharp angle and pushed Callie against her seat, as it shot up into the firmament.

She lost her breath, and her eyes widened with fear and exhilaration.

Darn you Captain Wilde! You are a devil, but, oh, I love this, I do love this.

The air rapidly grew colder, and she began to shiver, but the plane gently slanted back down, reversing direction back toward Columbus.

She marveled at the endless forms and designs of the landscape,

47

the delicate tracery of the drainage patterns of creeks and arroyos, and for the first time really appreciated the strange beauty of the desert landscape.

As they approached Columbus, Callie sat back, loosened her grip and relaxed. At that moment, Casey banked sharply and the plane tipped almost ninety degrees. The seat belt held her firm, but she let out a protracted scream anyway. As much as she was terrified, she was that excited.

Strong wind gusts convulsed the little plane as he struggled to set it down in the blowing dust. A moderate bump was all Callie felt as they touched down and came rolling to a stop.

Casey killed the engine. Callie basked in the relative silence of the wind and her astonishment. She gazed up at the sky she had just come out of. Casey hopped out and stood by her, on the wing.

"You look drunk," he said.

Callie let out a sigh. "You made a new woman out of me, Captain."

"Well, I'm glad it was me and not someone else, Miss Masterson."

"So, is this how you impress the girls?"

"Seems to have worked. Why don't you take these off?" He gently slipped the goggles over her head.

"Oh, I forgot I was wearing them," she said, still a little giddy. "Isn't that funny?" She raised herself and climbed out, shakily.

"Steady now," cautioned Casey.

"Oh, I'm fine," she said, and nearly slipped off the wing.

"Whoa!"Casey caught her in his arms, and seeing something inviting in her eyes, held her for a moment, but she shied away.

"Trying to take advantage of a girl in a vulnerable state, Captain?"

"Just trying to improve morale, miss."

"Mine or yours?"

They remained there, motionless, in the dusty wind, equally smitten.

Filming the action

Chapter 6

The private stood by the plane. He cleared his throat. They both turned and looked down at him.

"Sir, an important message from General Pershing arrived. The Squadron is ordered to report to the base at Casa Grandes for immediate duty."

Casey's eyes brightened. "Thanks, Private."

"And so it begins," said Casey, jumping off the wing. He helped Callie off. "I better get back to Camp. Why don't you walk there with me?"

Callie said nothing as they left the airfield. After they had gone a little way she stopped. "Casey, isn't there a way I could go with you?"

"You are a crazy girl. There's a good chance we'd crash, get shot, court martialed, or a combination of all three. What do you think of those odds, Miss Aviator?"

Callie frowned. "Don't say things like that."

"Besides, there are no seats available. Oh I know-we'll just tell Captain Foulois to walk." He smiled and shook his head.

"Darn it all. There has to be a way."

They continued walking, and Callie conjured up possible schemes. They reached the gate, and Casey took her hand. "Listen, I have a lot to do, but we should have some time later on, before the squadron takes off."

"You're thinking about all those pretty senoritas you can flirt with down in Mexico. Isn't that so, Captain?"

He couldn't tell whether she was joking or serious. "Are you going to meet with me or not?"

"When?"

"Around three, at Headquarters."

"Okay."

Callie crossed the tracks and walked back through town. The flight had transformed her in some unknown way. She was always gutsy, but now she was ready to play fast and loose with the rules to get where she needed to be.

As she passed the saloon she noticed a Ford convertible, with

BIOGRAPH MOTION PICTURE COMPANY printed on the side. She stopped and stared at the words, then rushed into the saloon.

The same bartender was there and regarded her nervously. Two men at the bar, in business attire, obvious newcomers, were having an animated conversation.

She went straight up to them.

They ceased talking as she approached. "Gentlemen, welcome to Columbus, New Mexico," she said, in her most gracious voice.

They looked at her quizzically.

"Pardon me for interrupting, but I take it that you will be heading south to film the action down in Mexico, with that notorious PanchoVilla."

They looked at each other.

"That's correct, miss. And who might you be?"

"Callie Masterson, correspondent for the *Houston Chronicle*," she answered, shaking their hands.

"I'm Chester Moon and this is Lazlo, my cameraman. Will you join us? We can all sit at this table."

He led her over to a corner table and they all sat down. "What's your pleasure, Miss Masterson?"

"I'll have a brandy, and call me Callie, please."

Chester was a dapper fellow, with a thin mustache and receding hairline. Callie sized him up as a ladies man right away. Lazlo, who remained silent, was younger, short and wiry, with a worried, Slavic-looking face and in need of a haircut.

"Callie, I have feeling that you are here with a proposal." He said this with a knowing smile.

Callie sipped the brandy. "How intuitive of you, Chester. I'll come right to the point. You see, my fiancée, Captain Casey Wilde, is set to fly off soon to rendezvous with General Pershing on the Punitive Expedition-"

"In pursuit of Pancho Villa!"

"Exactly."

"Did you say fly?"

"I most certainly did. Namely, the First Aero Squadron."

"And where will he be flying to?"

"I believe it's Nuevo Casa Grandes, about 150 miles into Mexico.

And seeing as there are no seats left on the plane, I will need some transportation to get down there."

Chester and Lazlo looked at each other, then back at Callie. Chester's eyebrows were frozen in the raised position.

"Now Callie, isn't that somewhat dangerous territory for a woman?"

"I'm a reporter sir, first and foremost. I go where the story takes me. I have already survived Mr. Villa's attack on this town, and I have no doubt I will continue to survive. I can shoot a gun and ride a horse, so do not fret about me."

"You were here...during the attack?"

Callie nodded, solemnly. She pointed to burns on her neck and arm.

Chester took a drink and rubbed his chin. "Well now, we are on a rather tight schedule, and have budgetary constraints, as you can imagine."

Callie pulled a fifty dollar bill out of her blouse and slapped it on the table. Lazlo jumped.

"I am a friend of General Pershing, Chester. He runs the whole show. I can open doors for you. And I speak tolerable Spanish. I'll pay my own way and help you boys out in the bargain. Well? What do you say? Que dice?"

Chester looked at Lazlo. They both looked at the fifty dollars. Lazlo went to grab it and Chester slapped his hand.

"I was going to see if it was legitimate," Lazlo said in his thick accent, looking slightly offended.

"Hold on now," said Chester. "How long do figure on riding with us? And what about your fiancée? How's he going to take this little arrangement?"

"Just get me down to Casas Grandes. And don't worry about the Captain. He'll think it's just swell."

Chester put up a little more resistance, but Callie won him over, and they shook hands on the deal.

She ran all the way back to Lucille's place.

"Lucille! Are you here?" Callie shouted, out of breath, running into the bedroom to pack some things for a journey of undetermined duration. She removed her dusty clothes and sponged herself off, for her next bath might be many days off.

She brushed her long black hair and smiled at herself in the mirror.

Callie Masterson, this is the most outlandish thing you have ever done. But I can't stop now, can I? Chester and Lazlo are sweet. Always wanted to see a how a movie camera works. Casey will be so surprised. I hope he won't be angry. Silly girl, he's in love with you.

She heard the front door open. "I'm in here, Lucille."

"Well, hello, Callie. Have you had lunch yet?" She noticed the packed suitcase. "Are you leaving us, dear?"

Callie put her brush down and went over to her friend. "I am, Lucille, at least for a while. Casey, Captain Wilde, has received orders to fly down to join the troops, and I'm going to be right behind him. Some nice gentlemen from a movie company have agreed to provide me with transportation. Oh, Lucille, don't look so upset."

"Well, I don't like the sound of that. How well do you know these men?"

"I'm a good judge of character, Lucille, especially men. We had a very nice talk just now, in the saloon."

"Oh my Lord."

Callie took her hand. "Now don't fret about me, all right? I'm a big girl. Besides, if anything does happen, Casey and General Pershing will be there. I need to go and tell Casey my plans. And the movie fellas want to leave soon."

"I can see nothing I say will change your mind," Lucille said resignedly, "but let me at least fix you a lunch to take."

Callie wrote notes about her first airplane flight while Lucille prepared the food. She grabbed the suitcase and walked into the kitchen.

Lucille was putting a sandwich and some fruit into a small bag. Callie took the bag and embraced her.

"Thank you for everything you have done for me, Lucille. My own mother could not have treated me with more kindness. You are a wonderful friend."

"I know," she murmured. "I will miss you, Callie. And so will Randy. I will be forever grateful to you for saving my only son's life. May Jesus watch over you."

They stood facing each other, tears streaming, these two accidental friends, who had become so close, so fast.

"Say goodbye to Randy for me. Give him a kiss. And Lucille, I *will* be back. You haven't seen the last of me."

Callie kissed her on the cheek and hurried out, waving without looking back, running toward town.

She took a shortcut to avoid the burned rubble downtown. As she reached the train station, one of the Curtiss Jennies flew right above her, toward Mexico. Her heart jumped, and she ran faster. The station clock said three.

She caught sight of Casey, leaning against a fence, a cigarette in his hand. Callie slowed down immediately and walked casually up to the steps.

"You catching a train?" he asked, eying her suitcase.

Callie put her suitcase down and sat down next to him. She took his cigarette out of his mouth and had a drag.

"You're just full of surprises, aren't you?" he said.

She put the cigarette back in his mouth. "I have one more for you. I'm going down to Casa Grandes too. With a movie company," she said matter-of-factly.

Casey did a little double take. "Movie company?"

"Yes, and here they come now. Be nice to them."

He peered at the convertible heading toward them. "That's no movie company. It's just two guys in a convertible."

"Hush." She waved at the two men. "Hi there, boys!"

The car pulled up and Chester got out, smiling his best PR smile. Lazlo remained in the car.

"Captain. Chester Moon here," he said, extending his hand. "Director for the Biograph Motion Picture Company.

Casey shook hands, reluctantly. His lips tightened around the cigarette, which burned fiercely.

"That's Lazlo, in the car," said Callie. "He's the cameraman. Look, Casey-they took out the back seat and put a piece of plywood down for the camera platform. Isn't that clever?"

Casey walked over, casting a suspicious look at Lazlo, who was eating peanuts from a bag and following Casey's moves like a cat watching a dog.

"What do you fellas plan on photographing?"

"Whatever we can find, hopefully a battle or two. The public is hungry for newsreels on the Revolution, and now this Pancho Villa expedition has caused more commotion."

Casey walked to the other side and inspected the camera equipment. "And how does Callie fit in with all this?"

Chester looked at Callie.

"Why, being that we're both covering the Revolution," she explained, "we can help each other. They get me down there and then I-"

"Pay them?" said Casey, sarcastically.

"Yes, my fair share, but I can speak Spanish, and that will come in handy. And I'll introduce them to General Pershing."

Chester nodded in agreement, still smiling. Lazlo ate his peanuts, his thick eyebrows furrowed in a frown.

"General Pershing? Callie, he's got an army to command. Do you think he's going to talk to a couple of-"

"Casey, we'll work this out when we get there. Now I know you have to leave, so may we have a few moments alone?"

She took his hand and led him away. He stared at Lazlo as they left. Lazlo stared back. Callie winked at Chester.

They walked to the railroad station and sat on bench.

"I don't like the look of those two," said Casey. "How do you know you can trust them? Especially that little guy in the car. Is he a Bolshevik?"

"Casey, we have a business arrangement, that's all. And now I'll have access to maybe the biggest story of my life. It's only a hundred and fifty miles. I thought you would be happy."

Casey took his hat off and ran his hand through his short blond hair. "Well, I guess I am, but you sort of sprung on it me, Callie. Of course, it's none of my business who you travel with."

"Don't worry about me," she said. "But please be careful in that flying machine of yours."

"Okay."

"Chester wants to leave now, so that we can get there before nightfall."

"Good idea. I'm gonna try that too." They were both silent for a moment, and then walked back. Casey watched them drive off, toward the Mexican border, and then he headed toward the airfield.

First Squadron flying liaison with the US cavalry in Mexico on punitive expedition in pursuit of Villa

Chapter 7

Eight Curtiss Jennies, the entire Air Force of the United States in the Spring of 1916, took off just after five p.m. and headed southwest in a loose formation. The planes had no lights, maps or navigation equipment, but the pilots made use of the moon, the North Star and the lay of the land.

Soon they were forced to land. Casey and Foulois, Carberry and Bowen put down at Ascencion. The others became separated by darkness and landed elsewhere.

Six planes finally showed up at Casas Grandes the next day.

Casey and the others made their best guess at where they should land, and the graded dirt road seemed the best choice. Once down, he searched for General Pershing.

It was a strange and chaotic gathering-thousands of soldiers, horses, mules, wagons, and a small contingent of trucks and cars, all enveloped in a moving haze of dust. The Sierra Madre foothills were just to the south, but the immediate country was rugged enough. It was exceedingly arid and noticeably hotter than New Mexico.

Casey checked in with Pershing's aide, a cocky young first lieutenant by the name of George S. Patton. He learned that one plane had returned to Columbus with engine trouble, and the other was missing.

He went back to his plane and found the ground crew refueling it. Casey walked around the flimsy machine. It was literally made of spruce and linen, held together by wire and bolts, and powered by a small ninety horsepower engine. The pilots had misgivings about how the Jennies would hold up to the rigors of the high altitude flying in the mountains.

Someone grabbed his shoulders from behind. Tired and hungry, he wasn't in a playful mood, and turned to confront the jokester.

"Glad to see me?" said Callie, with a childlike smile. She wore riding pants, a blue blouse and a red bandana around her neck. Her hair was partly pinned up, and partly falling across her face from the gusty winds. Her big eyes and pursed lips gave her an innocent look.

"I was expecting you were gonna be kidnapped, and we'd have to pay a ransom, but you made it through. Where are the movie boys?"

"Oh, they're busy as bees, going around filming the troopers and such. I was taking a nap in the mess tent, just to get out of this heat and dust."

"Now what?"

"Well, I had a talk with General Pershing, and he was rather angry with me. So, I told him that I could travel with Chester and Lazlo, but he didn't like that idea at all, said it would be unsafe, not to mention improper." A coy smile came and went. "So, he said I could ride with the other correspondents in his group of cars, if I didn't make any trouble."

Casey let out a long sigh. "I swear, you are the wiliest woman I have ever come across. When do you think he's going to figure out that he's been hoodwinked?"

"What a thing to say, Casey Wilde. You offend me, sir." She put her hand over her heart.

"Glad to hear it," he said, trying to hide a smile. "You're getting a little out of control."

"Better get used to it." She knocked the hat off his head.

"Now you're in trouble." He grabbed her by the waist and pulled her to him, waiting for a reaction. There was that look in her eyes again, but she twisted away and headed toward the tents.

"I may just report you to General Pershing, soldier" she said prancing off.

"Better get used to it," he yelled back.

That night General Pershing spread out his map on a makeshift table beside a lantern. A small group sat around a blazing campfire, as the heat of the desert dissipated rapidly into the clear atmosphere. The wind had died and the dust settled.

Callie sat next to Rolley Garble of the *New York Times* and Floyd Terrazzo of the *Chicago Tribune*. She watched the fire flicker and pop, taking notes as General Pershing explained his strategy.

"We'll be in Colonias Dublan tomorrow. We believe that Villa is near Guererro, a hundred and fifty miles to the south. Captains Wilde and Foulois will undertake a reconnaissance flight at dawn and look for any sign of the bandits. Majors Tompkins and Howze, and Colonel

Allen, are already riding south in three different columns."

Callie watched the General go over the flight details with Casey. She knew they wouldn't be seeing much of each other on the expedition, but she was dying to go up in the airplane again.

Two White Mountain Apache scouts were also in the circle-Corporals Big Sharley and B-25, veterans of the Apache campaign with General Pershing in New Mexico Territory, some thirty years before.

They wore slightly tattered US Army uniforms, but whatever military bearing they displayed was canceled out by their brooding glare, dark weathered skin, and long black hair, around which they wore white headbands.

B-25 seemed interested in Callie, but remained taciturn. His friend spoke instead. "He likes you. He thinks you pretty."

"Well, tell him thank you."

Big Sharley continued. "He wonders why you out here all alone with the soldiers. Me too."

These remarks were drawing snickers from the two male reporters. Callie put her pencil down. "I work for a newspaper, like these men. I write about what the soldiers and Pancho Villa are doing, so that people back home will know what is going on."

"And maybe write about us too?"

"Of course."

"I'm Big Sharley. He's B-25. He's lookin' for a wife."

"Tell him I'm married."

Big Sharley whispered the news to his friend, who nodded.

"Why is he called B-25?"

"Nobody knows." They both got up and left. Callie wrote some notes.

"Now I heard you were a single gal," said Terrazzo, of the Tribune.

"I thought it would make things less complicated if they thought I was married."

"Smart move, miss. These Apaches are still half savage. But I'll look out for you."

"Thank you, sir, but I can look out for myself. And I don't agree with that opinion. What white men call savage is really the native people's keen awareness of their environment, unlike white folks, who have become stiff and clumsy in the wilderness. These Apaches see things we can't. Why do you suppose the Army hires them as scouts? We'd be lost without them."

"But, Miss, these Indians have no conception of goals or purpose-they live in the moment."

"And isn't that wonderful? I believe that the Apache, the Comanche, and a few other tribes who haven't been ruined by our civilizing efforts, still regard the world as their ancestors did-the past, present and future are all the same." She grabbed a stick and drew a circle in the sand. "Circular, not linear. The way a child sees things, before they too are civilized."

The men looked at her like she was mad. Floyd shook his head. "That's a foolish philosophy, young lady."

"But it's mine, sir, and I'll keep it."

Callie was overcome by fatigue and excused herself. The General had some men set up a tent for her, with extra blankets. She slept with the flap open, so she could see the stars, and fell asleep in seconds.

They moved out just as the sun came up. Callie rode in the back of a sputtering Model T Ford that trailed Pershing's contingent of four Dodges. They were followed by supply trucks, wagons and pack mules, and thousands of troops.

She observed the soldiers as they passed. Each one carried a Springfield rifle, an automatic pistol, and ninety rounds of ammunition. The horsemen also possessed sabers.

The sun ascended into the sky and the heat intensified as the wind began to blow. The infantry walked in a continual cloud of dust behind the horse soldiers. They soaked their bandanas in water and wore them across their face. Callie copied them.

A few lucky soldiers had their own sand goggles. The ones on horseback kept their eyes shut, but most of them were nearly blind by the afternoon.

The motorcade came to a halt at the Santa Maria River. Even though it was nearly dry, the soft bottom was like quicksand. Engineers went to work constructing a wooden track for the vehicles.

Callie stretched her legs and walked a bit. She heard a horn toot behind her. It was Chester and Lazlo.

"Good day to you Callie," said Chester as he came to a stop.

"Well, hello boys. Where are you off to?"

"We hear that one of the squadrons has located a small band of *Villistas* not far from here, near the village of Santa Cruz. We can't miss a chance like that."

Callie was instantly energized. "Please wait while I get my things." She ran off before Chester could protest, grabbed her gear out of the Ford and hurried back.

"It may be a little risky down there, Callie," warned Chester.

"Good!" she answered, jumping into the back and throwing down a blanket on the camera platform. "All right gentlemen, I'm ready to go."

Chester started the engine. Lazlo turned around and looked at her. "You remind me of the women in Hungary-they're a little crazy, like you." He smiled broadly and offered her some peanuts.

"Why thank you, Lazlo."

They approached a rise and stopped. Down in the valley below shots could be heard. Chester stood up and scanned the view with binoculars. "I see our boys, all right. It looks like they are on the chase. There's too much dust to see up ahead, but I'll wager the quarry is close at hand. Lazlo, get the camera ready."

Callie watched as Lazlo went to work. He lifted the camera out of a black case lined with red velvet as if it were a baby. It was a technological marvel, with a square black body and a turret of three cylindrical lenses of shiny silver and gold chrome-the Bell and Howell 2709 35mm motion picture camera.

Lazlo set up a large wooden tripod, which he secured to the car frame with brackets, and several sandbags for stability. He then attached two large circular film magazines to the camera and affixed it to the tripod.

Callie was fascinated by the exquisite craftsmanship of the thing.

"Lazlo, this is so beautiful. I've never seen anything quite like it before."

Lazlo stroked it with pride, as if it were a racehorse. "This is the very same camera that Mr. Chaplin uses. But I am very concerned about all this dust." He covered it with a blanket and looked back at Chester. "Okay, camera is ready."

"Hold on kids. Here we go."

They caught up with the galloping troops, but stayed back because of the billowing dust. Then the horses turned off to the right and they got a clearer view. The bandits were firing from some low hills.

Callie was writing nonstop.

Near village of Santa Cruz. Troops pursuing Villistas hidden in some hills. About 200 of our mounted soldiers. Hot, with blowing dust. Brown, desiccated land. Pop of rifle fire. Our boys are gathering. Some have dismounted and are returning fire. The energy in the air is electric. This is the real thing!

Chester stopped the car and jumped in the back. Callie had to stand up to make room.

"Okay, Lazlo. Get a wide shot of the scene. And then close up on the horsemen. Get one of them rearing up."

Lazlo cranked with his left hand and swiveled the tripod with his right, as he panned the battle scene. Suddenly, the cavalry charged toward the hills, pistols firing.

Chester jumped back into the front and moved the car down the road a few hundred yards, parallel to the action. The bandits broke for their horses and took off across the plain.

"Get footage of the bandits Lazlo!" Chester yelled as he increased speed. Callie was hugging the tripod to keep it steady.

The bandits split into separate groups that went in opposite directions.

"Uh-oh," said Callie. "They're coming our way, Chester."

Chester kept driving.

"Chester!" she yelled.

"Don't worry," he shouted. "They'll see our camera. They won't bother us."

Callie quickly pulled her Colt out of the suitcase and loaded it.

The bandits, about ten of them, were heading for the road at an angle that would cross directly in front of them. The Army troops were in hot pursuit, firing intermittently.

Lazlo was cranking the Bell and Howell for all he was worth. Chester was hunched over the wheel like a race car driver.

Callie watched them approach, like an ominous storm growing bigger by the second. One of the bandits in front had his pistol drawn and began firing. Bullets whizzed over their heads.

Chester swerved in surprise. Callie bit her lip, took careful aim, and fired off a quick shot, knocking the bandit backwards off his mount. The cavalry thundered by soon after.

The car slowed to a stop. The soldiers and bandits disappeared over a rise. Hot dust and silence settled over the car and its occupants. Chester fell limp against the seat. Lazlo finally pulled his face away from the camera. "I heard a shot in the car," he said.

Callie shyly held up her gun and shrugged.

"You?" said Lazlo. "I saw someone fall. It was a fine shot." He slowly collapsed into a crouch. "Oh my, it's very hot, isn't it?" he said, with a dry swallow.

Chester turned around. "Miss Masterson, I am indebted to you for such quick thinking. You may have saved our lives. Funny, they've never shot at us before." He furrowed his eyebrows into a hurt expression.

Callie wiped the sweat from her forehead. "I'd love to take credit, but I think our troops being right on their tail had a lot to do with it."

Lazlo sat down and took a drink of whiskey out of a flask. He offered it to Callie. "Thanks, Lazlo." She took a swallow, grimaced and coughed. "Whoo! My goodness, I think that did the trick." She handed it to Chester, who was staring at her gun.

"Where did you learn to shoot like that?"

Callie arched her back and put out her arms to stretch. "Oh, back in Comanche Springs, my Daddy taught me how to hunt before I was ten years old. I didn't really ever enjoy the hunting part, but I've always liked the feel of a gun in my hand. Isn't that the strangest thing?"

Chester took another swig of whiskey. They all just sat there, sweating, grit between their teeth, contemplating the silence of the primeval landscape. The wind rose up and whined like a mournful song.

Chester looked up. "Someone's riding this way."

Callie grabbed her gun. Lazlo took his camera and put it in the case.

"It's okay," said Chester, peering through binoculars. "It's just a horse."

The rider-less pony trotted right up to the car, confused, and moved a little distance away.

Callie got out and approached the uneasy animal "He must have belonged to that fellow who shot at us. Hi there, sweetie. Are you an orphan now?"

The horse backed away, unused to hearing English.

She held out her hand. "Yo soy tu amigo." He twitched his ears at the sound of his own language. He let her come closer, and she stroked his head

"He might not be used to women," said Lazlo.

"Well then, I'll just do this real slow." Pobrecito. Está   bien. Vamos a ir a buscar algo de comida"

She took the reins and moved to his left side, still stroking him, talking softly, then put her foot in the stirrup, and eased herself into the saddle.

"Well done, Callie," said Chester.

"I told him that we're going to get him some food."

"That's one of Villa's for sure," said Chester. "He looks half-starved. You just made a friend."

"I'm going to ride this little guy back to the camp."

Chester started the car. "We'll follow you, Callie. I'm sure not about to let you ride alone out here."

Callie checked the saddle-an empty leather scabbard and a faded blanket tied on the back.

The horse was a tough little paint, with a solid black chest and face, except for a white stripe that ran from forehead to nose. His hindquarters were white and his tail a solid black. He was in rough shape, had been ridden hard, but the bright eyes told her that he was an intelligent animal.

"Let's go get you some grain and water, boy. C'mon!" The horse broke into an easy trot. Callie found herself a horse and was jubilant to be living some unspoken fantasy from her childhood. Even the horse perked up with this strange new rider on his back.

Chester drove slowly behind, while Lazlo pulled out a harmonica and began to play Hungarian folk songs.

Callie rode a little way ahead through the quiet desert and thought about everything that had already happened to her since getting off that train in Columbus, all by pure chance. Out here, life was intensified-the heat, the sun and the wind, the poverty and cruelty, all of it took its toll on a person, but it also made her tougher. She had felt a force building inside of her since Villa's night attack, and she didn't want to lose it. That sense of physical self-reliance she had as a kid, but somehow had lost in the city, had come back to her, and she felt like she could take on anything and get through it.

And riding this Mexican pony in the middle of the Chihuahuan desert and the Mexican Revolution, was the best place she could possibly be.

The camp was just ahead and she urged the horse into a gallop to show off her new prize, Indian style. She sprinted down the road, leaning into the wind and letting out a whoop, and came to a dusty halt in front of General Pershing's Dodge.

He was studying a map with his aide. "Callie, what are you doing on that horse?"

Callie was grinning like a ten-year-old. "I adopted one of Villa's ponies, sir. He practically begged me to."

Pershing came closer to inspect the bedraggled horse and its Mexican saddle. "Well, I'll be damned," he said under his breath.

Just then, Chester and Lazlo drove up. "General. We got some amazing footage of that last battle, but one of the bandidos decided to fire at us. Callie returned fire and saved the day. Ain't that something?"

Pershing gave her a quizzical look, took off his hat, and shook his head. "Callie, maybe you should put a uniform on. We could use a few more soldiers like you."

"No thanks, General. I'll stick to reporting. Excuse me, but I better go and take care of my horse, sir." She wheeled the animal around and rode off.

"Reporting? So that's what you call it."

After the pony was fed and watered Callie borrowed a brush from a soldier and gave her new horse a good grooming. She then led it out to graze with the other horses.

One of the planes was about to leave for Columbus to deliver various messages, including dispatches from the correspondents, so Callie prepared her notes and enclosed them in an envelope addressed to the Chronicle, and also some written dispatches to be sent by telegraph to Mr. Shaughnessy.

She wondered how Casey's flight had gone, but there was no way to know.

As sunset approached, the rich warm light, diffused by dust, transformed the barren land into a soft and surreal landscape of saturated gold. She had found an isolated hill and was reading Shakespeare's Sonnet sixty-five.

She put down the book. "'That in black ink my love may still shine bright.' Perhaps some young woman in the next century will read the words I write about this adventure, and be inspired to go on one of her own. It's a fine thought, that our words can carry our feelings long after we are dead and gone." She looked at the page. "But, William, you express it so much better than I."

A barely audible, high-pitched drone distracted her. She put down the book and tried to locate the direction of the sound. Then she saw a tiny glint in the southern sky.

She scampered down the hillside and arrived at the airfield, where she waited. The plane's engine grew louder as it approached. Callie was smitten with the dashing Captain Wilde, but the growing inevitability of America's entrance into the European conflict weighed heavy upon her. Would he disappear before she ever got to really know him?

The plane circled low and came down, tilting this way and that, touching the ground gently, with hardly a sound at all. She saw the white scarf blowing in the cockpit and ran up to the plane.

Captain Foulois jumped down first. "Hi there, Callie," he said wearily. "Rough day." He walked off before she could respond.

Casey slid down off the wing and removed his cap and gloves. He was a few shades darker from sunburn and dust. Callie gave him a hug. He seemed too tired to respond.

"So, how are you, Captain?"

"Pretty darn worn out, miss."

"What did Captain Foulois mean by a rough day?"

"These planes aren't working out too well. They're too light for the altitude. We got caught in some whirlwinds that I thought were gonna tear the plane apart. It was pretty close, I want to tell you."

They began to walk back to the tents as the mechanic checked the plane's condition.

"Is it the engine, Casey?"

"Heck yeah. Those little ninety horsepower jobs can't hardly get above eight thousand feet, and Cumbre Pass over yonder is above nine thousand." He sounded frustrated and looked exhausted.

"Well, should I write about that? Would that help get something done? It sounds very dangerous."

"I don't know, maybe. I have to put in a request for better machines."He looked at her, put his arm around her shoulder and smiled. "How was your day?"

"Oh, just another day on the trail."

"You look like you're hiding something."

"I am. Casey, I got my very own horse- a stray from Villa's gang. A pretty little pinto. He's kind of thin, but he's got spirit."

"Like you."

She put her arm around his waist and they kept walking, in silence.

They both ended up at General Pershing's campfire again that night. He shared some of his special recipe, called slum beef jerky, with potatoes and carrots. While they ate, some Mexican women in black *rebozos* moved silently among them, selling warm fragrant tortillas wrapped in cloth, and *biscochitos*, anise flavored cookies.

Callie handed them some coins. "Muchas gracias, señoras. Donde vives?"

They hesitated at being asked where they live, for they feared the possibility of reprisal from Villa's men if it were known they had helped the gringos in any way.

"Santa Cruz," one of them answered, softly. Her older companion pulled her away, and they disappeared into the night.

"Some of them are nervous about coming here," said Pershing, "but this warfare has so devastated their villages that they will risk it to get some hard cash."

After they finished the main course Callie gave out some of the cookies. "They're so soft and warm, they melt in your mouth. She must have just made them. I remember a Mexican lady back home used to make them at Christmas. I haven't had one since."

"These are mighty good," said Casey. "They taste like licorice."

"It's the anise, my dear" explained Callie, giving his arm a squeeze.

Pershing revealed that Villa was said to be in Guerrero, a day's ride south. "Colonel Dodd's regiment is making a beeline for the town and hopes to corner him. Captains Wilde and Foulois will attempt to make contact and determine whether reinforcements are needed." He lit up a pipe and took a few puffs. "We're getting close."

Long days in the saddle on Villa's trail

Chapter 8

Callie wrapped herself in a green army blanket, grabbed a bag of biscochitos and walked to the airfield in the tenuous dawn light. It was just below freezing and the planes shone with a coating of sugary frost. She saw Casey and the mechanic preparing the Jenny for take-off.

"Take these cookies for Colonel Dodd and his men," she said. "I have a feeling they could use a little sugar," she teased.

He busied himself with inspecting the Jenny's landing gear and engine. Callie followed him around the plane, shivering. They crouched together beside the big tires, Casey feeling the rubber for any flaws. Callie watched him, all caught up in his military world. "How in the world do you stay warm up there?"

Casey looked up with an impish grin. "I think about all my old girl friends."

She gave him a shove and he fell back on his behind, laughing. "You're awful serious in the morning," he said.

She stood up, arms folded, looking down at him. "Darn it, Casey. I worry about you up there. General Pershing told me one of the pilots crash-landed yesterday."

"Oh yeah, that was Darque. He broke his nose and had to walk quite a ways, but he's okay."

"These planes aren't safe at all, are they?"

He dusted himself off and came close to her. "They're just like a woman. Gotta treat 'em with kid gloves."

"I could use some of that too. Don't be so mean."

He took both of his gloved hands and gently enclosed her face with them. "There. Is that what you want, miss?" She slowly put her hands over his. "Yes, Captain, that's what I want." They stood staring at each other, forgetting where they were for the moment, and the chaos that lurked in the hills and arroyos.

The sun edged over the horizon and brand new rays of light, sharp as glass, cut through the still morning air, which was suddenly jarred as the plane next to them fired up with a harsh whine.

Callie said something, but she saw that he didn't hear. He was in the cockpit and moving away from her in mere seconds, and the planes became airborne and were gone. "Vaya con dios," she whispered under her breath.

She stared at the sky for a few moments, and then walked away.

She went to check on her little Mexican pony, her *bandido*, she called him. He had already gained some weight and she was anxious to ride him, but there was work to do. Callie needed some serious distraction to keep her from fretting about Casey. She proposed to Chester and Lazlo that if they drove at a steady pace they might catch up with Colonel Dodd near Guerrero. Villa would then be very close. "There's potential for some great footage and an exciting piece for the paper."

They left unnoticed in the Ford, as the huge camp was still getting itself together and preparing to move out, men, animals and machines merging into a lumbering dinosaur of an expedition.

They drove into the foothills of the Sierra Madre and the air grew cooler, the vegetation more lush. Callie went in and out of sleep, curled up on some blankets on the plywood camera platform. She happened to open her eyes and gazed up at five hundred-foot walls of golden sandstone in some nameless canyon. As the walls closed in she noticed petroglyphs of geometric figures and humped-back flute players from some long-ago tribe. She asked Chester to stop so she might have a closer look. One section ran along the canyon wall for nearly a hundred yards, often filled with reddish hand prints that seemed to say, "Look, I was here once, alive, just like you."

They decided to take advantage of the deep shade of some big cottonwoods to enjoy a break from the tiring drive. Lunch consisted of beef jerky and the rest of the cookies. Callie lay on the sand, looking up through the massive branches that broke up the sky into blue slivers and sighed with the wind. Canyon wrens serenaded them with descending trills that echoed off the stone walls. It was a little paradise they had stumbled into. But Chester was worried about lingering too long and they soon left. She soon nodded off into a dream:

I love it up here, Casey. I love flying and floating in the stars. And tonight there's no engine noise, just soft wind and silence, and your blue, blue eyes. If I'm up here with you, I know you're safe. Hold my

71

hand. So silent, so nice...

"Wake up, Callie! The troops are up ahead," said Chester from the front seat.

She awoke from her dream with a start, disoriented. She sat up and blinked. Rounded rear ends of cavalry horses were moving just ahead, forming a long sinuous line of 400 khaki-colored troopers. This was Callie's first look at the "front line" troops, who were moving fast and set on engaging the fleeing bandits. They had been on the move for fifteen days and had covered 375 miles, crisscrossing mountains and deserts on Villa's trail, and were nearly worn out.

Chester drove alongside the mounted soldiers and honked, waving and brandishing his infectious mustachioed smile. Lazlo stood up and saluted each soldier they passed. Callie leaned out over the door and waved enthusiastically, sending her beaming smile out to the appreciative, and surprised, troops.

Dusk was approaching and a command was given to halt.

Colonel Dodd, a cigar stub in his mouth, was conferring with a group of officers when the trio drove up. He was a craggy West Pointer of sixty-three, had twice been cited for gallant conduct under enemy fire. Chester jumped out and went right up to the Colonel.

"Chester Moon, Colonel, of the Biograph Motion Picture Company. A pleasure, sir." They shook hands. It was plain Dodd didn't know what to make of Chester and his sidekick, shyly munching on peanuts by the car. Callie approached slowly, not wishing to interrupt, but Colonel Dodd spoke up when he saw her, removing his cigar to improve his enunciation.

"Miss Masterson, your reputation precedes you. Welcome, although I must say I am a bit surprised to see you so close to the action."

"Thank you, sir. Chester, Lazlo and me are endeavoring to cover the action, and we seem to make a good team." She held her hands behind her back, in the manner of a shy adolescent, perhaps intimidated by the grizzled, battle-hardened veteran.

"I have news of your friend, Captain Wilde."

Callie felt her heart jump.

"You look worried. He flew in around noon with some messages and a bag of your cookies, that's all. He's just fine. But we most

72

certainly enjoyed them. Thank you, ma'am."

"I was glad to do it, sir. You and your boys have been through so much."

"You're correct on that account, miss. The supply trucks still haven't caught up with us. And General Pershing dispatched a message saying he's sending fresh troops and supplies and that we should stop for a few days and rest."

"Well, that must be wonderful news."

"But here's the thing." He took her by the arm and led her in a little circle as he explained. "You see we captured one of Villa's recruits, and he informed us that his boss was wounded in the leg near Guerrero not far from Carranza's boys. He's probably less than thirty miles from us, getting medical attention. This could be our big chance to bring the scoundrel to justice."

The Colonel and his cohorts debated their next move well into the night. Just before eleven p.m. he decided on a forced night march of thirty-six miles over an unknown trail through the mountains. He was determined to catch them by surprise with a dawn attack. It was a grueling night for the troopers. Without Mexican guides they literally groped their way through the darkness. The column was forced to halt repeatedly so that the army's Apache scouts could dismount to examine the lay of the land. During each stop the exhausted soldiers practically fell off their horse, grabbing naps on the cold ground, holding the reins all the while. Eventually, it was easier to just walk and lead the horse.

Chester's car was unable to negotiate such a rugged trail. Since they all needed some sleep, a sheltering circle of junipers was found where they could bed down undisturbed through the night.

Callie lay wrapped in two heavy blankets in the back of the Ford. The Big Dipper hung vertically in the springtime night sky and it was easy to pick out Polaris, the North Star. They had come over 400 miles from New Mexico, her body ached and she desperately wanted a bath, but sleep came easily in the cold high-desert air.

She became dimly aware of the soft dawn light, but was also of a strange chewing sound. She lifted her head and peeked over the car door. A doe was munching on the bag of peanuts Lazlo had left on the hood. The deer's eyes observed Callie while it kept on eating. Once finished, it stared at her, sniffed the air, and bolted away.

She wanted to go back to sleep but knew they needed to depart. The air was so bitterly cold that she was inspired to build a fire, for there was plenty of kindling around the trees. Soon she had a good blaze going and crouched in the glorious warmth. The sky had come to life in soft morning colors and she imagined herself an Indian, just as she had done as a little girl. She managed to heat some water in a metal cup and pulled out a precious bag of black tea saved for just such an emergency. She sipped the tea in great contentment and would have been satisfied to stay there the rest of the morning.

The crackling wood and fragrant smoke roused Chester and Lazlo. They mumbled incoherently, finally getting out of the car and going off to relieve themselves.

They headed for Guererro on a smoother track and reached it by six a.m.. The white dome of a colonial church rose from a cluster of brown adobe buildings, which were spread along either side of a small river.

Callie stood up, frowning with concern. "There's some commotion going on down there. Look-those men, riding away fast. I'll wager they're with Villa."

Chester was pointing his binoculars the other way, towards the mountains that overlooked the village.

"I see metal shining in the sun. I see horses and cavalry hats up there. That's why those boys are running. The U.S. Army has arrived. Lazlo, my boy, prepare for action"

Chester grabbed a rifle off the floorboard, making sure it was loaded. General Pershing had provided them with two army Springfields after hearing about their close call.

Dodd's detachment descended into the valley. A large group of Mexican soldiers rode out of town, carrying a flag, but he wasn't sure if they were Carranza's men, their supposed allies, or Villa's, masquerading as government troops. As they moved closer, the Mexicans broke and ran. Dodd ordered an attack.

The Army horses were so spent that they could only manage a listless walk, and two simply crumpled to the ground under their riders. The soldiers then dismounted and fired from a distance, with rifles and machine guns.

Chester drove slowly to a higher vantage point. Lazlo began filming. It was a panoramic scene, with the rugged mountainous backdrop and the peaceful village erupting in gunfire and smoke, people yelling and horses charging this way and that.

All Callie could think about were the innocents who always get caught in the crossfire of such battles. She spotted small groups of women and children scurrying for shelter down in the near-empty plaza.

It wasn't much of a battle and was soon over.

They drove into the town with the troopers right behind. Callie got out of the car and saw for the first time the effects of the "Revolution" up close. The town was devastated. Any house or store of value had been sacked by the *Villistas*. As the villagers reappeared, Callie was shocked to see their ragged state, the men in filthy serapes, the women with their babies, bedraggled and in tears.

She walked slowly across the plaza, as the soldiers inspected the buildings on the slim chance that the wounded Villa might be hiding. Dust and smoke mingled in the cool air, and the ubiquitous smell of corn tortillas made her mouth water. She was famished. But then she came upon a sight that froze her in horror. A dirty toddler was playing atop his dead mother's body, smeared with her blood, her warm body still a familiar comfort to him. The child looked up at Callie with blood dripping from his tiny fingers. She could not face it and started to run off, but then stumbled back, scooped up the baby and found a woman to take her. She looked at her bloody hands and washed them off in a horse trough. She felt faint and sought relief from the heat and dust in the village church.

She pushed open the old heavy wooden door. It was as if she had crossed into another universe. Hushed and dimly lit with candlelight, the graceful interior fulfilled its purpose admirably-a sanctuary from the bleak and violent existence outside. Callie leaned against the cool wall and stared at the glittering altar, the spiritual heart of the village. The rustic wooden crucifix was somehow comforting.

Objects of great beauty surrounded her, even though her eyes focused on nothing in particular. She breathed in the smells of old wood, candle wax, incense, and closed her eyes.

She was sleepy and very hungry.

I wonder where Casey is. I wish he was here, with me. I wish we could sit here, in one of the pews and listen to them singing some sweet Mexican hymn. Like it was some ordinary Sunday. I wish this war was over.

She felt someone tugging on her sleeve and was jarred back into the present. A small boy, wearing a brown poncho over his white shirt, looked up at her with sad, serious eyes. He was holding his hat in his hands. She slowly knelt down to his level and took his small hand. "Que quiere, muchacho?" she whispered.

He looked around, assured no one else was there, and whispered back to her, "Pancho Villa quiere verte." He waited for an answer with big inquisitive eyes.

Callie could not believe her ears. Pancho Villa wanted to see her? "Estas seguro?" she asked.

"Sí, señorita." He handed her a small piece of folded paper. She unfolded the dirty note. The scrawl was barely legible:

"I want you to tell some truth about me. You are going to be safe here. Pancho Villa."

The boy explained that Villa was hiding up in the hills, not far off, and that he would lead her there.

Callie hesitated, looked into the eyes of the child, and then knew she would go before anyone could tell her how crazy she was. She told the boy, whose name was Pablo, that she needed to get her notebook. He would wait for her behind the church.

Callie pushed open the heavy wooden door and winced at the bright glare of the plaza. She hurried over to the Ford to grab her bag and jumped at the sight of Lazlo lying in the back, sleeping soundly. She smiled and rushed off.

They crossed a small creek over a footbridge and followed a trail that went up a canyon full of cottonwoods, and therefore invisible from the town. It was cool and fragrant along the path, and Callie felt reassured for reasons she could not explain. Maybe she felt like she was giving in to Mexico, yielding to its sad beauty, taking a risk, a young white gringa, tempting fate.

Vamos a ver, she said to herself. We shall see.

Pablo related how Villa recruited him as a temporary messenger. He was to receive fifty pesos for his task. His father was dead, and his mother depended on him to take care of their small herd of goats. The money would be a small fortune to them.

They reached a ridge after about a half hour and followed another trail, lined with tall Ponderosa pines that smelled of vanilla. A fresh northerly breeze revived Callie. The blue shapes of the Sierra Madre rose from the desert just to the west. From up there, Mexico was a Shangri-La. The trail descended into a small mountain creek and went along the water on a well-used path.

Pablo put his hand up and they both stopped below a cliff. He gave out a soft whistle. A soldier moved from behind a tree only ten yards away. He held his rifle at the ready and looked back down the trail. He motioned for them to follow. No one said anything.

A steep trail led up to what looked like a sheer rock face. Callie spotted a cave opening behind thick shrubbery. Pablo was told to wait. Callie smiled at the boy, gently squeezed his shoulder, and followed the soldier into the darkness.

Some of Villa's gang

Chapter 9

The blackness swallowed her. She extended her hands to find the cave wall.

The air became cool and damp on her skin. Taste of fear in her mouth.

Why did she agree to this? They could slit her throat and no one would ever find her.

The cave narrowed into a claustrophobic passageway. They had only walked about ten yards.

Were those statues? No-rigid *Villistas* glared at her on both sides of the sweating walls. She smelled the grease on their bandoliers and pistols as she brushed by them

Everyone was very close. Faint glow of a lamp from somewhere. Faces of the revolution.

One of them was a woman with a long black skirt and a high-necked white shirt that tapered tight around her narrow waist. A holstered pistol hung midway across her torso and two belts of cartridges made a wavy "X" across her chest. A sombrero covered her thick black hair.

The woman came toward her and mumbled something that Callie could not understand.

Callie backed away nervously. "No comprendo."

"She must check you for weapons, señorita." A distinguished looking man with a mustache and cultured voice spoke from behind the young woman. "She is a *soldadera*, one of many who fight with their men, para la revolución."

Callie stood still while she was searched, ill at ease with the hot glare of the bandits' eyes upon her in the cramped space. Strong odors of sweat and kerosene hung in the close air.

She held her hand out to the woman. "Mi nombre es Callie. Cómo te llamas? "

The woman was surprised that Callie wanted to know her name and looked back at the man who had spoken. He nodded his approval.

"Mi nombre es Elena, señorita," she answered faintly.

Callie smiled and shook her hand. "Con mucho gusto, Elena. Es un nombre muy bonito."

The young woman, hardly out of her teens, smiled with embarrassment. "Gracias," she said, barely audible, backing away into the darkness.

"Miss Masterson. I am Ramon Fernandez. We are pleased that you come. General Villa would like to...how you Americans say it...set the record straight. Please, this way."

He ushered her into a small dead-end passageway, where more soldiers stood on either side of a cot, upon which General Pancho Villa lay. He wore a dirty shapeless sweater and was sitting up against a wall. His right leg was stretched out, wrapped in bloody bandages and immobilized by a primitive wooden splint.

A lantern sat on a ledge and filled the space with pale yellow light. A small candle flickered in a niche in the wall. Villa puffed on a thin cigar. A bottle of liquor sat on a small table beside the cot. She was offered a chair, so she sat down. Now smells of melting wax and cigar smoke mingled with the sweat and kerosene.

The lack of any conversation made Callie nervous, and then Villa spoke. "Buenas días, señorita. My English...it's not so good, pero General Fernández, he help us."

Now Callie was close enough to get a good look at the infamous Villa. He had a large head and thick neck, but a baby face, a little pudgy. His mustache made a long flat triangle under his nose, and he had short black, wiry hair, with a high forehead. In spite of the coolness, beads of sweat glistened on his face.

The prominent brown eyes held all his secrets. They were restless and seemed to speak to Callie before he had uttered a word. He was pale and looked fatigued from the ordeal of his serious leg wound, but the fire in his eyes spoke volumes about his inner strength, and cruelty.

He made her feel uneasy, as he puffed on the cigar.

"What do they think of me en los Estados Unidos? They think Villa, he's alive or dead?"

Callie chose her words with care. "It is most people's opinion that you are still alive. I must say, General, that before the attack on Columbus you were considered a hero, a Robin Hood-you know of him?"

Ramon explained.

"Sí, claro, the English bandido. We are much alike," he said, smiling broadly.

"But, because of the attack, and the Americans who died, they are angry with you, which, of course, is only natural."

"I tell you. In Columbus... my hombres, they get a little loco. But that man, Sam Ravel, he sold no good stuff...bad bullets, don't fire."

"Sam Ravel? I stayed at his hotel. I met his son Arthur. Your men nearly killed him, but he ran off. He was only sixteen." Callie had anger in her voice, in spite of her vulnerable situation.

Villa turned to Ramon for clarification.

"El hijo de Sam tenía dieciséis años."

"It was not me that said to kill the son. But our time is un poco... I must speak of other things. I hear you are una mujer valiente, una mujer de honor...how you say?"

"Yo comprendo. A brave woman and a woman of honor. That's very kind of you, General."

Villa seemed pleased with himself and enjoyed his cigar for a few moments.

"Asi, what I want to say to you, to los Estados Unidos, is this: We fight for the people, la *gente*, we don't fight for us. You understand, sí? I am just a campesino. No, I am *all* of them. I become a bandido when I was young- my jefe, my boss, he rape my sister. My father, he was dead, mi madre she work for us kids...we had nothing, señorita. Nada. No derechos, no justicia. Comprende?"

"Sí. No rights, no justice." Callie wanted him to hear the words in English.

Then Villa began to rant with emotion and gestured dramatically with his hands, wincing in pain from his swollen leg, too fast for Callie to understand, about Porfirio Diaz, an oppressive dictator during his childhood, and how Carranza, whom President Wilson now backed instead of Villa, would establish another class-based society that would keep the peasants trapped in poverty. He hated the Spanish upper class for enslaving the Mexican people. He had even less use for the Church, which was just as corrupt, he exhorted.

Ramon patiently translated.

The outburst visibly tired him. Callie surmised that he hadn't slept much, with the wound and the constant harassment of Pershing's troops.

"It is too bad for the killed gringos, pero we fight for *nuestras vidas! Nuestras vidas,* señorita."

"Sí, General. For your lives."

"The land of Mexico...it is rich...los minerales... mucho gold, mucho silver... mucho oil. We sell to gringos, the Germans, everybody, but where all that money? Dónde está el dinero? He rubbed his fingers together. "We don't see. Nada. señorita, we are still poor as when bastard conquistadors took our gold. Nada ha cambia. No change. For trecientos anos, nothing changes. They rape my sister. They rape Mexico. Y asi, luchamos, we fight, por una vida mejor. It is our right, no? It is a right for everyone. Para toda la gente!"

"A better life. It is your right," Callie said quietly, moved by his eloquence.

Nevertheless, she bit her lip and decided to challenge his words. The lantern illuminated her womanly profile, this young woman with her tumbling black curls and thin, graceful neck, such an unlikely person to be challenging a violent outlaw, who had murdered men, and women, point blank, for daring to disagree.

"Some of the people I have met say they see no difference between what Carranza's army does and what your men do. They live each day with much fear. They suffer. Their animals, their crops, even their sons, are taken from them, *their* women also raped, and they get little in return. Sometimes, they are shot, in front of their children, if they protest. I myself have seen some of these things." She paused. She was nervous, but her voice remained steady. *Steady girl, don't let them see you shake.* "General Sir, where is the justice in fighting, if there is no compassion, compasion por los pobres? If you do not discriminate between the victim and the enemy?"

She waited uneasily for Ramon to translate. As he did, a wave reaction of passed through the soldiers, who mumbled threateningly, indignant at this gringa's words.

Villa remained calm as he took in her words, but his eyes flashed like silent lightning. "Mexico...she is not like your country," he said, wagging his finger for emphasis. "From when the Spanish

82

conquistdadores come, till now, Mexico she is wet with blood. La sangre. Is like...una lengua, a bad language we are taught, por la fuerza...how you say?"

"By force."

"By force, sí" His voice had weakened to a whisper. "Señorita, it is not what we want, la violencia, but it is what we have."

He slumped with fatigue and waved his hand, as if to say, enough.

"We will not give up, until we kill every one of those bastards, Carranza and his dogs. And then, we are free. Tell them what I say."

He sighed heavily and crushed his cigar out on the damp cave floor, sending a smoky hiss into the air.

Callie got up. Villa raised his hand, as if to hold her there for something he forgot to say.

"Señorita Masterson. What I hear of you...it is true. A brave woman." He looked at his men. "Mira amigos-una mujer muy, muy bravo. La dejó pasar." They stepped back to let her pass.

She walked out carefully, as if she were leaving a church, smiling at the soldadera as she passed. Ramon told her that Pablo would lead her back to town, but that they must wait at a certain place on the trail for an hour, before continuing back down.

Pablo led her to a small meadow, where they were to remain until Villa was long gone from the hideout. Callie had been in somewhat of a daze during the remarkable interview, but as she sat down in the grass it suddenly hit her that she had not written a single word of Villa's conversation.

She whipped out her notebook and began to write nonstop for the next hour while it was all still fresh in her mind.

The walk back down was much quicker. Callie wished she had said more, had asked more pointed questions. Her feelings were mixed, her viewpoint had shifted. She no longer thought of Villa as a hero or a villain. All that she knew was that he was very human-hurt, weary and probably scared.

They entered the plaza and she realized at once that everyone had gone. Not a soldier, truck or mule was in sight. "Chester must have assumed I had gone with the army." She got a sick feeling in her stomach and sat down on the sidewalk and put her head on her knees and groaned.

83

Pablo put his hand on her shoulder in alarm. "Que paso, señorita?"

"Mis amigos, se fueron," said Callie without looking up. "All my friends have left me."

Pablo stood by her uneasily, not sure what to do. Then his face brightened. "Ven conmigo, a mi casa."

Callie slowly raised her head. "Sí?" she asked.

"Sí!" said Pablo smiling. "Está muy cerca."

Callie's spirits lifted a little. This little boy, a complete stranger, invited her to his home.

She followed him down a narrow side street. The young American woman, tagging behind a Mexican boy, attracted attention. Two rough looking men came up behind her. One grabbed her arm.

Callie turned and jerked her arm away. Pablo ran up. "No se moleste a la señora. Ella es mi amiga."

They looked at each other and snickered. One of them roughly shoved Pablo aside.

When the man turned and looked at Callie, she was aiming her Colt 45 between his eyes.

"Soy un amigo de Pancho Villa. Usted es un hombre *muerto*," she announced with great emphasis.

They backed away, smiling uneasily.

She pulled the hammer back and the sharp click of the metal in the quiet alley sent them fleeing down the street.

Pablo's home was only a little ways, at the edge of the village, adjacent to a cornfield, a modest one-room adobe. Callie had to bend down as she followed Pablo through the low doorway. It was very dim inside. A small, dark Indian woman was patting tortillas and throwing them on a small grill, under which some burning coals glowed red. Her eyes grew wide like a surprised cat when she saw Callie come in behind her son.

Pablo whispered something to his mother, who immediately produced a plate of beans and some of the just cooked tortillas, and motioned for Callie to sit at the table and eat.

Callie hesitated, not wanting to take any of the little food they had, but knew it would be impolite not to. "Gracias, señora."

Pablo ate beside her, all the while relating his role as guide for Callie's interview with Villa. He then stood up and triumphantly pulled out the fifty pesos. "Mira mamá!"

She touched the money to confirm it was real. "Madre de Dios!"

When he made her understand that it was because the gringa agreed to be brought to the cave that he had gotten the money, his mother thanked Callie profusely.

Toward sunset Pablo went out to gather their small herd of goats into a shed, and Callie tagged along. He said that lions were prevalent in the mountains, and since he lost his dog, he had to keep the herd inside. When she asked him if the dog had run away, he replied the *Villistas* had shot him.

She knelt down beside a gurgling irrigation ditch and splashed her face with the icy water. Crickets began chirping in the cool dusk as the first bright stars appeared.

They went back inside. Pablo's mother served them a deliciously rich hot chocolate, with a strong cinnamon flavor. Her name was Luisa, and she was from the Tarahumara tribe up in the Sierra Madre in the neighboring state of Durango. She told Callie of her old home deep in the Barranca del Cobre, where she and her husband grew fruit trees and farmed by the river. They were very happy until miners and loggers drove them out. They had no official deed to their land, so the Mexican government ignored their pleas.

After they moved to Guerrero things were a little better, until her husband died from typhoid fever. The revolution had made life very difficult, she said. They feared the Mexican Army as much as the *Villistas.*

Pablo then reminded her of the fifty pesos that Pancho Villa gave him. "Yes," she said, "but if we do the wrong thing, he might shoot us tomorrow."

Callie did not know what to say. She sipped her hot chocolate.

Now her "adventures" seemed rather foolish. What good was it doing these people? What would be the result of all the suffering and death? She could go back home, have her job, make choices, sleep in a clean bed, not worry about violent intruders banging on her door in the middle of the night. But they were trapped in this chaos. They had nowhere else to go.

You were right about one thing, General Villa. Nothing changes for the oppressed.

She leaned back and closed her eyes, thought about Lucille and Randy back in Columbus, wondered when she would get to see them again, and was about to doze off, when she was bothered by the whine of a mosquito in her ear, but the whine increased in volume and soon became the familiar drone of a Curtiss Jenny biplane.

She let out a squeal, jumped up and ran outside. She couldn't see anything, but could tell it was getting closer. Pablo and Luisa came out and looked up into the sky with her. The plane made a big circle and then seemed to be flying right over them. Luisa made a sign of the cross, while Pablo ran about shouting, "Un avión! Fantástico!"

"He's looking for a place to land, that's what he's doing," said Callie. She stood still, trying to pinpoint where the pilot was coming down. The pitch of the engine changed, the plane was lower in the sky, and she knew it was landing and began to run toward the sound. She guessed it would be the road they had come into town on.

"Senora!" cried Luisa. "Su bolso." Callie ran back and took her bag from Luisa, then gave her and Pablo a hug.

"Gracias por todo," she said, stuffing a bunch of pesos into Pablo's hand.

Callie ran along the irrigation ditch, crashing through brush and setting off a chorus of barking dogs. She nearly ran headlong into a very surprised cow.

The yellow grass of the fields reflected more light, so that she could make her way a bit easier.

She could still hear the engine whine. It was getting closer. She crossed another field and saw it, about a hundred yards distant, sitting in the road, the cloth wings reflecting what little light there still was.

She had to go down and up a ravine, lacerated her leg on cactus, but finally stumbled onto the road.

She was so out of breath that she had to slow to a walk. She began to wave and yell. "Hello! Hello!" She squinted through the darkness, her head thrust forward in concentration. A lone figure appeared out of the darkness. "Callie? Is that you?" Casey was suddenly in front of her, and she stopped, sweat rolling down her face.

"Well, who do you think it is?" she said, her voice cracking with emotion.

They embraced each other with great relief.

86

"I'm mighty glad to see you, miss."

"What took you so long, Captain?" she said, laying her head on his shoulder.

Casey straightened up. "We can't stay here. C'mon."

"Oh, goody. I get to fly again."

He lifted her up on to the wing. She jumped into cockpit and he made sure she was fastened in. He got the engine started and taxied down the road

People on horseback were approaching fast. "Keep your head down, Callie!" he yelled.

Casey gave it full power and lifted off, just as the riders were about to catch up. They opened fire, but the copious dust from the takeoff prevented them from seeing anything to shoot at.

The plane banked to the south and quickly gained altitude. Callie looked down on the Mexican landscape and made out the shapes of the mountains and a few tiny yellow lights in a vast canvas of black. The cold air immediately reminded her of how under dressed she was.

She stuffed her hands under her arms and was thrilled to be airborne again. They seemed to be at the very edge of space, so peaceful it was.

Then the engine died.

Callie stiffened and stopped breathing.

"It's okay," yelled Casey. "Sometimes she stalls like this, but she always comes back." All she could see was his dark profile, hunched over, furiously working the controls.

She was too terrified to answer. They were floating in near silence, surrounded by a glittering universe, and it was the most wondrous and terrible thing she had ever experienced. A mixture of awe and fear put her in a trance, and she wondered if it was another dream.

The little plane gently undulated and creaked in the invisible air currents, as if it were perfectly capable of staying aloft without an engine, but they were steadily losing altitude.

"Damn you!" muttered Casey. "C'mon now, baby, wake up. Get us back home."

Callie saw the isolated lights below grow larger and wished she could touch Casey. She breathed in short little inhalations and tears streamed out of her eyes as the Jenny descended with a whine and dove for the desert.

Callie was filled with rage and fear, screwed her eyes shut and cried in silence.

I already dreamed this and I woke up...I woke up...I woke-

A loud backfire made Callie scream and the Jenny woke up.

Casey pulled her out of the dive with less than a hundred feet to spare, kicking up a cloud of dust on the desert floor and sending a jackrabbit scurrying for its life.

Callie buried her face in her hands. She finally lifted her head as they came over a ridge and gaped at the sight of a thousand campfires glittering below in the darkness. Casey banked the plane in a long falling curve that brought them to the ground.

His fellow pilots came rushing up, but Casey ignored them, unfastening himself, then jumping on to the wing beside Callie. He placed his hand on her shoulder.

"I'm sorry that happened, Callie? Say something. Speak to me."

She was hunched over, huddled in the cockpit. She looked up and couldn't really see anything, but imagined she was looking into his fierce blue eyes. She whispered weakly in a hoarse voice. "Nice flying, Captain."

Casey took her hands, warming them in his. "I wouldn't let anything happen to you, miss. You can count on that."

Callie nodded. "I'm cold." Casey draped his jacket over her trembling shoulders and helped her out of the cockpit.

His comrades were cheering and slapping him on the back as he lifted her off the wing. They walked back to camp, their arms around each other.

Callie stayed close to camp for the next few days. She said little about her disappearance in Guerrero, except that an Indian family had invited her to their home. In light of her brush with death, General Pershing did not press the issue.

Captain Foulois was about to fly dispatches and mail up to Columbus, and she entrusted to him an envelope stuffed with her articles and notes for the Chronicle. The wind was picking up and he was anxious to take off.

"You be careful, Captain. Take care about those air currents."

"Yes ma'am, I intend to. I believe someone else requires your attention," he said, looking behind her with a smile.

Callie turned around and saw Casey leaning against his plane with a basket, his legs crossed and a cigarette dangling out of his mouth. She walked over to him. They had seen each other only intermittently since her rescue.

"Captain, whatever do you have in that basket? Flowers for me, I hope?"

"Not quite, miss, but almost as good". He pulled out a bottle of tequila, a salt shaker, and a lime. "There's a nice little overhang down in the arroyo, out of the wind and shady."

He led her down a dry stream bed sprinkled with scarlet Indian paintbrush. There was a small alcove, cool and inviting against the bank of the arroyo, and they sat down on the dry sand.

"Now you'll have to explain exactly how this is done, sir, as we didn't drink too much tequila back in Comanche Springs."

"Well, it's pretty simple." He cut the lime into small wedges and produced two heavy shot glasses from the basket. "You lick your finger like this and sprinkle some salt on it. Got that so far?"

Callie smiled and nodded enthusiastically.

"Okay. Now I'm pouring us equal shots of tequila, and this is good stuff, you know. A sergeant procured it in Chihuahua City. So, you lick the salt, drink the tequila, and bite on the lime."

"Lick, drink, and bite. Okay. I think I got it."

"Okay. Let's give her a try."

They both held up their glasses. A gust of wind blew Callie's hair in her face, making her giggle. They clinked the glasses together, sucked the salt, drank the shot, and bit on the slice of lime. The assault of tastes made Callie grimace and the sting of the tequila made her gasp.

"Whoo!" she exhaled strongly, fanning her face. "That's got quite a kick, yes it does." Her eyes brightened. "But I like it."

"I thought you might," said Casey. "One more time?"

"Practice make perfect."

This time Callie half kissed and half sucked the salt with a loud smack, threw back the liquor, and bit into the lime with great gusto.

"Ha! That one was even better," she cried, wiping her mouth and throwing her head back in delight. "You stop laughing at me, Casey. You're turning red, you know."

Casey caught his breath. "You're a wild woman, Callie Masterson."

"You're darn right I am, and you better not forget it."

Casey held up his empty glass. "You know what they say about tequila, don't you?"

Callie leaned in close and looked him in the eye, in mock seriousness. "No, Captain, what do they say? Tell me."

"They say… that the third one is the charm."

Callie slapped her leg. "Well then, gosh darn it, what are we waiting for? Hit me again, handsome."

Casey almost let the bottle slip out of his hand.

"Control yourself, sir."

"I'm trying, ma'am."

Callie performed the third one with such fluidity that she looked as if she had been doing it for years. She let out a long "aaah" and fell on her back in slow motion. "How come you don't make any noise?" she asked Casey, while staring up at the brilliant blue sky.

"Cause I'm an army pilot and we're real good at these things." Casey leaned over and looked down at her.

Callie's eyes were glassy and moist as she gazed back up at him. "Thank you for rescuing me, Casey," she said softly. "I don't know if I ever-"

He interrupted her with a no nonsense kind of kiss, and they had no inclination to stop, and every reason to prolong the pleasure for as long as they dared.

The sky darkened and one of those sudden high desert thunderstorms rushed across the sky, slapping the ground with big, cold raindrops and stirring up dust, and then it was gone. A buzzard circled for a closer look at the two lovers, but flew off, uninterested. Colors deepened and the air cooled as the sun lowered, but this only drew them closer.

He lay on his back, with her head nestled on his chest. He caressed her hair with his fingers. The effects of the tequila had subsided and their mood shifted to the serious.

Casey cleared his throat, for they hadn't spoken for quite a while.

90

"I have to fly to Namiquipa in the morning."

Callie stirred out of her reverie. "That's your job, isn't it?"

"Yes. And you have to cover the revolution."

"Yes. We both have our jobs. And they're good jobs, not the boring, everyday sort. What if you hadn't pulled the Jenny out of that dive?"

"We wouldn't be here, talking."

"Exactly." Callie sat up. "And that means something. It means you're a wonderful pilot and we get another chance." She stared down at Casey.

"Callie, everything's so uncertain out here. And the war in Europe isn't going away. Things are going to change fast."

"I know that. It frightens me."

Casey sat up and embraced her. "Frightens you? I didn't think anything frightened you."

"Oh, don't be too sure. It's easier with you around. Do you think we'll get into that darn war over there?"

"It sure looks that way."

"Yeah." Callie drew circles in the sand with her finger. "Well, they better give you decent planes." Casey didn't answer. "Casey, what's the most important thing in life to you?"

"Right now, the army is my whole life. Aviation saved me. I would have been a good for nothing lout, but now I have a purpose. Same as you. Writing gives you a purpose."

"It's more than that. It excites me. I think I could write stories, fiction I mean. I think that's my future."

"So, there you are. We both have our work cut out for us."

"It's deeper than that. I can't express myself properly... must be that tequila. What I mean is...I crave intensity in my life, and it kept eluding me. That's why I came out here, don't you see. Maybe you did too. Neither of us has any use for a safe, predictable existence. I feel like I'm answering a call, but I know this is only my first attempt."

She paused, trying to recall something. "I have these dreams of journeys. I'm riding across a grassy plain that goes on forever. There's dark mountains, bluish and distant, just like the Sierra Madre over there," she said, pointing to the west, "but they never get any closer.

91

You know how it is in dreams, your body not working quite right, and there's no sense of time, just a kind of forever that I keep chasing."

Casey picked a twig and chewed on it. He looked at her with what could only be called an admiring gaze. "You know, when I first caught sight of you at that train station, I knew right away you were a different sort of girl."

"I'm glad."

"So, you found some of that intensity in the revolution."

"I did, but I also found it just now, with you."

Casey gave her a wary look.

"Why does that make you uncomfortable, Casey?"

"Look here, I enjoyed what just happened as much as you. But nothing's for sure in this life, especially *our* lives."

Callie had no response.

Casey gathered up the glasses and bottle. "We better get back. How'd it get dark so fast?"

They climbed out of the arroyo and headed to the campfires under a star-filled sky.

Tenth Cavalry charges Villa's men

Chapter 10

The next morning there was news that two of Villa's lieutenants were staying near the town of Cusi. Pershing directed Major Robert Howze to investigate with a squadron of six mounted troops and a machine gun troop. This time Callie rode with the two other correspondents at a safe distance behind the soldiers.

The Apache scouts, headed by First Sergeant Chicken, studied the ground carefully to pick up a trail. Loco Jim and Big Sharley fanned out to check the brush and arroyos. Callie was fascinated by their ability to pick out the smallest details. Big Sharley would rest his head on the ground in line with the track and close his top eye. Callie noticed that he always kept the tracks between him and the light source, in this case, the low morning sun. She surmised that under these conditions he could catch the slightest sign of compression in the dust. His long black hair and wiry limbs gave him an animal appearance as he lay upon the ground, using all his senses to pick up clues invisible to a white man.

He stood up and pointed to the west. Then he threw some dirt into the air and watched where the wind blew it. He closed his eyes and sniffed the air, humming a quick little chant. He pointed to the west again. The squadron moved in that direction.

A small ranch appeared in the distance. Loco Jim went ahead and studied the adobe buildings with field glasses. He came back and reported that many *Villistas* were in the area, some on top of the building, some hiding behind a stone wall.

Major Howze cautioned the reporters to remain in the car. The squadron charged, firing their weapons and catching the Mexicans by surprise. There was a brief pistol fight which lasted several minutes, after which they chased the bandits off the ranch and engaged in serious combat, eventually killing forty-four, with no casualties on the American side.

First Sergeant Chicken came galloping back in triumph with one of the bandit's rifles. "Damn fine fight!" he yelled to the reporters, with a big smile. "We can't take no scalps, but I got this here gun." He let out a war cry and galloped around the car with great excitement.

It was 1916, but Callie couldn't help thinking that she must be seeing much the same scenes as General Pershing did thirty years earlier, during his tenure at Fort Bayard in New Mexico Territory. There were no better trackers than the Apache.

When they arrived back at camp, Pershing was greatly pleased to hear of Howze's success. One of the Mexican prisoners was to be interrogated by Hell Yet-Suey, another Apache scout who was adept at extracting information. Before any words were spoken, the waiting prisoner was unnerved by the very appearance of the Indian: dark, fierce eyes, magnified by his dust goggles, wild, unkempt hair blowing in the wind, and white teeth bared like a wolf's. The captive revealed that Villa was most likely heading for Parral, a beautiful colonial city further south, where he had many friends and sympathizers.

Callie met Chester and Lazlo at the end of the day and related the skirmish at Cusi. They sat around the campfire as the light faded. It was nearly June and the evenings were now more comfortable in the mountains. The spring winds had finally ceased blowing and everyone was in a better mood. Soon, the local villagers appeared with fresh food and treats. The last plane had landed and Casey appeared, dusty and sunburned. He sat next to Callie, obviously worn out from the day's mission.

There were burritos, hard boiled eggs and fresh garden carrots to feast on. And biscochitos, of course. Even the normally taciturn Pershing looked relaxed, chatting with his troops.

A rickety wagon, pulled by mules, rolled out of the darkness and stopped beside the gathering. A group of musicians, on their way back from a wedding, asked if the gringos would like to hear some music. General Pershing gave the okay and they quickly set up around the wagon. The band was a mix of guitars, trumpets and violins, which varied from decent shape to nearly worn out. They played sweet love songs, full of pathos and yearning, the lead tenor giving his all for this unexpected audience. Then some quick-tempo *bailes* that made Callie want to dance. Even the Apache scouts seem to enjoy the music. B-25 was keeping time with a spoon and metal cup, nodding his head with the rhythm. They launched into some *corridos,* one of which hailed the exploits of Pancho Villa, and another glorifying the medicinal effects of marijuana.

Casey disappeared and came back with the half empty bottle of tequila. There wasn't much light, but they still took care to conceal it from General Pershing, since it was technically illegal while on active duty. It was the perfect touch. Callie swayed to the music as the warmth of the liquor infused her body. She laughed with the up tempo pieces, and nearly wept with the sad ones, the *canciones tristes*. Casey had his arm around her waist and was trying to sing along, but made a mess of it with his lousy Spanish.

As if on cue, a big yellow moon rose above the horizon. The musicians immediately launched into *La Luna de Baranquilla,* and everyone fell under the spell of the bittersweet melody of lost love, even if they understood little of the actual words. The emotions of the band were so sincere that one felt the melody, as well as hearing it.

Big Sharley and B-25 jumped up and did a little jig around the fire, and were encouraged by the claps of the soldiers. They let out little yips and squeaks as if they had been raised on the songs and this provided no small delight to the musicians, who looked at each other in amazement to see their ancient enemies dancing to their mariachi music.

The mix of guitars and horns brought visions of matadors, vaqueros and dancing senoritas to Callie, and she fell madly in love with Mexico then and there. She looked at Casey and whispered in his ear. "Cómo estás hombre?"

"Muy bien, señorita," he said, with his funny mid-western accent.

The band then performed the melancholy *La Paloma Blanca.* Callie squeezed Casey. "Oh." She cupped her ear to concentrate on the lyrics.

"What's the matter?"

She turned to Casey. "A dove singing a sad song on a summer evening, reminds a woman of how her sweetheart also flew away, but still she waits, she waits…"

Casey put his arm around her.

"Everyone's looking at us," she whispered. Although the firelight was dim, she blushed, as she remembered that she was a lone gringa, surrounded by thousands of soldiers.

"Who cares?"

As the musicians began to climb back on the wagon, one of them passed his big sombrero around and everyone threw in a few pesos. Callie and Casey walked away from the crowd, following the meandering road in the moonlight, saying nothing. Wild ideas whirled inside her head and she wondered how it would all play out.

The next morning a small group of soldiers were to leave on a routine mission to purchase corn at a nearby ranch near Rubio. Callie, Chester, and Lazlo were huddled in a small circle discussing the possibilities. Chester spoke first.

"There's a ranch house at San Miguelito. One of Villa's most trusted aides might just be hiding out there, according to a couple of scouts."

"So, there might be more to this little trip than buying corn," said Callie.

"That's how it looks. How's the camera, Lazlo?" he said, looking at his cameraman. "Lazlo let the camera get wet during that thunderstorm we had the other day."

Lazlo looked peeved and quickly responded in his thick Hungarian accent. "The camera is doing very well."

Callie looked back toward the corrals. "Chester, I'm going to fetch Bandido and ride behind you."

"Do you think that's a wise idea?"

"He needs some exercise, and it's a beautiful morning. Besides, I've heard Rubio is only a short distance away."

"But, Callie, don't you think you should clear it with Lieutenant Patton?"

"Chester, if I asked permission for every little thing, I wouldn't have any fun, now would I? I'll be right back."

Chester looked at Lazlo and shrugged.

Lazlo hit his chest with his fist. "This is a woman who follows her heart. She don't need no damn permission."

Callie trotted over on Bandido, and they were off. This time she carried her Colt in a holster she had procured from the Quartermaster.

Lieutenant Patton, accompanied by ten soldiers of the Sixth Infantry Regiment, led the caravan, along with Big Sharley and B-25, riding in three Dodge open-top touring automobiles. The media trio followed in the Biograph Ford. It was a fine June morning. The recent rains had brought the desert back to life. Prickly pear cactus sported bright yellow flowers and creamy white yucca blossoms arose out of sharp, dagger-like leaves. Even the lowly creosote was spotted with delicate yellow blooms.

Callie leaned back in the saddle and enjoyed the fresh summer breeze and, once again, the company of Chester and Lazlo. She cherished her time with Casey, but relished getting out in the back country on another potential adventure. She had to admit that anytime she took a ride in Mexico, it was liable to end in an adventure. She was glad she had brought her horse.

The army cars stopped. Patton got out and warily approached the ranch. The other soldiers fanned out in a circle to surround the place.

Lazlo already had the Bell and Howell set up and was peering through the lens, when three horsemen exploded out of the brush about fifty yards away, pistols firing. Patton, an expert marksman, returned fire and killed one of them on the spot. They wheeled around and caught gunfire from the rest of the regiment, then headed toward the mountains. Patton again fired, and this time shot the horse out from under one of the riders, who somersaulted off the animal and somehow managed to land running. Patton took aim and shot him dead at a hundred yards.

It was all over in five minutes.

The dust slowly dissipated and everyone walked up to examine the bodies. Callie was right there beside Patton, who was questioning one of his guides. "Is this the man, Miguel? Is this Cardenas?" barked Patton.

"Sí, Lieutenant. It is he. Villa will miss his amigo," he said, turning toward Patton and Callie with a broad smile.

Patton slapped his thigh. "Damn, we got the bastard!" He ran back toward the Dodge and parked it close to the bodies. "Okay boys, we're gonna strap these hombres on to the hood, just like a couple of deer. Get to it!" While this was done, he removed Cardenas' silver-studded saddle from his horse and threw it in the Dodge.

Lazlo was filming the entire event. All the troopers were buzzing around with excitement at such a coup. The sight of the bloody men

98

splayed out on the scorching metal of the car sickened Callie, and she walked away. She sat in the car and solemnly wrote about what she had just witnessed.

On the way back the sight of the dead men tied to the car elicited considerable agitation from surrounding villages. General Pershing would be quite pleased that one of Villa's right-hand men was eliminated. He dubbed Patton, "The bandit", from then on.

Callie became disgusted with the whole affair. Chester reminded her of where she was, and also reminded her of their first meeting back in Columbus. "You must have suspected things like this would occur in what is essentially a small war. Back then you seemed eager for action, ready to do anything for a story."

Callie eyed him curiously. Just when she had dismissed Chester as a lovable but dim-witted huckster, he would surprise her. "You're right, Chester. I allow my emotions to get the best of me, when it really does no good at all. I must grit my teeth and let the soldiers be what they are-soldiers. I just wish they hadn't put them on the car like that."

"We had to get that on film, Callie. The folks back home will eat it up."

"Yes, I know. And the same exact thing will probably happen in Europe, a thousand times over. It seems we are born to kill. It goes on and on. The century is only sixteen years old, so young and new and full of promise. I see everything changing, except for that. Pancho Villa even seemed saddened by it, *la violencia* he called it."

"Pancho Villa? Have you talked to Pancho Villa?"

Callie was about to change the subject, when a Mexican woman, waving a yellow scarf, suddenly jumped out on the road from behind some brush. Chester slammed on the brakes and Bandido reared up in surprise.

"Por favor. Mi hijo es gravemente herido. Puede usted ayudarme?"

"She says her son is badly wounded," said Callie. "They need help."

She followed the woman a little ways down an arroyo. In the shade of a cottonwood tree laid a young man, perhaps sixteen, or seventeen, with a blood-soaked bandage around his shoulder. Callie saw at once that he was pale from loss of blood, possibly in shock.

She looked at the tearful woman and tried to reassure her, although she wondered if there was enough time. "Esperar aquí. Encontraré a un doctor."

She rushed back to the car. "Her son has been shot. You two must stay with her-it's just a short distance down the arroyo. Big Sharley and B-25 can be lookouts. I'm going to inform Lieutenant Patton and then ride back to camp for Doctor Stevens."

Chester protested, "Now wait-", but Callie galloped away. Patton's car was only a mile or so ahead. She rode up alongside his car.

"I must say this quickly, Lieutenant. A young man is badly wounded back there. My friends are with him and I am off to fetch Dr. Stevens. I can make much better time if I cut across the valley here. Adios, sir."

"That's a no man's land out there, miss!" he yelled as she charged away in a cloud of dust.

Bandido was well-rested and she gave him full rein. They tore across the flat sun-baked desert. Callie leaned forward, her head against Bandido's neck, whispering encouragement. The scent of sagebrush and creosote, the fresh wind in her face as they galloped through the fierce Mexican landscape, made her giddy.

They had already covered half the distance when Callie saw three riders approaching rapidly from the left. She saw the puffs of smoke and gave Bandido a kick as the bullets whizzed over them.

She became enraged. "You bastards try and shoot my horse, will you!"

There was a slight rise ahead, and once over it she swerved Bandido off to the left and doubled back. The bandits came over the rise and suddenly she was gone. They slowed. "Donde esta la gringa? Que-" A bullet ripped through his heart before he could finish.

Riding parallel to their path, a hundred yards away, was a rider-less pony. The bandits squinted and saw the glint of gunmetal under the horse's head.

Callie lay astride Bandido, exactly like the Comanche she learned it from, her left leg hooked over his back, her left hand grabbing the saddle horn, her right leg controlling the horse with quick little movements, leaning forward and firing from under his neck, all but invisible to the bewildered Mexicans.

100

"Ride steady, Bandido," she spoke into his ear, "I won't let them hurt you".

She realized she probably had only a few bullets left in the Colt's chamber. She had to make them count.

The two riders split up and began to ride at her from different directions. "Matar el caballo!" the larger man shouted.

She drew a bead on the bandit, pressing hard against the horse's neck to steady herself, constantly reassuring him into a steady gallop, and squeezed off the second shot.

The big Mexican somersaulted backwards out of his saddle, just as the third bandit advanced and fired successive shots, the last grazing Callie across her shoulder and back.

She screamed half in pain, more in rage, clutched her back instinctively and lost her grip on the saddle, hitting the ground hard, then bouncing back up, grabbing Badido's neck with both of her arms. The horse slowed down, enabling her to regain control.

When the remaining rider saw his other comrade go down, he beat a fast retreat.

Callie went after him.

Bandido didn't need urging. He flew across the sand and brought her within fifty yards of her terrified quarry.

She was erect in the saddle now and twirled the gun in her hand to get a better grip, extended her arm and fired. It was an easy shot at that distance.

The man probably died from fright at the sight of this female demon of death bearing down on him like some crazed renegade Indian, before the bullet shattered his skull. He struck the ground and tumbled for twenty yards, and slammed against a dagger plant, impaling his chest

Callie circled her vanquished enemy, thrusting the Colt into the air and letting out a shriek of joy and blood lust. When she squeezed the trigger there was only a click.

She rode in tight circles around the body, howling and whooping, calling up something inside her she never knew existed.

She brought Bandido to a halt, leaped off the horse, and fell upon her dead enemy in frenzy, kicking him repeatedly, shrieking curses. She seized a large knife stuck in his belt and held it poised above the body.

Bandido snorted and stomped the ground, surprised at the actions of this suddenly strange woman.

She glanced at the horse. The sensation of blood soaking into her blouse and running down her back jolted her out of her hysteria.

"Andele, Bandido!" She jumped into the saddle. They whirled away and sped across the valley.

The desert hush returned. A golden eagle, riding the thermals, floated over the scene and looked down-three horses grazed the sparse grass, three bodies sprawled in the dust, the wind blowing the scent of blood into the air. His keen eyes took it in and he swerved away.

She reached the camp in minutes and alerted the doctor. While he fetched his bag Bandido could not keep still, kicking and whinnying, rearing up in agitation. "Cuidado, Bandido!" yelled Callie, "You nearly threw me."

He finally mounted his horse and followed her down the road back to the Rubio, barely able to keep up with them. Bandido leaped off the road and hit the ground running into the arroyo. The doctor followed more cautiously.

When they reached the boy he was still conscious. The doctor hopped down and went to work.

Callie crouched down in the shade, accepting the canteen offered to her by Lazlo. She sweated profusely, was covered in grime, and she had a look on her face that unnerved Chester.

"Callie, are you all right?"

She didn't seem to hear him, fallen back into the giddiness of the kill, a warrior's bliss.

The doctor stood up. "He's going to make it. The bullet passed through, don't think it hit anything vital or he'd be dead. Lost a lot of blood, but his youth saved him. We'll take him back to camp and make sure he's all right."

Callie looked up at him, dreamily. "Doctor Stevens," she said softly,"I believe I have been shot. Would you kindly have a look at my back?"

They were all taken aback. Doctor Stevens dropped down and cut away part of her wet blouse with scissors. Her back was covered in blood. "Damnation child, why didn't you speak up sooner?"

He grabbed the canteen and washed off the blood to determine the extent of her wound. "She's been grazed, pretty deeply." He examined her closely. "Must have hurt like hell. A few more inches, it would have gone through your neck, girly. You're a lucky one."

Callie said nothing as he stitched the gash the bullet had left and applied a bandage. "This will do for now. You lost a fair amount of blood too. You'll need to take it easy."

The mother was very concerned that Callie had received such an injury on the ride to save her son. It was inconceivable that a complete stranger, let alone a gringa, an American lady, had risked her life in this way for a *campesino*. She took both of Callie's hands and cried over them, head bowed in deep emotion.

Callie, still not quite herself, smiled, patted her on the back and pointed toward Bandido. "Senora, gracias a mi caballo, Bandido, no yo." She grinned at Chester. "He did all the work." The horse snorted at the mention of his name.

All of this made the woman cry even harder.

Dr. Stevens ordered her to remain in the tent overnight so that he could check for any sign of infection. He asked her if she wanted anything, but she declined. In the solitude of the tent, she tried to grasp exactly what had occurred out there on the desert. But she had a visitor.

General Pershing peeked in, smiling, unsure as to her condition. "May I come in?"

"Of course, General," said Callie drowsily.

"I know you're a bit weak, so I won't stay long. What happened out there?"

Callie took a deep breath. "Well, sir, Bandido and I were riding back here as fast as we could," she began, weakly. "A young Mexican was badly wounded near Rubio.I suppose he got caught in as crossfire, and out of nowhere, I was attacked by three men."

The general sat down beside her, shaking his head. "Callie, Callie. You seem determined to disregard all proper caution that common sense would warrant. This is wild country. There are all sorts of desperate characters out here. And you, twenty-four-year-old American journalist, decided to ride unprotected right into the heart of that very real danger. You completely disregarded Lieutenant Patton's warning."

"There was no time, sir. The boy's life was at stake. It was no time to consider proper procedure. Surely, you, who have been through so much conflict and performed so gallantly, realize the situation."

Pershing knew he would come out on the short end of this discussion before he had even started. How could he find fault with this remarkable young woman with the piercing dark eyes, the disarming smile and the confidence of an armed battalion? She had enchanted him and everyone else she had come across from the very first day. A man could only wish for such a wife, such a daughter, such a friend.

"How are you feeling?"

"I'm fine, just a little tired, but I hope someone remembered to brush and feed Bandido. He rode hard."

"I'll see to it. One more thing, Callie. I found this tied on your saddle." He handed her a large tuft of black, greasy hair. "Did you do this?"

She took it in her hand, mesmerized, as if it were a shrunken head from some cannibalistic tribe. "I've never been attacked in such a fashion. I had to protect my horse. He's been through so much, General. He will do anything I ask of him. He trusts me like a child. When the bullets came close to him, I lost my head."

"For the horse, not yourself."

"Yes sir." She looked at the hair. "I did do this. I might have done a proper job of it, if there had been more time."

A slight tremor ruffled his military demeanor. He rose up, hesitated, gently touched the top of her head, and exited the tent.

June 21, 1916. Troopers of the 10th Cavalry who had been captured at the Battle of Carrizal, upon release to the U.S. Army at International Bridge, in El Paso, Texas

Chapter 11

Captain Charles Boyd was a cocky West Point graduate who commanded the African-American Tenth Cavalry regiment. He was one of several officers set out on patrol to check for the presence of *Carrancista* soldiers east of the base camp. After a meeting with General Pershing he was in high spirits, displaying a sheet of paper with his orders. "I've got peace or war right here," he said to his troops. Some of the soldiers looked at each other with quizzical expressions.

Captain Lewis Morey, with Troop K, was to join Boyd at a ranch near Villa Ahumada.

Accompanying the regiment was Lem Spilsbury, a Mormon scout who had signed on to catch Villa, but was now a reluctant participant in what might become an all-out war with Mexico.

Upon reaching the ranch Boyd conferred with his officers. Reports indicated a few hundred soldiers in the little town of Carrizal, about seven miles distant, and three hundred more at Villa Ahumada. Captain Boyd was keen on marching through Carrizal, even though he was warned they would be fired upon.

"These aren't *Villistas* on the run," interjected Lem Spilsbury. "They're Carranza's men, under orders to fight. There's another road that bypasses Carrizal, and it's shorter, Captain. We'd be asking for trouble if we rode through that town."

Boyd bristled at the notion of avoiding a fight. "We'll go through the town, and if they fire on our rear guard, we'll go back through the town and clean them up."

His officers advised him to request permission first, with handwritten notes to the mayors of the villages. The next morning they saddled up and headed toward Carrizal, stopping at an irrigation ditch to water their horses and check their weapons. They could see the adobe houses and a small church just beyond some cottonwood trees. Some Mexican interpreters delivered the request notes. While awaiting an answer a small group of Mexican soldiers rode out to meet them.

"I am General Gomez," said a heavy-set man leading the troops. "I have orders to stop any American forces going east, west or south."

Lem Spilsbury interpreted.

"And I have orders to go through the town," asserted Captain Boyd.

"If you do this, we will have to fire on your men." He thought for a moment. "Let me confer with my commandant to see if an exception could be made."

Boyd thought he was stalling and became impatient. "Tell the son of a bitch that we're going through," he commanded Spilsbury.

Gomez reddened in anger. He did not need an interpreter for that comment. He abruptly turned and led his men back to Carrizal.

The regiment spread out on either side of a dirt road leading to town. They could see Mexicans taking positions behind trees, along with two machine guns, and snipers up on the roofs of houses. They advanced, and then Boyd yelled for them to dismount and fight on foot. The machine guns started firing from the trees.

"Commence firing!" yelled Boyd. He rushed forward and was shot in the hand. "I've been wounded! Go to 'em boys!"

He waved his hat at Captain Morey to move forward. A second bullet went through his shoulder, but he took no notice and advanced toward the gunfire. He turned back to his troops. "C'mon K troop! Let's take-"

Before he could finish, a bullet slammed into his eye, instantly killing him.

There was panic and confusion. Wounded horses shrieked in pain and soldiers started falling from the intense return fire.

They dropped to the ground and began firing back with their Springfields.

Captain Morey's troops became separated from the rest. He saw Boyd's horse running confusedly across the field. Suddenly there were Carrancistas charging at them from the left.

"Sergeant Page! Good God, man! They're right on top of you! Fire your guns!"

"Captain, we can't stay here!" responded Page.

A bullet hit Morey in the shoulder and knocked him on his back. He lay there dazed, then got back up and ordered a retreat. "Scatter out, men!"

He re-crossed the irrigation ditch and made it to an adobe house, along with several other soldiers. A trumpeter sounded retreat.

"You boys make your getaway if you can, because I'm done for," he said weakly.

A few troops stayed with him, and at dusk they began the trek toward the ranch, but Morey couldn't keep up and gave them his map and compass, with orders to go on. He then slept for some hours, woke up refreshed, and made it back to the ranch, where he found an abandoned meal and a pot of warm coffee in a small kitchen.

Eventually, the Mexicans captured the soldiers who had not ridden away or hidden, twenty-four in all, including Lem Spilsbury. Shoes, hats, money, and jewelry were quickly confiscated, and then they were marched to Villa Ahumada, where a train transported them to the penitentiary in Chihuahua City. Passengers swarmed around them threateningly, but the soldiers held them off.

President Wilson heard about the Carrizal fiasco from newspaper boys on the streets of Washington. Twelve Americans had been killed, fifteen wounded, and twenty-four captured. He dreaded that this incident would lead to a more serious confrontation with Mexico. He demanded that the prisoners be released. A few days later, Carranza, also wanting to avoid all-out war, agreed.

Eventually, it became clear that Captain Boyd had been responsible for the incident and some of the tension eased. At the Press Club in New York, on July 1, Wilson spoke forcefully:

Do you think the glory of America would be enhanced by a war of conquest in Mexico? Do you think that any act of violence by a powerful nation like this against a weak and distracted neighbor would reflect distinction on the annals of the United States? I have to constantly remind myself that I am not the servant of those who wish to enhance the value of their Mexican investments, that I am a servant of the rank and file of the people of the United States.

The American prisoners were released on the International Bridge in Juarez. Reporters crowded to photograph the men, who were wore a motley assortment of clothes, from serapes to yachting caps. Their clothes were burned and they were then taken to a building, where they were fumigated with kerosene.

The weary black soldiers of the Tenth Regiment were handed fragrant bouquets of sweet peas by the African-American residents of El Paso.

General Pershing asserted that he had specifically ordered Boyd to be cautious and avoid a fight with the Mexican troops, unless absolutely necessary. But the damage had been done, and this embarrassing defeat essentially ended the Punitive Expedition.

The battles were over, and the next six months would be the most difficult for the taciturn general, but it would open up new possibilities for Callie.

Army campfire in the Chihuahuan desert

Chapter 12

While the powers that be debated the fate of General Pershing and his ten thousand troops, they were ordered confined to the base camp at Colonia Dublan, the Mormon settlement in northern Chihuahua. The camp soon took on the aspect of a bustling town, as numerous Chinese merchants opened food stands and laundries. Liquor was prohibited in camp, but cantinas existed just outside the fence, as did an approved prostitution area, for Pershing once again decided this was the best way to handle the "woman question." Areas for boxing, wrestling, and ball games were also provided. Lest the troops fall prey to idleness, Pershing established daily drills and maneuvers

Callie was now able to ride Bandido to her heart's content, for the surrounding area was deemed safe.

Not far from camp were the ruins of Casa Grandes, a Pre-Columbian site that was nearly a thousand years old. Callie could ride there in twenty minutes. The maze of adobe walls was somehow very soothing, for their soft rounded forms blended perfectly with the desert landscape. A talkative little man named Pedro would show her the secrets of *las ruinas*, like the two mummies clothed in linen, found in a tomb surrounded by jewelry and pottery. He even had names for them, Guapo y Feo, Handsome and Ugly, though Callie couldn't quite see the distinction. He kept the pair in a small adobe barn next to a mule stall. His prize possession, however, was a five-hundred pound iron meteorite. They were guarded by a small wooden statue of Our Lady of Guadalupe on a nearby table. Pedro didn't require Callie to pay the usual fee, because she was "muy hermosa", but she insisted on giving him something.

Bandido was a wonderful source of solace. She had greatly missed the company of animals in her life and the perky little horse had come to her in such a strange and accidental manner that she considered him a good omen. She was sure that he would have starved or been shot had she not adopted him.

He was just the right size and smart as a whip. He was also barely out of adolescence and would sometimes surprise Callie by bucking out of sheer mischief and trying to throw her in the middle of a trot.

He would rear up and let out a long whinny in pure exuberance or shake his long pretty mane in mysterious frustration.

"Bandido, "Qué quieres? Usted está loco!"admonished Callie, only halfheartedly. She could never get truly angry with him, for it was his wildness that she cherished above all.

He responded instantly to her whenever she spoke to him in Spanish, his ears twitching and the flash of perception in his eyes.

"Andale, muchacho!" she would cry, and he would at once break into a spirited gallop. "Rapido, rapido!" she yelled, her exhilaration escalating with Bandido's reckless spirit as he raced across the wide-open desert just for the joy of it. All the riding tricks she knew as a girl in Comanche Springs came back to her, like leaning way off to one side and grabbing a flower at breakneck speed or surprising a jackrabbit flushed from hiding.

In her youth, small groups of Comanche on hunting trips from the Oklahoma reservation would sometimes camp near her house-some had sold horses to her father-and the young Indians would show her riding tricks that had been passed down from the warrior days. Those tricks had saved her life on the day of her ride to fetch the doctor. Even though she was just a youngster Callie quickly learned the Indian's riding methods. She often wondered why they were so kind to her, a scrawny little white girl.

Sometimes, they would find themselves atop a rise with a grand view of the rugged Sierra Madre rising to the west, and when the wind was right she caught the sharp scent of pine from the Tarahumara country, and she would pat Bandido's neck. "Someday we'll ride up into those beautiful mountains, mi querido." Her eyes picked out mesas that were a hundred miles distant and she wondered if she could ever tolerate the confines of a city again.

They continued on and found an old hunting path that followed a meandering creek, the trail crossing and re-crossing the shallow water many times, before they broke out into open country, where meadows strewn with wildflowers reflected the brassy sunlight. Groves of junipers and pines provided shade and relief from the blustery wind.

Callie was thirsty, and so was Bandido; she had absentmindedly forgot to fill her canteen. They came to a tiny creek in the woods and she dismounted, and Bandido immediately began to slurp up the cold water. She splashed a little on her face and then submerged the canteen. She was watching the bubbles float to the top when Bandido jerked up his head.

"Que esta mal?" said Callie, looking around warily. It was very quiet, only the sound of the water over the rocks, and Bandido's breathing. She looked behind her, then stood up and looked all around. Bandido snorted and backed away from the water.

"Qué es, Bandido?"

She followed his gaze, toward a wall of brush on a small cliff. She squinted, panning the area. A pair of yellow eyes returned her gaze. She emitted a quiet gasp.

She took hold of the reins. The woman and the horse, frozen like statues, stared intently at those eyes.

Minutes went by.

The eyes vanished; a flash of tawny brown came and went, but not a sound. Their eyes darted around, trying to locate something.

A jay squawked and made her jump.

Callie slowly looked behind her right shoulder. An adult mountain lion sat ten feet away.

"Oh!" She grabbed the reins tighter. Bandido tensed, sniffing the air, ears twitching, eyes flashing.

"Tranquilo, tranquilo," she whispered, stroking his face with her free hand.

The big cat sat there and they saw curiosity in its eyes, not threat.

Callie leaned closer to the horse, whispered in his ear. "Mira, Bandido. Es muy bonito, no? Que hermosa! So pretty. Un gato…un gato grande."

The reassurance in her voice and the non-aggressive stance of the lion transformed Bandido's mood. He shook his head and hunched down like a dog who wants to play.

"No, no Bandido." She held him there, gripping the reins with both hands. "I don't think he wants to play."

The cat then slowly fell over and began to roll in the dirt.

Callie smiled, astonished. "Well, maybe he does. Would you look at that?"

Bandido bolted forward a few feet, jerking Callie with him.

"Alto, Bandido!"

The lion leaped up and lashed out at the horse, missing his nose by inches. Crouching low to the ground, ears flat, fangs bared, the big cat growled threateningly. Callie pulled mightily on the horse to make him back up a few steps. "Está bien," she whispered loudly. Bandido tilted his head, unable to comprehend the lion's reaction.

After a few moments, the lion slowly calmed down, bounded into the trees and disappeared.

Callie drooped in relief and let the reins drop. Leaning against her young horse, she let out a grateful sigh.

By the time they trotted into camp it would often be near dusk, the smells of campfires, beans, bacon and coffee filling the air, reminding her how famished she was after a day of riding. But she would always brush Bandido and make sure he was fed and watered before she had her own dinner. She admired how responsible the troopers were about taking care of their own mounts and Callie seemed to blend right in with army camp life. Brushing her horse, she could not help but smile.

I have never felt this happy in my twenty-four years, and it has come about because of my involvement in this brutal revolution. Such a strange thing.

She felt everything tenfold-her youth, her sex, her femininity, her power, and her fear. And that thrilled her. Out here in the desert there was nothing to filter sensations-everything came to her potent, intact, just the way a fox or a hawk might receive it. Far away from stifling crowds and mindless chatter, useless information to distract her.

The very best times occurred when she turned off her mind and ran on pure instinct.

One typical sweltering afternoon the soldiers decided to cool off by washing cars and trucks, and even hosing down the horses. She walked toward the airfield and spied Casey and his pals cleaning the Jennies. Casey had on his regular pants and leather boots, but had discarded his army shirt for a white undershirt.

Callie leaned against a truck and watched him from a short distance away. He was tall and lanky, but had broad shoulders. The undershirt was a little snug on his torso. She felt herself becoming aroused. His muscles rippled as he moved a cleaning rag in circles over the plane's surface. His hair had gotten somewhat shaggy, and she liked that too. He also had acquired a beautiful golden tan.

I guess he's been without his shirt quite a few times. Wish I could do that. Casey, darlin', you are most alluring to me in that undershirt.

The sexual urge came on fast. Callie touched her breasts, ran her tongue across her dry lips, felt constricted and hot in her clothes, wanted to pull them off, throw them aside, wanted to be touched, wanted Casey.

One of the soldiers noticed her behind the truck and nudged Casey. He turned and saw her there, flashed his fine smile and waved. Then everyone began to wave.

"We see you, Callie, spying on us," they cried out, snickering.

Callie put her hand to her mouth, turned this way and that and tried to look like she was doing something else, but she was caught. What could she do? She turned around and waved without looking and hurried away, mortified, but then laughed. *Callie, you little fool. If you're going to be a voyeur, then don't get caught!*

The formidable heat of the Chihuahuan summer descended upon the camp like an iron hand. Callie rose early to ride Bandido in the morning coolness and then took a long siesta in her tent, writing short articles and long journal entries about her feelings for Casey and all the marvelous and terrible things she had witnessed since leaving on that train for Fort Bliss in March. She still read her little book of Shakespeare's sonnets that would comfort her when nothing else could. After writing in her journal, she picked up the book and singled out a passage in Sonnet 108:

"What's new to speak, what new to register,
That may express my love or thy dear merit?
Nothing sweet boy; but yet, like prayers divine,
I must, each day say o'er the very same.

She put down the book and stared into space. "What's new to speak? Nothing sweet boy; but yet, like prayers divine, I must, each day say o'er the very same..." It's true, Casey. Your blue eyes, strong

115

arms, and dashing manner, they keep showing up in my journal because they're my favorite things about you. And now, those big shoulders. It's nice to have your lover all wrapped up so neatly."

And yet, here she was, a twenty-four year old woman in the prime of life, full of plans and dreams, stranded in a forsaken desert with ten thousand soldiers, her lover with a war to fight, but she without a real purpose.

One evening around the fire, she, along with Casey, Chester and Lazlo, decided that they would drive down to the town of Galeana the next day for some relief from the dusty camp and have a proper Mexican dinner, some good Mexican beer, and maybe even some mariachi music.

It was calm Sunday morning when they piled into the Biograph Ford, sans movie camera, and headed south. Everyone was in good spirits. Lazlo played some Mexican songs he had recently learned on his harmonica, which further lifted their spirits.

They drove into the modest plaza and parked in front of a prosperous looking little café called El Milagro. There was a park in the center of the square filled with lavender blue jacaranda trees and an old stone fountain, around which gathered young couples in spotless white shirts and dresses, hands entwined, soft love-struck smiles on their brown faces.

Callie lingered by the car and couldn't help staring. "This is so pretty, so peaceful. Why haven't we come here before?"

Casey took her arm. "Oh, something about having to catch a bandit I guess," he said with a straight face, leading her inside. The place was brightly painted with blues and yellows and filled with families in their Sunday finest. A lone guitarist played sweet ballads. The tangy aromas of tortillas, refried beans, onions and cilantro permeated the warm air and everyone's mouth was watering. The waiter greeted them and suggested the courtyard, which would be cooler and quieter.

There was a weathered old splashing fountain in the courtyard which freshened the air and invited customers to make wishes, for it was filled with hundreds of coins that sparkled on the bottom

As Callie sat down she gazed around at the hanging baskets of scarlet geraniums, an undulating brilliant purple bougainvillea vine

116

that climbed up to the roof, and all manner of tropical plants flourishing in huge oblong pots. The courtyard was surrounded by bright yellow arches, above which was a second story with balconies and more flowers, and lines of just-washed clothes flapping in the wind. Cages of chirping canaries were suspended here and there.

"Who would have guessed such a charming little place existed here?" exclaimed Callie, squirming in her seat with anticipation. She glanced at Lazlo, who had a goofy expression.

"Never have I smelled such smells," he uttered quite seriously. "It is almost as if I could eat the aromas."

Chester tucked a napkin in his shirt and just nodded his head good-naturedly. He had been traveling with Lazlo for months and was used to his Hungarian quips.

Baskets of warm tortilla chips and bowls of thick spicy salsa and guacamole were set before them. A round of chilled beers were soon brought to drink while they decided what to order.

Each one in turn proposed a toast, according to the vagaries of his or her mind at the moment Lazlo began. "I toast to my beloved homeland of Hungary, which I have not seen for five years, and my perfect mother, and brothers and sisters, my departed father in heaven, and to my precious Bell and Howell camera that brought me to this strange and beautiful land."

"Here, here!" chimed in everyone.

Chester then raised his glass, looking natty as always, this day attired in a white suit and red bow tie, straw hat and perfectly trimmed mustache. "My friends, here's to the magic of cinema, which, like it did for Lazlo, brought me out here too. And, to my beloved Annabelle, whom I left forlorn back in California, but who knows, I shall return and make her my wife in the near future, when my ship comes in, God willing."

"Oh, that's so sweet, Chester. To Annabelle!"

"To Annabelle!"

Casey remained silent, seemingly hoping they would overlook him, but Callie gave him a nudge.

Instead of a uniform he sported a simple white shirt and khaki pants. The deep bronze tan he had acquired made his smile even brighter. He cleared his throat. "Well, you boys are all right and this was a swell idea. I haven't had too much time for socializing and all that, so I appreciate it all, every darn bit of it." He shook his head, as if to agree with himself, smiling at the two men across the table. "Another thing-I'd like to thank you fellas for looking after Callie. I guess we've all had some close calls on this expedition, and, well, we have to look out for each other, don't we?" Finally, he turned to Callie, sitting next to him. "And here's to you, miss, the best darn co-pilot a man could ever want."

Callie was beaming as they touched glasses.

Callie poured some more beer into her glass and watched it fizz and felt the bubbles tickle her nose. She looked up at each of the three men in turn. "I didn't really know what to expect when I came out here. I guess I somehow trusted things would work out, and I guess they have, thanks to you Chester for accepting a crazy reporter's wacky idea, to you Lazlo for never failing to make me laugh and see the bright side, and to you Captain, for saving my life several times, and teaching me how to get drunk on tequila in an amazingly short time."

Casey blushed and shook his head, grinning.

"Cheers!"

They ordered another round of the delicious Mexican beer, but now Callie's mood turned wistful. She was a little drunk, put her elbow on the table and rested her chin in her hand in the manner of a child. "What's going to happen to all of us? I don't know if I want to continue with the *Chronicle*. And, my God, I'm so scared we're going to war. Chester, what will you do now?"

"Well, Mr. D.W. Griffith, who was the head director at Biograph, is preparing for his next film with Mutual Studio. I might possibly be assigned as an assistant director. That's where my heart is, you see. These newsreels pay the bills, but there's little art in it. In fact, I'm waiting for a telegram from the studio that might shed some light on when they will start shooting. It's rather exciting. And, I'm certain they can use a cameraman with the talents of Lazlo here."

"That's terrific news, Chester. I had no idea. Isn't that wonderful news, Casey?"

"It's swell news."

"And, if I may be so bold, there may be a job for the likes of you, young lady," added Chester. "Since they moved the studios to Los Angeles, a little village called Hollywood actually, why things have just taken off. They need all sorts-script girls, carpenters, extras, people who can ride horses. All sorts."

Callie perked up at this. "Ride horses? I can do that darn well. Do you suppose they'd hire Bandido, too? That would just be terrifically neat."

"Well, you might just have to go out there and find out for yourself. Los Angeles is a sleepy little Spanish town, but has a great deal of charm. And the climate is excellent, groves of oranges and lemons in the valleys, and a short distance away, snowy mountains. You could do a lot worse, Callie," said Chester with a wink.

"Well, well, maybe there's a career in motion pictures for our Callie," said Casey, with his teasing grin.

"Oh, I don't know fellas. I used to think I knew my calling, but since I've been out here and seen what I've seen, I'm not so sure anymore. There's so much beauty in this country. I might just stay here for a while." She lifted her arms as if to encompass the courtyard. "Just look around us-the color, the flowers, the little canaries singing, and, my goodness, the smells. You don't see this back home. Why it's downright drab in comparison. These people don't have much, but look how they celebrate life with what they do have!" She took a sip of beer and her youthful face had a pensive frown. "You know, Mexico has awakened me...that's what has happened. For all the violence I've seen, I think I've seen even more beauty and bravery. These people teach us how to live. Whatever happens tomorrow, we must live for today. *Viva para hoy!*" She held up her glass and so did the rest.

"Viva para hoy!" they all shouted.

Casey leaned over and gave her a kiss on the cheek, at which she promptly blushed.

Everyone ordered something different: Chile rellenos, enchiladas verde, tacos con chorizo, and pollo con mole de cacahuate.

It was a fine Sunday outing.

119

Chapter 13

A week later, as Callie was writing in her journal, Chester and Lazlo appeared in front of her tent. They looked a little melancholy.

"Hi there boys. What brings you to my neighborhood?"

They looked at each other. "Callie, my dear, Lazlo and I are off to California. I received a telegram that Mr. Griffith can indeed use the both of us in his next project, so we've decided to throw in with him."

Callie put down her journal and jumped up to hug the both of them. "I am so happy for you. I know this will be a splendid opportunity. But how I will miss the both of you, my two brothers-in-arms." She was already teary and patting both of them on the shoulders, as if they really were her own brothers, about to venture out.

"I want you to think about my suggestion. A woman of your talents might make a very excellent life for herself in California. It's a wide open country with grand possibilities, just like our twentieth century." He put a card in her hand and closed her hand over it. "Keep my card and if you should decide to come out, just let me know and I will help you get settled. And one more thing." He turned around and took something from Lazlo. "I want you to have this. It's a Kodak Autographic."

He presented her with an elegant black camera, with a folding bellows and smooth black leather body.

Callie opened her mouth and widened her eyes in one astonished gesture. "Oh Chester," she said in a low whisper, "this is so lovely."

Chester smiled. "I've been watching you fussing over Lazlo's camera and helping him load it and set it up. The company gave me this in case I wanted to take some publicity stills, but I don't have the knack. I think you do. And there's an instruction manual in the case to go with it."

"And these are for you too señorita Callie." Lazlo produced a bouquet of wildflowers from behind his back, like a Hungarian magician. Now she was totally undone.

She held the camera and the flowers with tears in her eyes. The two men beamed proudly.

"And I have nothing for either of you," she said, drooping.

Chester put the camera in the case and set the flowers in a can of water that he brought along. Then he took both her hands in his. "Callie, you have never stopped amazing us. Your friendship has been an endless source of delight for Lazlo and me. What better gift could we have asked for than your sweet company?"

Lazlo inched forward. "All this is true, and much more," he said, shyly.

She hugged each of them numerous times.

"We must get to Nogales by dark, so, farewell and good luck to you. Godspeed, dear lady."

They walked away and Callie felt a tug in her heart, for it was only then that she realized how deep her feelings were for them.

A Fourth of July barbecue and dance was to be put on for the troops, and in no time a plywood dance floor and stage were erected, and long, mess-hall type tables were set up. A small band was organized and a multitude of flags and patriotic hangings festooned the stage. General Pershing approved a fireworks display to be held at 10p.m..

Callie had long ceased to be the sole woman on the expedition ever since the chase for Villa was abandoned. Mexican and Chinese cooks, Mormon wives, and even some of the "official" prostitutes all mingled in the huge encampment. Lieutenant Patton had brought his wife, and sister Harriet, down from Texas for the special celebration. General Pershing had met Harriet before the expedition and the two were very fond of each other.

By sundown the band was playing waltzes and fox trots, and the huge disparity between males and females did not seem to dampen anyone's enthusiasm.

Vaqueros from neighboring ranches sat on their horses, sharing cigarettes with the American soldiers, trying to understand what each other was saying. Some of them pranced around on fancy stallions with shiny saddles and showed off their equestrian abilities, urging their horses into a high-stepping routine.

Callie wandered over to the airfield and found Casey talking with Captain Foulois. The men concluded their conversation and Casey came up to Callie, who was dressed all in white, with yellow flowers in her long black hair. Every soldier within seeing distance was riveted upon her willowy figure

"Why look, it's Cinderella, out here in the Chihuahuan desert."

Callie sashayed teasingly around in a circle. "Haven't you heard, Captain-there's a little party going on?"

"I was wondering what all that ruckus was about? How's a soldier supposed to concentrate when...you look so darn beautiful?"

"Well then, you had just better accompany me to the ball and show me off."

"Well, I guess I have my orders. Shall we, miss?" He offered her his arm and they walked to the celebration. Casey was half starved, so they got their plates of grilled beef and fixings and sat near Pershing and Patton. Callie was glad to see the general relaxed, with a smile on his face. He had a daunting task to keep ten thousand troopers busy and well-drilled when there were no more battles to fight, or anywhere to go until President Wilson decided their fate.

Just as they finished, the piano player launched into a rousing version of the *Maple Leaf Rag.* Callie pulled Casey to the dance floor, which was crowded with couples, soldiers dancing by themselves and with each other, and a squealing bunch of Mormon kids from nearby farms. The Apache scouts joined in. Big Sharley and B-25 managed to coax some of the Mexican madams on to the floor and attempted to emulate the dance steps of the gringos, with mixed results.

Casey surprised Callie with his adroitness as he led her around the floor. The tinkling rhythms of the Scott Joplin tune got their shoulders and hips in motion as they trotted about, barely in control and giggling like children, having the time of their life. When the tune ended the crowd called out for more and the band played several more lively encores.

"Oh Casey, I'm so thirsty. Go get us some of that ice-cold lemonade. I'll wait for you here." Callie fanned and dabbed her perspiring face with a handkerchief. She looked over the milling crowd and the thousands of brown uniforms and could only think that this was a cruel interim before a much greater conflict would put all these young men in harm's way. All she knew was that some archduke was shot and ancient rivalries were rekindled, and suddenly a terrible war was spreading like a wildfire all over Europe. She wanted no part of it, but it would not let her go.

"Here you are, miss," said Casey, handing her a tall glass of lemonade. Callie drank it down in one long swallow.

"Dance with me, Captain. I like it when your arms are around me."

They put their empty glasses down in the warm dust and began to dance to a rendition of one of Callie's favorite songs, *Beautiful Dreamer*, by a fine young tenor, backed by violins.

Beautiful dreamer, wake unto me,
Starlight and dewdrops are waiting for thee.
Sounds of the rude world heard in the day,
Lulled by the moonlight have all passed away.

They glided softly in a small circle in the cooling evening air and held each other as lovers will, who are about to be parted. Callie felt pulled by forces she could not control and tried not to think about the future. "Viva para hoy," she mouthed silently.

They wandered off and found a little rise, from which they watched the fireworks. The horses were greatly unsettled by the bedlam and the artillery-like booms further darkened Callie's thoughts. She suddenly turned to Casey. "Tell me something. Tell me something you know. I've heard rumors. I know we won't stay neutral for long. How long do we have, Casey?"

Casey lit a cigarette and gazed at the exploding colors. "I'm supposed to report to Fort Sam Houston next week. We finally got those new planes."

Callie let out a long sigh and looked at the ground.

They spent as much time together the next six days as was humanly possible, given their surroundings, but the eve of Casey's departure arrived agonizingly fast.

At sunset the air was still and warm. On the horizon huge cumulonimbus clouds, reddened by the sun, mushroomed up into the atmosphere and seethed with faraway, silent lightning. Callie walked deliberately to Casey's tent. He was eating dinner, but when he saw her, he put his plate down and came over and took her hand. They walked a little ways into the darkness. She looked into his eyes. "I don't know what will happen after you leave. But I will not miss this chance to be with you tonight. Will you stay with me, Casey?"

Casey drew her to him and felt her soft hair against his face.

A thunderstorm roared over the desert that night with powerful winds and slashing lightning, but like all desert storms it moved quickly and was soon gone. The dawn was washed clean and fragrant. The desert would soon bloom with new life.

Callie didn't wait for the sun as she hurriedly saddled Bandido. Casey had already left to bid farewell to General Pershing and his army buddies. She waited for him by his plane. They said very little and she sent him on his way with a long kiss. As he taxied away she jumped on the horse and rode out to her favorite hill near the ruins. Casey made a big circle in the awakening sky and passed low, right over Callie and Bandido, who excitedly reared up and kicked with his front legs, as she took off her hat and waved, like some Rodeo Queen. The plane answered with a little jiggle, the wings catching the first rays of the rising sun, and then disappeared into the blue.

San Miguel de Allende

Chapter 14

San Miguel de Allende, June 1917

Callie wrote the date in her journal as she sipped a cup of strong Mexican coffee in the restaurant of the Hotel Vicente. The golden Gothic spires of La Parroquia, San Miguel's colonial cathedral, were framed by the window she gazed through, her eyes following a gaggle of uniformed schoolgirls as they made their way down a narrow, cobble-stoned street.

She was recalling her trip to nearby silver mine the day before, for an article she would send back to the *Chronicle*. After Casey had departed the army camp the previous summer, she had convinced Mr. Shaughnessy that she would make a more valuable contribution to the paper by traveling through Mexico and observing the changes wrought by the new Carranza government, as a semblance of stability began to return to the country. She was desperate to escape the dreary conditions at the camp and had no inclination to return to the states. She wanted to go deeper into Mexico and explore the hidden corners of its villages and the hazy mysteries of its turbulent past. And now she was sending back photographs, as well as articles, thanks to the camera Chester had given her. She would write her observations in a journal style, which she preferred, since she had been keeping personal journal since her youth in Texas.

Thus far, she had traveled to Zacatecas, Aguascalientes, Gunajuato, and now, the peaceful town of San Miguel de Allende. It was pure joy for her to be on her own, recording what she saw and felt with pen and camera. And there was so much to see that some days she would collapse in her room with exhaustion, having forgotten to eat while searching out an obscure museum or historic site

Walking down any street was an immersion in rich colors and weathered architecture. A two-hundred-year-old facade would be an ocean blue on its top half and lemon yellow on the bottom. Everywhere were warm ochres, siennas, and ambers, along with spicy bright violets, limes and electric blues, and all of this blended in with the heady piquant aromas that floated out of markets and tiny eateries, along with the sharp smell of burning pine or charcoal.

Callie was fascinated by the endless variety of doorways, often framed my heavy old stone lintels and sporting an endless array of metal knockers. And windows, barred with ancient wrought iron, with pots of geraniums, and a sleeping cat.

Callie was fascinated by all of it. She had seen glimpses of Mexico's beauty during the hunt for Villa, but now she was overwhelmed by it. All of that overflowed into her journal, as she wrote page after page of her day's adventure, and often a philosophical observation or two:

To think that I am getting paid for my adventure, for awakening each day with a smile on my face because I know I will be discovering something entirely new, talking to someone whose life is entirely different than my own, and therefore fascinating to me.

I see few American women my age who travel alone. In fact, there are few American women my age that don't live at home or have a proper "woman's" job, until they might marry and engage in their true calling of raising a family. Well, from this perspective, that sounds pretty dreary. I find that I am beating the system and am glad to do so. I have this fear that the police will find me out and haul me back to the states. The charge-having too much fun!

She put down her pen and flexed her hand, sipped some coffee and looked at a young couple lingering on the street, whispering sweet nothings to each other.

I'm not at all certain where Casey is at this moment. Probably flying high above Texas in one of his shiny new planes. One hundred and sixty horsepower, he boasted.

General Pershing is to arrive in France by next month. Imagine that-he's practically in charge of the entire American force. Soon, the boys will follow. We are in the war.

I wish I could fly with Casey again. I shall never forget that first day in Columbus when we went up in that rickety old Jenny.

But I can't think about it too much. I know he's where he wants to be. And, I suppose I am too. No, I know I am. So, let's leave it at that. Except that I do so miss his blue eyes and bright smile, and all the rest

128

of him. Damn it all!

It was not yet nine a.m., so Callie went up to her room, left her journal and took her camera to see what she might discover. She liked to roam the back streets, especially the narrow alleys, where light and shadow would create small dramatic vignettes: a boy leading a burro or gray-haired woman selling fruit on the curbside.

She came to one of her favorite places-the outdoor laundry basins, where for generations women had washed their clothes in such stone basins, through which fresh water flowed from the mountains. Rust-colored walls festooned with violet blooms of hanging bougainvillea provided a backdrop for the simple labor that took place there every day, as well as a lively social gathering of *mestizo* women, exchanging gossip, recipes, the price of tortillas, and perhaps their fate under the new Carranza government. She passed a small *churro* stand and bought one without thinking. She had become addicted to them. They were little more than long, tube-shaped, fried dough snacks, with sugar and cinnamon, but in Mexico even the simplest foods were delectable.

She came to a small plaza where flower vendors gathered under shaded archways, out of the sun. Shafts of light slanted in and fell upon bouquets of daisies, dahlias and zinnias, colors bouncing all over, dazzling Callie's receptive eyes.

She stood a short distance away, composed the scene, and got her shot. It was best to be as unobtrusive as possible, so she blended in with crowd and walked to the opposite side, where the different angle changed the entire scene. From there, it was the graceful Mexican women who caught the light, which fell on their red and blue *rebozos* in which they were wrapped like placid Madonnas. Some of the younger ones, with their coal black hair and flawless skin, took Callie's breath away. One of them noticed her photographing them and leaned over to whisper to her friend, and both of them broke out in radiant smiles, causing the whole group to turn and look at the crazy gringa.

Callie walked over, feeling guilty, and bought a bunch of daisies.

"Voy a volver con las photos," she said, promising to return with their pictures. They smiled shyly, nodding their heads, but not taking *la Americana* seriously.

She came to a large indoor market, *el Mercado,* where unending slopes of fresh fruit and vegetables, along with herbs, meat, fish, and articles of clothing were on display. There were pots full of different grains, seeds, and beans. "Mijo rojo-now what does that mean?" Callie pondered. She looked closer. "Ah, red millet." Then, a *carniceria*, where whole cow carcasses hung from hooks, along with chickens, rabbit, and sausage. A mariachi band was playing nearby and the smells coming from the food stalls reminded Callie of Lazlo's remark on their Sunday restaurant outing-you can almost eat the rich aromas. But she was there to photograph.

Everything she saw in Mexico was saturated in color. In passion. Some things were disturbing, but always primal, deep, close to the bone. *I want to take it all in, taste these colors, feel the joy and the sorrow of the campesinos. It's important and I'm not even sure why.*

She savored the raw scents of the dark roasted coffee beans, slabs of hanging meat, rich, pungent goat cheese, spicy cilantro, onions and chili peppers frying, burning wood, and the overriding, maternal aroma of warm tortillas.

Scents from the Aztecs, Mayans, Olmecs, and scores of unknown, unnamed tribes that stretched back into unremembered time.

After a while she needed some solitude and wandered through the Parque Juarez with its manicured jacaranda trees and balloon vendors, gray old men asleep on wrought iron benches older than they were. She kept walking toward the outskirts of town. It was, after all, a small town, with few foreigners and tranquility to spare. Once away from the main plaza, Callie only heard the wind and the birds. She passed under majestic trees that looked centuries old. Perhaps some weary friars had once paused under their branches for the cooling shade.

She kept walking, for the hotel clerk had told her that San Miguel's oldest church lay in this direction and she felt she was getting close. The road curved and a hundred yards ahead she spied a small structure all by itself.

"Ah, estoy aqui," she said, pleased she had found it so easily. It was a forlorn little church, next to a lush green field, with a line of trees and then the mountains in the distance. She passed under some willows and then through a stone arch that led into a tiny courtyard, enclosed by a stone wall. The exterior of the church was burnt orange and full of cracks and gouges, but the facade had an unassuming charm about it. A pair of wooden doors were flanked by two stone pilasters and topped by an intricate little wooden arch with carvings Callie had to stand on her tiptoes to decipher. They seemed to be round faces, connected by a snake-like vine, above which was a pair of angels with bright blue wings, who had been gazing at each other the past four hundred years. Above that was a small arched, recessed niche containing what Callie took to be an archangel, brandishing a sword above some unfortunate beings. A single steeple rose from the left corner.

There was a small plaque with the name, San Miguel Arcangel, Senor de la Conquista. Callie smiled. *Well, I got the Archangel right, but it has such a European look. Spain was still very much with them when they built this. It's an odd little church, an abandoned orphan. I could fix this up and live in it. No one around, not even close by. Such a peaceful place to live in. Leave the world behind.*

She walked back around and sat under the tree and closed her eyes. Sparrows hopped around her and gave out sharp little chirps. A horse was grazing way out at the edge of a field. She felt Mexico slowly revealing herself with the wind's breathing in the branches of the willow, in waves of euphoria and sadness. Callie had experienced this in different ways from her very first days in Chihuahua, and it was always the same-beauty and sadness in a strange dance of uneasy complicity. This little church was now the focal point, as she opened and closed her eyes in the drowsy afternoon warmth.

Why did they build their little European church in this Indian land four hundred years ago, where other, very different forces had endured? It happened all over the Americas, but there's something about Mexico. I can't put a name to it. It's hiding in this old church. Listen to the wind blowing around the church, Callie, what does it say? It says, Dejame en paz, leave me alone. And the church says nothing.

She got up and took one photograph of the church, so that she would have it to call up these feelings again.

131

Teotihuacan

Chapter 15

The next morning was uncharacteristically gray. Callie opened the hotel window and stuck her hand out into a fine drizzle. "Que extraño! What strange weather." She gazed in the mirror and brushed her hair, the softness of the moist air felt like a balm to her dry skin after so long a spell of Mexico's arid climate.

She wrapped a shawl about her shoulders, went downstairs into the lobby. She stood by the kitchen where the women were cooking and laughing, just to breathe in the aromas of frying eggs and chorizo, cinnamon rolls, and strong coffee,

The slender young girls bragged about their boyfriends, their *novios,* while the older stout women complained about their husbands. Callie chuckled and leaned in the doorway to say hello. "Cómo están las cosas en la cocina?" "Muy bien. Gracias, señorita! Gracias!" they responded with good humor.

Next to the hotel was a photography shop where Callie had left her film to be developed and made into prints. Since the film did not record color, she had concentrated on the play of light on surfaces and faces. The faces of the young Indian vendors were indeed wonderful-the film rendered them in rich grays and blacks. She had ordered extra copies and hurried back to the little plaza, for she was intent on keeping her promise.

With her flair for dramatics, Callie casually walked up to the women, stopped and smiled, then thrust a bunch of the photos in front of their faces, like a hand of cards. They eyes grew wide with astonishment and they squealed with delight. The girl whose pictures she held was in tears. "Ay, caramba! Creí que no vendrías!"

Callie beamed. "Estoy aqui. I had every intention of coming back."

They passed the glossy pictures back and forth to each other, twittering like sparrows, and soon the other vendors came over and joined in.

"La gringa!"

"Ella es un fotógrafo maravilloso!"

"Muy amable!"

"Qué fotos hermosas!"

The young woman who had expressed her surprise earlier got up and came over to Callie and embraced her. "Un regalo tan maravilloso. Muchas gracias, señorita. Son todos los americanos tan buenos?

"Yo espero," said Callie. They're gifts for me too, she said to herself. "Pero, éstos son también los regalos para mí, mis memorias de su país.

"Ah, sí."

"Que es su nombre?"

"Maria."

"Yo soy Callie."

As she was leaving, a child ran up to her with a bouquet of daisies. It was one of her best moments in Mexico.

She returned to the main plaza, entered the Post Office, and asked if there were any letters for her. "Callie Masterson."

The heavyset clerk shuffled through a stack of letters. Callie noticed a gold ring with a red stone on his finger and wondered if it was a wedding ring. Her eyes wandered to a large mural of Benito Juarez, rendered in florid colors. He loomed above his crouching soldiers, holding a Mexican flag. She thought of Villa and his soldiers in the cave, as if it had happened a long time ago, like this scene.

"Hay dos," he said, handing her two letters.

"Gracias, senor."

The first had Casey's handwriting. She stuffed the other into her pocket without looking at it and tore open Casey's as she walked over to a quiet corner by a window.

Dear Callie,

Como esta? Well, I hope. You must like it in Mexico, as you have been there for a while. I liked the postcard you sent of the Indians on the plaza in Zacatecas. They are beautiful people. I miss Mexico. But I really miss you.

They have been working us pretty hard. From what I hear, the French and English boys in Europe are way ahead of us in the aviation department. The idea is to get us over there so we can train with the veterans who have already logged a lot of hours in the air fighting the Germans.

134

Callie, you should see some of the planes they have-Sopwith and Bristol fighters that fly 120 mph and reach twenty thousand feet! We're all pretty excited and glad to be getting out of this hayseed army base.

We'll be leaving in a week or so, and this might be the last letter you get until I arrive in France.

Like I said, I miss you. I'll say it right now-you're the sweetest girl I've ever known. I'd like to dance with you again.

Take care of yourself, miss.
With love and affection,
Casey

It was too short. She wanted more. She needed to go somewhere and think. The drizzle had increased to a steady rainfall as she pulled the shawl over her head and walked into the plaza. The rain had washed all of the color out of the scene. The benches were empty and the park was deserted. Upon entering the hotel she took a seat at her favorite table by the window that looked over the plaza, and ordered coffee and rum. After adding some sugar and cinnamon she sipped the elixir, sighing. She gazed at the letter. *So, now what, Casey? You said what you needed to...maybe you were rushed, maybe exhausted. I can't know what you're going through. But a woman wants more. God, I sound like one of those pulp novels. Why am I upset?*

She thought about their experience together-it really wasn't a relationship, as much as a series of encounters. There were no commitments made, no promises. And yet...

She decided to leave for Mexico City in the morning.

Callie arrived in Mexico City on the summer solstice, but the chilly rain had followed her from San Miguel. She took a room in a small hotel near Chapultepec Park on the advice of friends in San Miguel. As she stepped out of the taxi a handsome bellboy rushed out with an umbrella, while others gathered her luggage, and she was escorted into the quaint lobby. Smartly attired guests were reading newspapers, cigars and brandy, perfume, and rosewater fragrancing the air, an air of efficiency and elegance, an altogether different world.

She approached the main desk, and a dapper fellow in a tailored black suit beamed a smile at her and said in perfect English:

"Welcome to the Hotel Dante, Miss Masterson. We received your reservation from Senor Lopez in San Miguel and are pleased to inform you that your room is ready and prepared for you. You will have an excellent view of the park, your own private bath, and a small kitchen. Simply sign our register, leave your passport, and we will take care of the rest. "Bienvenidos a México!" he concluded, and bowed to her in a grand flourish.

Callie, unprepared for such a welcome, blushed slightly and mumbled a gracias.

An elevator took her to the third floor and she was soon alone in her room. She had napped during most of the train ride and was still reeling from the sudden immersion into the raucous streets of the capital city. She sat on the bed for a moment.

The room was immaculate, with creamy white walls and a small balcony framed by billowing curtains that beckoned her to step outside and take in the grand expanse of the park and surrounding city. Streetcars clanged, newsboys hawked papers, trucks and buses rumbled by, mariachi music came and went from far away, and a strange blend of exhaust fumes and tortillas cooking floated into the room. She wondered if she had made a mistake.

She flopped down upon the bed and looked at a recent *New York Times* edition. There was a photo of General Pershing, with a caption below:

Upon his arrival in France in early June, General Pershing met with Lieutenant Colonel Billy Mitchell, who had been sent to Europe in March as an observer, and arrived in Paris just four days after the United States declared war.

Callie put the paper down. She put a call through to President Carranza's staff and was told they would respond within a week with an answer to her request for an interview.

The day was young and Callie dressed quickly, for she decided to rush headlong into the maelstrom of three quarters of a million people and take her chances. Standing on the edge of the front steps of the hotel, she watched an unending flow of humanity stream by for a few moments, and jumped in.

She waded past flower sellers with overflowing baskets, street vendors of every sort, peddling gewgaws and skeletons with top hats, street performers who juggled and pantomimed and encouraged their red suited-monkeys to shake hands. The calls and yells and laughter rolled through the crowds in an up-and-down musical cascade of Spanish, in a hundred dialects, accents, intonations, and pitch. Callie understood a quarter of what she heard, so rapidly did these city types speak.

There was only a light sprinkle falling, and some blue patches of sky could be seen. She left the crowded sidewalk and wandered into the park, reading snatches from her guidebook. One description of a ruin intrigued her more than any other, and it was not so far away. She lost no time in locating the appropriate bus.

After an hour's ride, Callie stepped off the bus and stood on the Avenue of the Dead. Opposite her, stood the Temple of Quetzalcoatl, the feathered serpent. She had arrived at Teotihuacan, the place of the gods, a somber, meticulously laid-out city that had come to life centuries before the birth of Christ. Only twenty-five miles from Mexico City, it was in another dimension entirely.

Threatening dark gray clouds hung low over the wide surrounding valley. There were only a few other visitors. Callie began to walk to the pyramid. The sound of the crushed gravel beneath her feet was sharp and loud in the repose of the countryside. The plaintive sound of sheep could be hear faintly somewhere in the surrounding fields.

The fierce heads of Quetzalcoatl were thrust out at ordered intervals along panels, alternating with Tlaloc, the rain god. To her eyes, it seemed half snake and half feline, aesthetically ugly, but with a raw power from the underworld.

She looked down the long straight Avenue of the Dead, which culminated in the graceful Pyramid of the Moon, a massive, rather rounded structure with a wide central stairway. Off to the right side of the road the even larger Pyramid of the Sun sat in ponderous majesty. Green fields lay all around, dotted with darker green trees and the surrounding blue mountains.

Callie moved slowly down the path, impressed, but not especially relaxed. There was a composed grandeur about the place, but there was also a dark undercurrent that seemed to echo the oppressive sky. She could see the tiny figures of people atop the pyramids, but down here she was alone.

The pamphlet in her hand was not very detailed. Whoever had built the complex and lived here for nearly a thousand years was a complete mystery. No trace of writing or language was left behind. They had appeared thirteen centuries before the Aztec, and vanished by 750 AD.

She had brought not much more than her camera and a canteen strung across her chest. There was a pungent scent that she could not place, something like sage. The feeling was strangely alien, as if she were slightly off balance, in a different gravity. She had never felt this way in Mexico, until now.

Well Callie, if you do nothing else, you must climb that gargantuan pyramid and see what there is to see.

She quickened her pace and soon reached the base. It looked like as if there were thousands of steps leading to the summit. A small side stairway led to a set of wide central steps, which turned into two smaller parallel stairs, which turned into a single set of steps that led to the top. Why did they design it that way, she wondered.

One step after the other on the rough-hewn stone, up and up she trudged, not looking up or stopping for a view, ascending upon the work of the mystery builders, on stones that were shaped at the same time as Hadrian's Wall, until she came to the last few steps, breathing deeply, feeling like she was suspended in the clouds, then raised her eyes to gaze at what lay around her.

A sudden wind chilled her sweating body, but it was the grandeur of the setting and the intimidating bulk of the pyramidal structure that sent shivers down her spine. She put her hands to her mouth and felt the surge of a silent power break against her. If it was meant to impress, it succeeded. She wandered around the top and rapid thoughts tumbled through her mind.

It's like a sleeping giant, that if awakened could crush us all in an instant. How could the people that conceived of this simply vanish? But I feel like it's sleeping, not dead, like a soft vibration down in the earth right beneath these pyramids. Strange, but that is what it feels like.

This was not "Mexico", just as Mesa Verde was not the "United States." Something that preceded all the mess and stuff of our civilization, leaner and purer.

She sat there, taking in the panorama around her, then noticed that, except for her, the pyramid summit was deserted. But she was not alone-hundreds of butterflies began to appear. They seemed to be coming up in droves from below, fluttering all around her in random movements. Then it dawned on her that their movements were not random at all.

Ahhh….Callie, you moron, they're mating, or trying to, or thinking about it. But it's all so fluttery and wispy, so graceful...they make little circles...they seem to be, I don't know, they could be...look at those two, they're touching. God, they are beautiful...drops of gold, and all so silent.

The butterflies increased in number, until thousands upon thousands ascended to the summit and filled the air with shimmering colors, gold, with black stripes, looking like half-daisies.

Callie, in her white dress, stood motionless in the center of the silent storm, Buddha-like, with her arms spread, eyes closed, perfectly still, letting the butterflies alight upon her hands and arms and shoulders, settle in her hair, cling tenuously to her dress. She lost all sense of time.

The way down was quite steep and she moved carefully down the steps, then walked back down the Avenue of the Dead. Everyone else had disappeared. The sun was lower now, the air cooler and a feeling of tranquility had replaced the earlier tension. A jackrabbit scooted across the road, stopped, regarded her, and sped into the grass.

There was one more thing to see-the murals. A guide led her into various chambers where shamans with elaborate headdresses were depicted upon blood red walls, with strange bubble-like forms floating in front of them. The guide informed her that these were speech bubbles, but no one could ever know what they were saying. Nearby, in the Palace of the Jaguars she saw pumas with headdresses, and in the Temple of the Plumed Conch Shells were murals of shells as musical instruments and birds painted green, blue, yellow, and red, spouting water. Finally, as if to present a grand climax, she was led to the Paradise of Tlaloc, the rain deity. A myriad of small figures diving and swimming, eating, picking flowers, and talking, so many talking, with their strange speech bubbles hovering in the air.

Callie marveled at the dark coolness of these secret places, the whimsical imagery, and those stately stone temples sitting above her in the sun-washed valley. Her senses were all used up. She plodded out of the temples to catch the last bus back to the city.

She welcomed the bustle of the metropolis, the smells and sounds and colors after the otherworldly experience of Teotihuacan, but the spell it had cast upon her would remain long after that day.

It was pure luxury to slide into a hot bath and be enveloped in soothing steam, cozy within the spotless white-tiled bathroom, with its sparkling chrome and shiny copper. She had been roughing it for a long time, so why not enjoy the good life while she could. Anyway, the *Chronicle* could well afford it and the articles she was sending back had gotten good responses.

The long soak left her pleasantly tired, so she decided to have a quiet meal in the hotel and turn in early to get a quick start in the morning. She extinguished all the lights in her room except for a candle, walked out on the balcony and leaned over the metal railing. The city sparkled and hummed with strollers, autos, and horse-drawn carriages. Again, the tantalizing aromas of Mexico wafted up to her on the cool evening breeze, along with the sweet scents of flowering jasmine that grew below in the hotel garden. She fell into the wide bed upon the cool sheets, blew out the candle, and fell asleep.

Xochimilco canals

Chapter 16

Callie spent weeks wandering through the streets of the city, waiting to be surprised, and she always was. She spent hours at outdoor cafes, writing pages and pages of impressions of these sojourns, of the people and the sprawling city. Her sense of history was sharpened by visits to the anthropological museum and the city library.

One morning she made her way to the Xochimilco district, its series of canals and gardens, the remnants of the ancient Lake Xochimilco. Floating upon the water were large roofed boats called *trajineras*, with room enough for entire Mexican families to picnic in and be serenaded by mariachis. A boatman propelled them along at a lazy pace by the use of a long pole.

Callie wandered along the shore, past the small cafes and walked through swarms of chattering children. She purchased a cone of lemon ice cream and felt like a kid herself, on a holiday from school. Wandering along the trails that ran along the canals she came upon a meadow and reclined in the soft grass to finish her treat and read some pages from her small book of sonnets. As she paged through the book, her eyes were attracted by a flash of white-nearby, a couple were teasing each other under a tree in the shade. Because of obscuring bushes, they couldn't see Callie, but she had a clear view of them. The woman wore a white sleeveless dress and her sweetheart a white shirt, which was half unbuttoned. She began tugging at his shirt, and suddenly he just took it off. She began to caress his smooth shoulders and he began to kiss her. They seemed to be the most attractive couple in Mexico to Callie at that moment, with their glossy black hair and bronze skin. They had no idea they were being watched and began to take more liberties. The woman lay upon her back, and he began to unbutton her blouse, her arms outstretched behind. He ran his hand over her breasts and kissed her longer and deeper, while she stretched out in obvious pleasure. Callie could hear her soft moans and his seductive whispers, until she too could feel his hands upon her and his tongue in her mouth. The eroticism was palpable, and Callie swallowed hard as a heat began to rise up in her breast, and she squirmed restlessly in her hiding place. A rush of passion flared up inside of her, but she abruptly jumped up and ran off before it overpowered her, the startled couple looking up at her fleeing form in the distance.

Instead of catching a bus Callie continued to walk without any idea of where she was going. On every corner it seemed there were lovers touching and kissing in a continual game of passion out in the open, for all the world to see. She berated herself for being so prudish, so easily overcome, but as she kept walking it dawned on her that the sexual electricity in the streets was not repelling her-it was attracting her.

She stopped in a small *mercado* and drank a cold orange soda, rubbing the chilled bottle across her sweating forehead. Her eyes wandered over to a book rack, where cheap paperbacks with tawdry images of half-naked lovers leered back at her. "Oh God," she sighed, and walked out of the store, trying to calm herself and figure out exactly where she was. She asked a passerby which way Chapultepec Park was, and decided to keep walking and exhaust the desires out of her body.

She sort of floated in a daze, for the sun had become strong and there was steaminess in the air that intensified all the smells of the city, not only the food and the cooking, the musty scent of horses and mules, but also the sweat and the perfume and the cologne, mingling into an exotic ambrosia. A weak smile spread across Callie's face.

There's some sinister plan to lure the innocent American, to destroy our morals and make us pure ladies into wanton harlots. Now everything's arousing me! Sombreros, bananas, guacamole, music and onions and colors, even the heat. Mexico is seducing me, and I like it. God, I am so thirsty and hungry and tired. I'm a limp rag. You will get through this, Callie, but I don't know if you'll recognize yourself anymore.

At last, the Hotel Dante came into view. She passed through the golden metal doors and felt once more the serenity of the genteel lobby. The hotel clerk shook his head as she entered the elevator, wondering why she always returned in such a bedraggled state. "Las gringas," he muttered.

The hot bath again performed its miraculous cure. Callie wanted something familiar to eat, so she requested a ham sandwich and a bowl of tomato soup, some lemonade, and a copy of *Collier's* magazine. She went over to the dresser and stood in front of the mirror, letting her blue robe fall to the floor. She looked at her reflection, her dripping black curls. She ran her hand over her breasts and was aroused, despite her fatigued state. She imagined what it must feel like to have a man caress her body in a public place, not only to let him, but encourage him, perhaps a man she had just met. There was an unsteady glimmer in her eyes that hinted of ragged, unspoken feelings that wouldn't go away.

I'm changing, by the moment. While I'm standing here, I'm changing, like in some Jekyll and Hyde tale. Mexico has opened a door inside me and the demons are let loose. Look-my hands are shaking. This is so odd. The night in the tent with Casey-that had something to do with it, surely, but it wasn't the same. What I'm feeling now isn't love, it's lust. By God, it's just pure lust, Callie. What are you going to do about it?

Her skin was pale, except for her arms and face, thanks to the months out in the open in Chihuahua. Soon, they would pale and blend in.

But why not darken the rest of my body-I like how it looks. With my black hair they would take me for a Mexican, sure enough. Funny, I used to be sensitive about my looks, now I'm perfectly *happy to be what...swarthy, dusky, who cares? Otherwise, I'd be just like every other fair skinned Texas girl.* She raised her arms and ran her hands through her hair. She felt good, really good.

A sharp knock at the door broke her dreamy state, and she quickly put her robe back on and opened the door. The handsome bellboy wheeled her meal into the room. Callie had a sudden urge to disrobe.

"Is there anything else I can do for you, madam?" he asked with great earnestness.

She stood there silently, her breasts heaving, her legs rubbing together.

"No thank you," she said, as calmly as she possibly could. "Oh wait." She retrieved some pesos from her purse and handed them to her fantasy. "Para usted," she said sweetly. "What is your name?" She wanted to keep him near her for a little longer.

"Francisco."

"Ah, como un santo?"

"Sí, pero, no soy un santo."

Callie fingered the loose knot that held her robe together. "No, I can see you're no saint, and I'm glad to hear it." It seemed as if another woman was talking.

Francisco smiled curiously and Callie could see that he was beginning to catch on, and she liked the tension, the feeling of being on the edge. She bent over to smell the soup, half exposing her breasts. The boy's mouth was partly open, his eyes riveted on her anatomy, and Callie's heart raced as she savored the thrill.

Another sharp knock. Callie straightened up. Fear immediately replaced desire in the boy's eyes. Callie tightened her robe and opened the door. It was the manager.

"Pardon, madam, but we have need of Francisco. Is everything satisfactory here?" he said, looking around suspiciously.

"Oh, yes. Francisco was most polite and efficient. In fact, you should give him a raise. He is very attentive."

There was an awkward silence. Francisco rushed out of the room and Callie shut the door, mortified that she might have gotten the boy in trouble.

"Give the boy a raise? Did I really say that? Did I really just try to seduce a bellboy?" She collapsed on the bed. "They are going to arrest you, Callie, you idiot," she chuckled.

Colonia Roma district of Mexico City

Chapter 17

When Callie awakened the next morning, a pleasing morning light suffused the room. The white curtains fluttered as the breeze brought in the usual scents, and a vague earthiness that had no name.

She was pulled in three different directions: A feeling of exhilaration from her outrageous flirtation, the ever-present moral standards instilled by her grandmother, always lurking deep inside, and, there was Casey.

She was angry that she even had to wrestle with such things. Why couldn't women embrace the power of their sexuality just as men did? The Twentieth Century was overturning the old ways-she herself had flown! Why not this? It was too slow. She wanted more: More comfortable clothes, more honesty with men, more choices in how she might live her life. She had been ambushed by the sensuality of Mexico, astonished at what it had unleashed inside of her, but that wasn't the reality. The reality was a veneer of moral rules that lay on top of that sensuality, like a lid closed over an unruly animal. She had to dance the dance, play by the rules, or pay a price. Until she sorted it all out, she must be wary and watch her step.

As soon as she dressed she walked to the post office and retrieved a letter from Casey, with a French postmark. She needed a secluded place to read it, found a small café with tables out front, and ordered a coffee.

She fingered the envelope and studied Casey's neat script, unlike her own rather wandering penmanship. "Miss Callie Masterson", it said. He always put that "Miss" in.

"Hola, senora. Te gusta?" A shy Indian girl stood before her with cheap trinkets to sell.

"No, gracias," said Callie, and the girl moved on.

She took the end of her spoon and carefully opened the envelope, almost reluctantly. She knew this would happen, the guilt rising up to the surface. Things had changed and she was no longer the woman that Casey said goodbye to.

She unfolded the letter and began to read:

147

Dear Callie,

Writing you from gay Paree. I can't really believe I'm here, but it's only for a day or two. We're stationed at a small airfield not too far from here. I've practically had to learn to fly from scratch. These French training schools aren't exactly the Ritz. We are up before dawn and only get some chicory to drink. But the planes are much faster than our old Jennies and can climb way above the clouds, and boy is it cold up there.

But the fellas are all swell, and soon I'll be flying a one-seater Camel-Sopwith Camel, that is One hundred and thirty horsepower, and she'll go nearly one hundred and twenty mph!

Everyone wants to be an Ace-that means you've shot down at least five Germans. This Richthofen fellow is on our minds-he's gotten at least forty of our boys. His photo is the bull's eye on our dart board. They have established an Aviator Headquarters here in Paris. That's where I'm writing you from. There's a bunch of pilots who don't even fly-we call them kiwis, after the flightless bird. We don't always get along so well. But there's Americans all over Paris. Some are AWOL, some are just lost.

The French can really cook!

I managed to get to the top of the Eiffel Tower, but the view ain't that grand after you've been to twenty thousand feet.

Gee, Callie, you would love it here. There are little food markets everywhere and a café on every corner, with the strongest coffee I've ever tasted.

Every time I sit down at a restaurant, I think of that little Mexican place we all went to that Sunday afternoon. You looked so pretty that day-that's how I think of you when I get down in the dumps-smiling and happy, in that little white dress.

I won't lie to you-sometimes I get scared, but as soon as I'm up in the air, everything's okay. You are always up there with me. Just like the old days.

You know, this aviation industry is only going to get bigger. I already heard they're looking for pilots up in Alaska and down in South America. Maybe you and I could do some exploring, once I get back. It's still a big world out there.

They are calling for me now. But I had to let you know that I was still in one piece. And don't worry about me. You write your stories and have some fun.

I miss you, a lot.
With great affection,
Casey

She put her journal on the table and began to write.

I am so confused and I am not even sure why. Nothing really happened. I have not been unfaithful to Casey. I just...thought about it. And yet, I feel like I have committed a sacrilege. His sweet words make me want to take a boat over there and go hold him. I wish we were still with General Pershing and chasing Villa. Somehow, with all the terrible things that happened, we still had fun out there in the desert.

I can't think about his situation too hard, can't dwell on the danger around him. Why are we even there? The Germans are no threat to us.

I'm not all sure what to do now. I need to work. I need to go interview Carranza. I need to stop being a silly tourist!

She abruptly closed the journal, left the café, and wandered restlessly. Callie realized the truth of the sentence in the journal-"*we had some fun out there in the desert*". Except that it was more than fun. When she left Houston on that train for West Texas, she began to change into someone else. Those three months of heat, dust and danger were the most exciting of her entire life. She was nearly killed several times, killed five men herself, saved some lives, talked to Pancho Villa, and fell in love with a handsome pilot. She wanted that intensity back. Perhaps that had something to do with her attempted seduction. Perhaps it had everything to do with it. She did not see how she could possibly go back to a life in the rigid society she had known. She would *not* do it. She would not give up all the power she had found. It was an unmistakable craving, a hunger to experience life on a deeper level, to give her feeling free reign and taste the sweetness of being utterly alive. She could live here, at least for a while. Underneath the Catholic formality, Mexico was seething, much like herself. It was as if she had been initiated into a secret order of ecstasy, had become a different woman. She wanted to wink at the

149

natives around her, as if to say, I know the secret too.

Paris sounded like a city that would suit her. Or Rome or Athens or Buenos Aires. Something about the Latin countries, with their heat, their colors, that made them feel voluptuous, where art merged into life and the lucky inhabitants were always surrounded by the continuity of their ancestors, the glorious past right there in the cathedrals and sculptures to provide sustenance and inspiration.

Callie looked up at the colonial facades surrounding her, with their graceful embellishments that bespoke of a time when craftsmanship was the order of the day. She passed the Presidential Palace and it occurred to her that Carranza's staff had never gotten back to her. Was it possible they had found out about her meeting with Villa, Carranza's ardent enemy? Callie let it go. She was never excited about the prospect; it just seemed like the obvious story to write for the paper, but her heart wasn't in it. She wondered where exactly her heart was these days.

She sat on the edge of a fountain and watched children wade in the cool water, giggling with delight as they splashed each other. She was simply glad to be at this spot on a beautiful morning in Mexico. She raised her face to the sun and closed her eyes and absorbed the comforting warmth.

"Hola, señorita!"

She opened her eyes and saw a pretty woman about her own age, smartly dressed, with an engaging smile.

"Hola."

"You are an American, no?" Callie nodded. "Yes, I thought so. My name is Paloma Vargas. I attended Harvard, in Boston, for my studies. I am very fond of Americans. I see you there by the fountain and I think-this lady is not the regular American tourist. You seem a little Mexican, with your long black hair. Que linda," she purred, as she playfully caressed a curl of Callie's hair. "I miss my American friends and I have wanted to practice my English, so I invite you to my home. It is only a short walk from here. Yes?"

Callie was taken aback at her candor, but immediately won over by her charm. "Why thank you. Yes, of course, I would be delighted. I'm Callie."

"Callie?" Paloma repeated it slowly. "Never have I heard this name."

"It was my grandmother's."

Paloma nodded in approval. "Que bonita!"

Soon they were winding through the tree-lined streets of the Colonia Roma neighborhood. Callie gawked at the opulent Beaux Arts architecture and tranquil plazas and parks. They crossed Rio de Janiero plaza and turned down a narrow lane, until they came to a handsome house of pink stone.

"Esta es mi casa," said Paloma. She opened the door and led Callie down a hallway lined with small, gold framed paintings, and then through a door which revealed an impressive library. A silver-haired, distinguished looking man sat at a small desk by a window, immersed in some ancient looking tome. He looked up over his glasses and smiled.

"Papa. This is Callie, my new friend from the states."

"Very pleased to make your acquaintance, Callie. I am Armando."

"It is a pleasure to meet you, sir. This is a most lovely home."

"Yes, we are comfortable here. It has been in my family for over two hundred years. Paloma, show her around."

"Sí, papa."

The library gave out onto an expansive living room, sprinkled with *objets d'art* and numerous vases of fresh flowers. A small fire flickered in the impressive fireplace, even though it was late summer. A severe looking woman wearing a shawl sat upon a white couch, leafing through a magazine. She had very pale skin and black eyes that made Callie uneasy.

"Mama, this is Callie."

Her mother merely nodded and continued reading. They walked past her and up an ornate stairway.

Paloma paused at the first landing and turned around. "She does not talk much. She is not well, I think."

Callie nodded and they continued up. It was somewhat dark, so Paloma took Callie's hand. "My room is at the end of this hall."

A door was flung open and a man aggressively confronted them. "Who do we have here, dear sister?"

Callie stepped back, startled.

"Ah, Carlos. You must stop your pranks. Callie, this is my older brother, Carlos."

He was a replica of his mother, pale, but with a crueler face, almost a sneer, rather than a smile. He was tall and thin, with straight black hair that partly hung over his face. He moved uncomfortably close to Callie. "You are very sweet, aren't you?" he said, in perfect English. "How is it this sweet gringa comes to our house, sister?"

Paloma pulled her away. "Don't call her that, Carlos! She is a friend of mine. Go away! No nos molestan!"

She led Callie to the next room. As soon as they entered she locked the door. Callie expected her to explain her brother's behavior, but instead she brightened up and led her to an enormous closet, filled with dresses.

"This is my little treasure house. I went to Paris this spring and found some most lovely things. But here are my very secret treasures." Half-hidden, under the hanging dresses was a small bureau with locked drawers. She produced a key and carefully opened the top drawer. Callie leaned in for a close look. Paloma lifted a silky piece of red lingerie in front of her. "Mira, Callie. Que bonita, no. So pretty. I put these on when I am not feeling so well, and like magic, I am a seductress, and all the men want me. Now you may try them on too."

She unfolded one piece after another, shimmery, diaphanous things, slips, chemises, camisoles, and the newly invented brassiere. Callie had never seen such an array of naughty underwear, and the idea of actually trying them on excited her, but she hardly knew this woman.

"Come. There's a large mirror by the bed."

"This is a bit unusual for me, Paloma."

"This is Mexico," she said gaily. "You can be more free here, be yourself, no? Aw, I can tell by your eyes that you are anxious," she teased. "It will be fun!"

Callie broke into a big smile. "All right then. Why not?"

They rushed out of the closet, giggling like little girls clutching their provocative prizes. Paloma joyously stripped her clothes off, throwing them on her enormous bed, and Callie followed suit. She had never done such a thing before, not to mention with another woman in the same room, but it felt absolutely wonderful. Unlike her towering brother, Paloma had a petite body, with small breasts and a lovely lithe figure. Callie, as always, was entranced by the smooth sienna-colored skin that all Mexicans seemed to possess. Paloma's lack of modesty was unlike most Mexican women Callie had known, no doubt due to her privileged social status and exposure to European lifestyles.

Paloma came up to Callie and touched her shoulder. "Que paso aqui?"

Callie had forgotten her old wound and turned to look at it in the mirror. "It happened up in Chihuahua, with the Expedition."

"Did you fall?"

"No, I was shot."

"Oh, mi Dios!"

"Seems like a long time ago."

Paloma struck a pose like a model, "What do you think, Callie? Pretty daring, no?" She then strutted around the room wearing a very short black camisole that was only tenuously connected over her breasts and a tight-fitting pair of abbreviated white bloomers. "The boys would love to see this. It's so light, feels so nice. Sometimes, I put these on and cover myself with just a coat and take long walks. Very exciting. You want to do that now?" She was nearly breathless with enthusiasm.

"I think we better just stay in your room, Paloma. Why, suppose we met with an accident and were taken to the hospital. They would remove our coats and all the doctors and nurses would see our scandalous under-things."

Paloma clutched her breasts. "Ay, Madre de Dios! My mother would murder me! Okay, we stay here."

Callie was actually tempted to say yes, but she didn't want to push her luck. She slipped on a blue sort of chemise that simply came to a halt at her upper thighs. Callie looked down and wondered if something were missing, and when she caught sight of herself in the mirror she gasped. "My lord, you can see practically everything." She turned this way and that, and was pleased how long and shapely her legs looked, and the enticing manner in which her breasts were half exposed.

"This is most amazing, Paloma. I love it. We are transformed!"

They broke into laughter and threw off what they were wearing and tried on things even more daring. Callie began to feel that power rise up within her, the energy of her sex, the force of her womanhood-lust, romance, love, seduction, all of it, the primal feelings at the core of her being, things she had somehow ignored and repressed for most of her life.

Callie collapsed on the bed. "Paloma, look at the mess we made. We have to clean up your room."

"Why? No one comes in here but me."

"Have you ever had a man come up here?"

"Impossible. I could never take such a risk."

"Don't your parents ever go away on trips?"

"Sometimes. But my brother, he hardly ever leaves, except to go pay for a whore. Even if he did, the maids are always here. They live downstairs, off the kitchen." She lay down next to Callie, face to face. "But I have my secret little rendezvous. I take tango lessons-you have heard of this new dance? It's from Argentina. *Very* sensual. One of the instructors, he is from Buenos Aires and *muy guapo,* very handsome. Sleek black hair, tight pants. We sometimes go to his place. I tell my parents I'm out with friends. I bring some of these things whenever I sleep with him. It arouses him very, very much." They started to laugh hysterically, until tears came to their eyes. "You know what, mi amiga? said Paloma, "Yo tengo hambre. Very hungry. Y usted?"

"I'm pretty darn hungry too. Sí, yo también."

"Okay. You wait here and I go down and fix some quesadillas, then I will ring the bell,"-she pointed to a gold chrome bell above the bed-"and you can come downstairs." She put on a robe and left the room.

Callie didn't want to get up. She luxuriated on the plush bed cover and squirmed with arousal at her barely clad body. She raised her legs up in the air and let the chemise slip down her body.

The bedroom door swung open. Carlos entered with his finger on his lips and was on top of Callie in an instant.

"My sweet little gringa bitch I'm going to have you." He pressed his mouth on top of hers to silence any screams, roughly fondling her breasts.

"I've been watching you try your little frilly things on, my sweet little whore, I knew you were ready for me," he whispered into her ear, trying his best to wedge his knee between her legs, trying to intimidate her with his black eyes. But there was more anger than fear

154

in Callie's eyes, and she struggled fiercely.

His weight initially overpowered her, but she turned violently from side to side, and finally threw him off the bed. He landed with a crash, but was up in seconds and grabbed her as she tried to get out the door. He held her from behind, in front of the mirror, attempting to enter her that way, his eyes ablaze with excitement as he watched his arms enfold her.

Callie reached back and pulled a gob of his hair completely out. He screamed in pain and hurled her away. As he clutched his head, she grabbed a small statue of the Virgin Mary and struck him across the forehead, sending him careening into the wall and causing three different pictures to come crashing down.

He wasn't moving anymore. The delicate camisole hung off her shoulders in ripped pieces.

Paloma rushed into the room. "Callie, what is going on? I hear all this crashing-" Callie pointed to the floor, where Carlos lay crumpled in a dark heap.

"Ay," she gasped, "I should have locked the door." She walked over to her brother and kicked him a few times. "Hijo de puta! Cobarde!" She went over to Callie, who was sitting on the edge of the bed, and embraced her. "I am terribly sorry this has happened. Please forgive me, Callie. Did he-?"

"No," said Callie, shaking her head. "But he came pretty darn close." She was still breathing heavily. "I'm all right Paloma. But he revealed something that might disturb you."

"What do you mean, disturb me?"

"He said he had been watching me, watching me try on the lingerie."

Paloma frowned, her thin black eyebrows furrowed in puzzlement. She stood up quickly and looked around, confusedly. "But how, where?"

Callie slowly rose and walked over to the wooden wall. "It would have to be here somewhere, the common wall you two share." The two women ran their hands over the smooth shiny wood, peering closely for any sign of a hole.

"I see nothing. How could I not have noticed such a thing?"

Callie looked higher. "He's very tall." She moved slowly toward

155

the door, then back toward the back of the room. "It's too dark. Have you a candle?"

"Yes." She lit a candle from her bedside table and handed it to Callie.

Callie lifted the candle above her head and crept along the wall. She stopped in front of a darker swirl of grain. "There!" shouted Callie. "Here, hold the candle." She stood on a chair and put her finger over the small opening. "Right here, Paloma.'

"I still can't see it."

"Exactly. He made sure it blended into the wood grain, so it was practically invisible." She peered into the hole. "Yes, I can see into his room all right." Callie stepped off the chair. They stared at each other, the mutual feeling of violation in their eyes.

Carlos began to stir, rising drunkenly, bleeding from the gash in his forehead.

"Paloma! Que paso? Estas bien?" called her father from the hallway.

Paloma grabbed Callie and whispered. "What do I tell my father?"

Callie looked at her, somewhat taken aback. "I would start with the truth.

Diego Rivera

Chapter 18

Paloma opened the door. Armando looked at both of them, then at Carlos. "Paloma, what does this mean? What has happened in here?"

Carlos was now standing, leaning against the wall, sullenly dabbing his head with a handkerchief. Callie had covered herself with a robe and stood with folded arms, awaiting Paloma's response.

"He attacked Callie. Your bastard of a son attacked my new friend, our guest."

Her father's face underwent a change from bewilderment to horror to disgust. He did not need her to give any details to grasp what had almost happened. He went up to Carlos and slapped him across the face, causing his son to cry out in pain. He then grabbed him by the collar, threw him out into the hallway, slapped him again, then pushed him into his own room, slamming the door. He pulled out a key and locked it from the outside.

He pulled a spotless white handkerchief from his coat pocket and wiped sweat off of his forehead, then walked over to Callie, his face disfigured with remorse. "My dear Miss Masterson, I am profoundly sorry for the heinous behavior of my son. If it is your wish to press charges, then I will summon the police immediately."

"What do you suggest, senor?"

Armando let out a deep sigh and quickly glanced at his daughter. "I have a ranch, far from here, in the high desert. There is no town within fifty miles of this place. The conditions are harsh, the isolation extreme. He would work at hard labor, cleaning up horse stalls and latrines as a virtual prisoner, for a very long time, perhaps the rest of his days. I knew he was bad, but never has he done such a thing. He is not fit for society anymore."

Callie remained motionless, arms still folded. Paloma's eyes were riveted upon her friend. Callie's face tightened, struggling with her feelings, staring down at the floor.

"That seems appropriate."

Armando bowed his head as if to secure the agreement. "I would also like to offer some sort of recompense for this terrible dishonor that has been done to you. I know nothing of your situation, but I want to assist you in some way, either monetarily or otherwise, to help you in your life's journey. Please think about this. There is no need for you to answer now."

"That is very kind of you, sir. What I would really like at the moment is a glass of wine, and some of those quesadillas Paloma cooked up."

He clasped her hands, managed a weak smile, and exited the room to deal with Carlos. Paloma gathered up the lingerie and threw into it the closet. They both got dressed and went downstairs, arm in arm.

After the meal, they had coffee outside in a small garden courtyard. Neither one said anything until Paloma spoke up. "You don't have to take my father's offer, you know. Maybe it is better if he goes to jail. I doubt he will ever change."

"I've grown up a lot in the past year, Paloma. If I hadn't gone through those three months in Chihuahua with the army, perhaps I would be angrier, more traumatized. I can assure you I am full of hatred for your brother and am happy to know he will be removed from society, but I was simply in the wrong place at the wrong time. He did me no lasting damage. I have already put it behind me."

Paloma looked at her with a mixture of awe and admiration. They were already fast friends.

Callie and Paloma remained at the table in the courtyard, drinking cups of coffee and reveling in the discovery that they were such kindred spirits. It was ten p.m. before Callie returned to her hotel room. She immediately grabbed her journal and began to write a sketch of Paloma's family, the beginnings of a short story, concentrating on Paloma's mother and Carlos, with their gothic bizarreness. She wasn't as unaffected by the assault as she made herself out to be. Her hand trembled as she put down details of his features, but she reasoned that to make him one of her own characters gave her a semblance of control, thereby rendering him less threatening. Her pen was tireless as she wrote page after page. She was creating a world, and it thrilled her more than any other story she had ever written as a journalist.

The next morning she received a call from Paloma, who had just talked with her father. Carlos would be taking a train that very day to his "prison" in Durango. They offered to put her up for as long as she might want to stay, as a member of their family. Callie hesitated, not because of the attack, but because of how strongly she cherished her independence and being on her own. Yet, she had grown close to Paloma in a matter of hours, and the thought of the doors that might open for her through such a friendship excited her.

Paloma picked her up in a sleek white Hudson Phaeton convertible. She looked gorgeous in a matching white dress that was daringly snug, and could not contain her enthusiasm as they drove.

"This will be *so* much fun, amiga. My city is full of strange and brilliant people, especially now, with the revolution."

"Carranza isn't exactly a revolutionary, Paloma."

"I don't mean just politics. There is a great outpouring in the arts, in painting, dance, writing. Many of my friends are artists. And many are expatriates, from France, Poland, Italy Spain. With titles! Barons, dukes, a count, even a marquess. Some are importing cognac. Some are selling fancy sport cars to the rich politicians. In fact, a very interesting couple is having a little party tonight, not so far from our house. We will go!"

"Oh my, what am I getting myself into?"

"Ha! You don't fool me, Callie Masterson. I can tell you're a party girl. And I know you really, really want to wear one of my Parisian dresses. Es la verdad, no? C'mon, admit it, amiga."

Callie was trying not to laugh, but did anyway. "All right, I admit it. But I don't have much experience in this line. You better help me."

"Ah, Sí, claro. I will hold your hand the whole time, *pobrecita*," emphasizing the last word, as if Callie were a child.

Paloma's house was empty, except for the maids, who had retired to their quarters. Callie and Paloma walked upstairs and entered Paloma's room. She turned around and looked at Callie. "Estas bien, cariño? You okay?"

"Yes, Paloma," she replied, putting her suitcase on a chair with business-like efficiency and removing some items. "I already told you, it's behind me. I'll let no man have control of me in that way."

"Sí, of course. And feel how much lighter it is in here with Carlos gone? I hope he never comes back."

They talked, had some lunch, then took a long nap during siesta, for the air was warm and drowsy. They slept close, like sisters, in the big soft bed.

Callie awakened first and crept into the closet to try on some of Paloma's French dresses. The softness and the elegance was unlike anything she had ever seen, or felt. She tried on a blue summery one, with narrow straps that left her shoulders bare. She tiptoed into the bedroom and looked at herself in the large, full-length mirror. She turned this way and that, and was pleased. *It's a bit risqué, but perfect for such a warm evening. It's nearly as light as the lingerie. I love it. I want it.*

"Pretty nice, sweetie. Los muchachos will like you very much, I think." Paloma was smiling, leaning on an elbow watching Callie.

"Do you really think so? I thought it might be too provocative."

"Provocative? You mean sexy? That one's tame. I'll show you provocative my innocent little *Americana.*" She jumped off the bed and ran into the closet, then came out triumphantly in a clingy satiny pink gown, the front of which plunged like the Grand Canyon. Frilly little tassels hung off the sides and thin arm bands, also tasseled, wrapped around her upper arms. Paloma's dark skin against the soft pink was striking to behold, and Callie could not help but gasp.

"Oh, my goodness gracious. Paloma, you look absolutely gorgeous, but quite wicked. You aren't really going to wear that out in the street, are you?" Callie walked around her in disbelief, but with a trace of envy in her eyes.

Paloma, pleased with her image in the mirror, twirled one of the tassels and gyrated a little to some imaginary music. "No. I'm saving it, for a really big party in the Hotel Primera next week." She went back into the closet and chose a silver dress with only a modest décolletage, but shorter and more girly. "Bueno. We look fantastic."

They promptly took off the dresses, experimented with Paloma's impressive collection of makeup, and finally drove off to the soiree. It wasn't quite as close as Paloma described. In fact, it was situated on the outskirts, where it was less urbanized, adjacent to the countryside of grazing fields dotted with coppices. Paloma drove onto a cobble-stoned driveway and stopped in front of a valet who bowed, smiled and opened the car doors. They were surrounded by huge old cottonwoods within a walled courtyard, the great branches seeming to droop with weariness, their silvery leaves brushing the stones. A row

161

of weathered dovecotes stood on tall wooden poles, and a hypnotic adagio of cooing rose and fell all around them.

Callie fluttered around in delight. "This is magical."

Rather than entering the large adobe house, they followed guests around to the back, along a lighted path, into an expansive garden and patio, where Chinese lanterns were strung between trees and a mariachi group was singing ballads.

They walked up to a small bar. "Que quiere, amiga?" asked Paloma. Mira, they have everything here for you-wine, rum, bourbon, scotch, even champagne."

"A glass of chilled, bubbly champagne is just what I need. Why, I can't even remember the last time I had some. I believe it was a wedding in Galveston a few years ago."

"Entonces, you have to catch up, no? Here's to you, my new sister, and all the good-looking men we are going to kiss. Salud!"

"Hola, Paloma."

A heavyset bearded Mexican man of about thirty, with penetrating oriental-like eyes stood beside them, smiling with a mixture of confidence and longing. "Aha, el artista!" said Paloma. "But help me please. Que es su nombre. I forget your name."

"I will forgive you. Diego Rivera, at your service señorita. And who is your lovely friend?"

"This is Callie Masterson, from...where are from Callie? California?"

"No, Texas."

"Oh, the other place you stole from us, huh?" said the artist, with a smile.

"I'm afraid so, Mr. Rivera."

"Please, no formality here. Call me Diego."

"I have not seen you at these parties for many months," said Paloma.

"I spent much time in Paris," he said between sips of a cocktail. "It is the greatest place in the world for an artist, right now. I became friends with Modigliani? Do you know him?"

Both women shook their heads.

"He is this short Italian Jew, with immense talent. Dedo, we called him. A crazy man. And Picasso, Cezanne. My God, it is the center of

162

the world. But, I am glad to be home in Mexico." He turned to Callie. "You have lovely deep black eyes, Callie. A man could get lost in those eyes. I should love to paint your portrait sometime."

"Diego, here you are." a small, intense looking woman with dark eyebrows took him by the arm, and led him away.

"Adios, ladies," he said, with a resigned look.

"Well, he liked you, I think," said Paloma.

"An interesting man, but not my type. But *he* might be." Paloma followed her gaze to a small table, where a young man in rather rough-looking clothes was engrossed in writing.

"Cuidado amiga, he looks strange to me."

"Hasta luego, Paloma."Callie had already begun to move toward him, trying not to seem obvious, but overcome with curiosity. Finally, she stood next to him, but he still took no notice of her. "Habla Inglés?" she said, nonchalantly.

He looked up, with dark sad eyes, a thin beard barely covering his chin. "English? Why, I'm American."

"Glad to hear it. I'm Callie. I'm very curious as to what you are writing."

"It's just a poem I've been working on." He closed his journal, somewhat protectively, Callie observed.

"I guess you're not going to let me see it."

"No, I'm not."

Callie sat down. He was almost gaunt looking, as if he hadn't been eating well, but there was a concentrated intensity about him which she found very attractive. She took a sip of champagne. "I wonder what people call you?"

Her candor began to soften him up. He turned around to look at her. "You know, I didn't come here to meet a woman."

"I can certainly believe that."

He leaned forward, wringing his hands, as if he had lost his train of thought.

"Don't you drink?"

"Sometimes," he said. "I actually prefer marijuana."

Callie was visibly startled. "Isn't that...dangerous?"

"Have you ever tried it?"

"Me? No."

"Then how can you have an opinion of it?"

"I guess I can't. What's it like? I suppose people don't really go crazy, like they say."

"It relaxes me. Everything becomes like *Alice in Wonderland*-a little silly and exaggerated. I get ideas for my poems when I'm high."

"High? Is that what you call it?"

"It's what they call it on the street. Oh, and it also causes one to laugh, hysterically, at just about anything. I once laughed like a fool just because I saw a lady sneeze."

"Really? It does that to you? Why, that's not so awful. But I do need another glass of this. Shall I bring you something?"

"All right. I'll have a scotch. Straight."

Callie fetched the drinks. She sashayed back to the table and handed him the scotch, with exaggerated formality.

"So, tell me your name again," she said, as she sat down.

He shook his head, smiling. "Max."

"That is a perfect name for a poet," declared Callie, with great certainty.

Max gave her a confused look.

"I'm sorry. This bubbly stuff is going to my head. I'm not always this silly. I guess I thought you needed cheering up. You see, I am myself a writer. So, we're comrades in arms, you might say." A phonograph began to play *"I'm Always Chasing Rainbows."* Callie put down her glass. She leaned closer. "Say, Max. How about a dance?"

"I'd rather not."

"Doesn't matter. It's a ladies choice." She stood up and took his hand, and he reluctantly acquiesced. Callie was just drunk enough to relax and not care what people thought. And that womanly desire began to rise up inside her as she responded to the lovely feeling of a man's arms around her and the romantic melody. Max looked as if he were enjoying it too and held her closer. Gay, well-dressed people moved around them, illuminated by the colored lights and animated by whatever type of liquor they had imbibed.

Callie suddenly drew back as they danced. "How old are you, Max?"

"Nearly twenty."

164

Callie slowly put her head back on his shoulder, saying nothing. The song ended and they walked back to the table. "Max, why are you here? Writing poetry at a party?"

"A friend told me about it. He said there might be some writers who could look at my work, maybe give me an opinion."

"Well, how did you end up in Mexico?"

"I'm fed up with the states. When Wilson entered the war, I knew I had to leave. They might well have drafted me. It's a stupid war. The fat cats will make a lot of money and the average Joe will just get shot dead. I want to create beauty, not death." He was practically ready to cry. Callie wanted to hug him but she didn't. She realized she was caught up in a moment, exacerbated by the champagne and Max's charming innocence. She sat back and gathered her wits about her, so that she wouldn't do anything ridiculous. Still, she had that desire rising within.

"I must go find my friend," she said, standing up, unsteadily. "Perhaps I'll see you later." She walked to the edge of an interior courtyard and turned around. Max was once again furiously scribbling something in his journal.

She wandered from one room to another in the hacienda. The party had broken up into small groups, some playing cards, some dancing to phonograph records, some in animated discussions. She finally spied Paloma on a couch, talking with a young, bohemian-looking couple, the woman clearly Mexican, the man possibly American. "There you are," said Callie, plopping down next to her friend.

"Callie, meet my friends, Harry and Luisa Holland. It is they who gave the party."

Harry stood up and shook hands. "Are you enjoying yourself, Callie?"

"Oh yes. You have created a wonderful atmosphere. I love the Chinese lanterns."

"Luisa is the genius behind the decorations. She attended the Art Institute in San Francisco. That's where we met. I have a fatal weakness for artists."

"She helped decorate our house," said Paloma. "Some of those those pieces of art in the living room-Luisa chose them."

"And my husband found them," said Luisa.

165

"Found them?" asked Callie.

"I have an import business in San Francisco. Have you ever been there?"

"Unfortunately, no."

"It's the most beautiful city in the states. You must come visit us, and we'll show you around. Where are you from?"

"A little town in Texas-Comanche Springs. But I've been living in Houston for some time."

"Houston? Why I just read about a race riot down there."

"Race riot? What do you know of it?"

"Well, I believe it was the 3rd Battalion, an all Negro unit that traveled to Houston, from New Mexico I think, to guard the Ship Channel-the war and all- they were evidently harassed by the locals. The battalion responded by marching on the town, and numerous white people were killed."

"My God, that is just awful. They are from Camp Furlong in Columbus, New Mexico. I knew some of those boys. They are fine people."

"It's a bad business."

"I hear such terrible stories about what happens to Negroes in the southern part of America," said Luisa. "Are these things true, in your city I mean?"

Callie wasn't prepared for such depressing talk at a party, aside from the fact that she was still a little tipsy. "Well, the citizens generally get along, but I cannot deny that some serious injustices have been done to the colored population. But these soldiers, I suppose they will be on trial soon?"

"I believe so. The strange thing is, they were all set to leave for the war in Europe. Pershing has called for three million soldiers. Had they done so, none of this would have happened."

"So, the situation grows worse in Europe?"

"Why yes. And Pershing, no doubt a sincere man, believes that our boys can fight the Germans the way they did the Apaches, with mobile warfare, sharpshooters."

"I got to know General Pershing," interjected Callie. "He is truly a fine man. He cares deeply about the troops."

"I'm sure that's true Callie, but warfare has changed, and the

166

reason, in two words, is the machine gun. It lays down a devastating field of fire against an enemy advancing on foot. If Pershing lets those troops operate in the open field, it will be tragic error. A disaster, I tell you."

Callie slumped down in the couch under the weight of Harry's warnings.

Luisa lightly punched her husband to break the somber mood. "Let's change the subject, shall we? We are giving a party, remember? The war is far away, *mi amor*."

"Don't let it get you down, amiga," Paloma whispered to Callie. "I am sure your *novio* is okay. You told me-he's muy bravo, no? "Está bien."

"Sí, Está bien," said Callie, without conviction.

Paloma and Callie left the party and began to drive around the city. Gliding through the streets in the white convertible refreshed them after the smoky heat of the party crowd. A crescent moon was rising as they drove around a lake in Chapultepec Park. The glassy reflection enticed them into stopping. The air was calm and filled with the soft hum of crickets.

"This is nice, just sitting here," said Callie, lying sideways in the seat. "Look how the moonlight is, shimmering in the water."

"Sí, it's true, amiga, and this will make it even better." Paloma took what looked like a hand-rolled cigarette out of her purse.

"What have you got there, Paloma?"

"Mar-ee-juana," she said, exaggerating each syllable in a lecherous voice. "It will loosen you up, señorita."

Callie sat up. "But isn't that illegal?"

"Not in Mexico, not in this car, not tonight." Paloma held a match to the tip and inhaled deeply. The curious fragrance surprised Callie. "You see, inhale it like this, and then hold it and take in a little smoke at a time." She handed it to Callie, who hesitated, then tried it.

She sucked the smoke in and held it, took a few quick breaths, and exhaled. "Hmm, interesting, but it's just like an exotic sort of cigarette, that's all."

"Wait a few minutes, amiga."

A remarkable scene began to unfold on the shore of the lake. An

167

elderly man in oriental clothing started to dance in slow, graceful movements as a young boy played a flute beside him, with long drawn-out crying notes that hung in the air like smoke. The moonlight silhouetted them with its silver backlight and the crickets pulsed steadily in the background.

"Paloma," Callie whispered,"are you seeing this too, or am I having a vision?"

"I see, I see. Es mas hermosa. Como un sueño."

"Yes, a beautiful dream," she sighed blissfully.

The man moved with exquisite balance and placed his arms and legs in precise positions, transforming himself into a tree, an eagle, a cat, and other life forms.

But Callie began to literally see these creatures, crouching, spreading their wings, dissociating into branches. The man had vanished. The flute emulated whatever next appeared in perfect resonance. She slowly opened the car door and walked a little ways toward the pair, stopped, crouched down by the water and stared all the more, desiring to take part in it. She could not remember how she came to be by the lake or whether the vision was being performed especially for her. She became convinced that she was one of the animals being conjured, for she could see far into the night and every single scent in the forest was discernible to her. Her memory of being human was some faraway memory. The young boy smiled at her. Looming above him, a huge cat, now yellow, now white, now black grew closer to her, and it's tawny eyes penetrated into her like sharp knives with such force that she moaned, backed away, until it leaped on top of her, and she screamed in fear.

Paloma was kneeling over her, brushing her hair out of her face. "Callie, it's all right. It's the smoke. Decir algo. Say something, please!"

Callie looked up at her like a lost child.

"Vamos, let's go home." Paloma led Callie back to the car. "Sit back now. Close your eyes and feel the wind as we drive. It's a beautiful night."

Noche de Ronda

Chapter 19

The two women sat in the courtyard. It was late morning, but they had just finished breakfast. Paloma stared at Callie, who had said little.

"I think I am corrupting you," said Paloma.

Callie looked up with drowsy eyes and a half smile. "Then I am doing it willingly." She brushed the hair out of her eyes and yawned. "It's such a pretty day-we should go for a walk."

"I shouldn't have let you smoke last night."

"I'm glad you did. It was a nice little adventure. I had no idea people could turn into animals. Max was right. I felt like Alice in Wonderland."

Paloma giggled. "You sound funny. Your voice is hoarse. Are you still seeing things? Am I turning into a serpent?"

Callie ignored the joke, her brows furrowed in thought. "When I woke up this morning I realized the revolution is still happening, but not out there in the Chihuahuan desert. In here." She pointed to her heart. "My old life has been overthrown. I keep getting caught in these skirmishes. I keep getting ambushed, and I don't know when it will settle down again. It's as if I'm on my horse, galloping and not caring where I am headed. This is my new life. I keep wondering what will happen next."

Paloma held her cup poised in midair. "Eres como un Pancho Villa femenino. Ha!"

Callie smiled and nodded. "Sí, es la verdad, amiga."

"Okay. Remember I tell you about the big fandango at the Hotel Primera? It will be this Saturday night. Eduardo, my tango *novio* will be there. And, I think you must find one too, because it will be filled with handsome hombres."

"And I suppose you are going to wear that shocking pink gown and drive all those hombres crazy."

"Claro. Of course. Es la guerra. Viva la revolución, querida!" Paloma broke out into riotous laughter and dropped her cup of coffee, shattering it on the smooth flagstone. One of the maids rushed in to investigate the commotion.

Callie jumped up and began picking up the pieces.

"Esta bien, Callie. Maria will clean it up."

Callie looked up. "No, Paloma, we will clean it up. It's our mess."

Paloma sighed, "Ay caramba, la socialista," and joined her on the floor.

Saturday arrived and Paloma eased her gleaming white Phaeton into the circular entrance of the impressive Hotel Primera. The Saturday evening breeze fluttered the tassels on her pink French gown as she adjusted a delicate tiara nestled in her hair. Callie sat next to her, attired in a simple white dress with a blue choker, the evening air laced with scents of smoke, perfume, and tropical flowers planted around the entrance.

She scanned the chattering crowd, her face animated with anticipation. Two valets rushed up and opened the car doors. Paloma pulled one of them aside and put some money in his hand.

"Here we go," she said, winking at Callie as they entered the hotel. The two women pranced up the wide marble stairs, hand in hand, smirking at each other.

They passed through the lobby into a spacious ballroom. The two of them paused and looked around-an orchestra played some banal old-fashioned tune. A few couples danced, but most were sitting at tables. Callie frowned. She could tell Paloma wasn't too impressed either.

"It will get better, you'll see," said Paloma, pulling Callie along, as they appraised the situation. Everyone seemed to be older and less avant-garde than Callie had hoped. Suddenly, Paloma squeezed her arm. "I see Eduardo," she squealed, and rushed off. Callie looked to see where she was going and saw a table with some younger men, one of whom stood up and hugged Paloma. He was indeed, handsome. They immediately took to the dance floor, and Paloma pointed at Callie and waved with a big smile, followed by a wave from Eduardo, as they danced around the floor. Eduardo moved his body with graceful assurance, tempered with a touch of *machismo*. Callie was only a little jealous, but as she looked around for prospective partners, no one aroused her interest. She attracted attention nevertheless, and had no lack of partners. Eventually, she walked out into the lobby, paged through some magazines, then bolted out the door.

She headed into the dark heart of the city, where few gringos ventured, letting herself be carried by the flow of the crowd through the narrow *calle*, until she heard an enticing melody float out of an open door, above which a lighted sign advertised "Café Paradiso", with a suggestive drawing of a dancing couple.

She strolled in and immediately had the feeling that she had left reality behind. A nattily dressed gentleman beckoned her in with a lascivious smile and offered a table, but she breezed right by him and walked along the periphery of the room. Callie always got the scent of a place right off the bat, and breathed in a heady melange of perfume, cigarettes, and whiskey. The place was a strange mix of the seedy and the elegant, the beautiful and the desperate.

The dance floor was half filled with couples of all ages, some casually dressed, some in tuxes and gowns. A small orchestra played a seductive song that urged Callie to dance.

She took a stool at the long bar and ordered a glass of wine. Single Mexican women were sprinkled about the club, but she was the lone gringa, and was getting looks from both sexes. She felt powerful, full of energy, well aware that she looked desirable.

A weird voice behind her cackled something lewd-sounding in Spanish. She looked around and saw a blue and yellow parrot in a brass cage behind the bar cocking his head at her. He began repeating the word, *"ferrocarril"* over and over, rolling his "r's" for all he was worth.

She felt good there. The wine tasted just right and induced a pleasant euphoria. She had turned twenty-five a few weeks ago, a quarter of a century. She was ready for anything.

The Mexicans danced with abandon. Men moved past her, trying to catch her eyes. A somber, dark-skinned woman with a cynical smile eyed her from the end of the bar. The vocalist sang love songs with a fervent yearning.

A striking young man, perhaps Callie's own age, stared intently at her from across the floor. She felt the warmth of his gaze before she caught sight of him. He was swaying his body to the music in a manner which Callie had never seen, rather like someone in restrained ecstasy. She put her glass down and returned his stare. He wore a

172

white tailored suit, had neatly cut, slicked-back hair and an assured expression on his face that said he had already made up his mind.

One song ended and another began, a tango. He moved directly toward her through the dancers, half dancing, half gliding. Callie was thrilled. Her mouth went dry and her heart fluttered when he came up to her with a sweet and slightly arrogant smile, and held out his hand. She took it, rising up to accompany him to the center of the floor, where he slid his arm around her waist and took her right hand high in the air and launched into the forward motion of something like a tango. He moved like a cat, in sinuous curves and dips, keeping a certain space between them, until he would bring her right against him to make a tight rapid turn that would take her breath away. Callie was only feeling, not thinking, for it was wonderfully easy to follow his strong lead. When he held her close the smell of his hair was sweet and masculine, and there was a smoky scent to his clothes.

They said not a word, but moved in a trance, as if he had been waiting to find a partner equal to him.

There were moments when he locked his eyes with hers, for the dance was as emotional as it was physical, and more intimate than she thought possible with a stranger. Someone shattered a glass, a knife blade flashed, some woman screamed, and a man was dragged away, but they kept dancing, until the song faded with a soft guitar arpeggio.

They stood there, her hands still clasped in his, perspiring, reading each other's thoughts. Callie caught sight of the dark woman, now glaring at her. She had an impulse to leave, but the music began again, this time with a familiar song-*Noche de Ronda*, and her partner swept her away.

It was a haunting song, a cautionary tale for lovers. The lover pleads with her not to go on the night of rounds and be taken by another man, for he waits for her to return, slowly dying of sadness.

Even as he pinned her close to his body she saw the back of a soldier in uniform, so resembling Casey that she was startled and fell out of step. He let her recover, pulled her closer and caressed her back, moved his legs within hers, held her like a lover, until she gave in to the intense pleasure of it all and let herself be taken.

She watched the singer smile at them, as if he approved, swaying to the music, pleased with himself.

173

Callie did not resist, for it was lovely to be seduced like this. She was living, following her instincts, blissful one moment, guilty the next. The predatory grasp of his body around her, which might have repulsed her at another time, fulfilled her need at that moment. Before the song had quite ended, he pulled her away from the floor. She looked back at the accusatory stare of the dark woman, as she was led out into the night.

At that moment Paloma appeared in the street and watched them walk away. "Callie, where are you going?" she yelled.

Callie glanced backwards with a carefree smile that silenced Paloma, who stood under a streetlight in bewilderment, as the seductive music from the club spilled out into the street.

Return to New Mexico

Chapter 20

Callie watched the day dawn in Mexico City through the window of the cab that returned her to Paloma's house. They passed a lonely little adobe that had somehow escaped the wrecking ball of progress. Multicolored hollyhocks swayed in the wind like gangly children and she thought of Lucille and Randy Sharp in New Mexico. She wanted to see them badly, along with Bandido, who was being looked after by Randy.

There was nothing to think about. It was settled. She explained as best she could to Paloma.

"I've lost my focus. I don't regret anything, but I need to get back into some kind of project, some undertaking that I'm passionate about. I've gone adrift. I shall write about what I experienced in your country, and perhaps make something of it. But I must move on. I have to recapture that fire I felt in the desert, chasing Villa. Can you understand, Paloma?"

Paloma tried, but could not fathom Callie's motives. She had been certain that her new friend, her *amiga*, was to become an integral part of her life. "You break my heart, Callie." She lay on her big bed, inconsolable. Callie moped in the courtyard, drinking cups of coffee, full of remorse, but unwavering in her resolve.

Paloma finally came downstairs, red-eyed, but composed. She sat next to Callie and took a sip from her coffee cup. "A true friend understands. She does not stand in the way. Somos verdaderos amigos, mi amor. Nothing will change that."

The next morning Paloma drove Callie to the railroad station in the white Hudson. They spoke little. Callie kept thinking about her first carefree ride in the beautiful auto when Paloma picked her up from the hotel. She understood her friend's reaction because Paloma was like Mexico-exaggerated passion and fierce beauty. She would miss her.

As soon as they reached the station Callie jumped out, grabbed her two suitcases and blocked Paloma from getting out.

"It is better if we say adios here."

Paloma looked helpless. "Sí," she whispered.

Callie bent over and embraced her, kissed her softly on the cheek and looked at her for a moment, then turned and ran into the station, just as a rush of tears streamed from her eyes. She made her way through the crowded station, bought her ticket to El Paso in a daze, and quickly boarded. She wanted to fall asleep and wake up in New Mexico. She wanted to hurry her life along. She wanted something to console her between the scenes.

Callie threw her baggage up on the rack and looked around. Everyone seemed normal-businessmen, mothers with children, young soldiers. Was she the only person there trying to manipulate her life, like a frustrated writer abruptly tearing a page out of the story if it doesn't work out? She collapsed in a window seat. It would be a long journey, nearly a thousand miles. She dreaded it, she welcomed it if it could be some sweet hypnotic oblivion from which she would emerge into the clean sharp air of New Mexico, and start over.

She slept long and deep and awakened in the late afternoon light, famished. She hurried to the dining car, ate a hearty meal, had a glass of wine, then some coffee, which brought Paloma to mind and a wave of sadness that passed. Now sated, the most pressing hunger still gnawed inside her. She requested another cup of coffee, grabbed her journal, and began to write, slowly at first, hesitant about where to begin, until a gust of inspiration lifted and carried her into the tale.

Sometime later the porter came up and informed her that the dining car had closed some time ago. Callie looked around at the empty car and rushed back to her seat so as not lose her train of thought. She wrote and she wrote by the weak yellow coach light as the invisible Mexican countryside flew by in the darkness. She never consciously stopped writing, but simply succumbed to sleep, still grasping her pen. Her dreams continued the story and it was out of this other world she awakened, slightly disoriented and blinking in the bright light of morning.

She uncurled herself and sat up, grimacing from stiffness and a dry throat. People were moving about, children were laughing, the smell of coffee floated in the air. The golden colors of the desert morning sun unfolded in a gently moving panorama through the window. As she stretched, Callie noticed a large ink stain on her blouse, where her pen had rested part of the night. Her journal was lying on the floor.

177

She had not yet separated her writing from her dreams until that instant, and she clutched the journal to her breast, ecstatic in the realization that she had indeed written all those pages of her adventures. She turned the pages, caressing them with great satisfaction. "It's only a beginning, but it's a lovely beginning," she murmured.

Callie leaned against the window glass and gazed out at the harsh desert landscape she had traversed with General Pershing and the 8th Regiment a year before. She experienced a succession of memories along with the rolling momentum of the train, faces of soldiers, Mexicans, Indians, and Casey. She tasted the fine yellow dust floating inside the train as millions of tiny illuminated motes, and experienced the familiar and powerful urge to be out there again, riding in the blazing sun and relentless wind on Villa's trail. She was sure she recognized a long pink mesa far off to the west.

She had been writing for some time when the train pulled into El Paso. The porter informed her he thought there was an eleven a.m. train to Columbus, but he wasn't certain. As they came into the station Callie was poised with her two suitcases by the doors, ready to leap off the coach. The train groaned to a stop and emitted a long steamy hiss of relief, and Callie hit the ground running, searching for a conductor. She found a bespectacled old gentleman who pointed her to right gate. "You've got about five minutes, young lady, so hurry along," he advised with a smile.

She rushed down the platform and arrived at the last "All aboard!", clambering up the steps, gasping, sweating, but bursting with excitement. There were few people in the car and she stretched out on two seats. The train began to move and she sat up, startled. "My God, I forgot to buy a ticket!" When the ticket collector approached she confessed. "Sir, I have just traveled a thousand miles up from Mexico City and neglected to purchase a ticket for the last seventy miles. May I purchase one from you?"

He looked at her quizzically, as if he was unaccustomed to any deviation from the normal routine. Callie gave him a sweet grin and he sold her a ticket.

She was lost in thought with memories of Columbus and curiosity about how Lucille and Randy had fared. She sat back and relived the night of Villa's attack. It seemed more like a movie than an actual memory. "If I can just write it down in story form, perhaps it will all make sense, and come to something."

She closed her eyes for a moment, and when she opened them there was the funny little red two-story train station of Columbus, dwarfed by the New Mexico desert.

Callie jumped out of her seat and descended to the platform. The hot wind blew her hair into her eyes, but she shook her head and walked toward the site of the burned down Commercial Hotel. There was a brand new building in its place. She wondered if Arthur still worked there, but was too anxious to see Lucille, and hurried off.

She had no time to send a telegram and warn her of her coming, but knew it wouldn't be a problem with Lucille. It was the hottest part of the day, and Main Street was mostly deserted. Callie spotted the tall red and yellow hollyhocks against the adobe wall and increased her pace, sweat rolling down her face and her arms aching from the weight of the suitcases.

She went up to the side door and knocked, then gently pushed it open, sticking her head inside the kitchen. "Hello! Lucille? Randy?" She put down her baggage and grabbed a glass from the shelf and filled it with water. She gulped it down so fast that she choked. Then she drank another. Then another. She caught her breath and wiped her mouth, peeked into the bedroom. Everything in the little house was as neat as a pin, just as she remembered.

Callie looked at the clock. "Twelve-fifteen. She's teaching. Of course, they're both in school. But Bandido isn't!"

She opened her suitcase, changed into riding pants and rushed out the door. There was no one around the stables. She stopped at the entrance to the stalls; all wound up with excitement she forced herself not to yell out his name. The other two horses looked up and regarded her with mild curiosity, but when Bandido caught sight of her he pricked up his ears and snorted, then let out a long whinny of recognition, shaking his head in great excitement.

Thus gratified, Callie dashed over to him, jumped up on the gate and hugged him with a years' worth of longing. "How are you boy? Como esta? How's my Bandido? Did they take care of you? Did Randy take you out every single day? Mi hermoso caballo." His eyes

179

sparkled, even though she was crying all over him. She held her head against him and caressed his face. "I really missed you, you know that? Now, let's go for a ride, amigo. Que dice?"

She went inside the stall and removed his halter, stroking his nose continually to calm his agitation.. "Okay Bandido, let's get the bridle on. Hold still now, I know you're excited. Here we go." She struggled to keep his head still. "God, Bandido, help me out please."

Throwing the halter away, she grabbed the bridle and positioned it, stuck her thumb in the corner of his mouth to get the bit in. "C'mon, Bandido, open up." He finally relented and she inserted the bit. She quickly slid the bridle over his ears while he was somewhat still and adjusted the chin strap.

She threw a pad over his back and when she carried the saddle over he began to paw the floor, then nod vigorously up and down. He suddenly kicked with his hind legs and sent a bucket flying into the next stall, causing the other horses to react. "Hold on now, I'm going as fast as I can, sweetie. You are *so* rambunctious. Chico tonto!" She lifted the saddle up and let it fall gently on his back, then snugged up the cinch and led him outside.

As soon as they were out in the sunlight, he reared up excitedly and bolted away. Callie was already sprinting alongside and threw her herself up on the saddle as he accelerated out of the corral. Bandido was not one to trot.

Callie guided him toward the open country where the familiar peaks of Tres Hermanas Mountain jutted into an azure sky. She stayed on the road to avoid prairie dog holes and leaned into the wind as the horse rocketed away like a thoroughbred.

They skirted the base of the mountain and entered wilder country, leaving a long trail of dust behind. Callie saw a flash of white off to her right. A herd of pronghorn, spooked by their sudden appearance, bolted in the same direction they were riding. Callie shook the reins and gave Bandido a little squeeze, and he launched into high gear. "Vamos muchacho!" she yelled.

Callie thought he was going to leave the ground they were moving so fast. She lay astride his neck like a jockey, with a crazy smile on her face. Off to the left she saw the red caboose of a slow moving passenger train. Bandido caught up with it. She waved at the surprised passengers, whose silent mouths opened and closed like puppets, pointing and waving back at the woman on the speeding horse, who flew by the train. A young girl of about eight, with long, ribboned pigtails also watched the black-haired woman, her blue eyes wide with fascination.

But even Bandido couldn't keep up with the fastest animals on the plains, and the antelope soon were out of sight.

On the way back to town Callie could not stop smiling, for she was in her element, on her pony, riding across the open country. She had no regrets about the past or concerns for the future, at least for this day.

They approached the house just as her friend walked up to her door. Callie let out a loud whistle. Lucille turned around and her freckled face expanded in astonishment. She put her hand over mouth, dropped her books and ran over to them.

"Did you ride here all the way from Mexico?" she exclaimed, ignoring all logic. Callie broke up with laughter and slid off the horse. The two embraced, then Lucille drew back and wiped her eyes. "We always seem to be hugging and crying. Why is that?"

Callie shrugged. "I don't know. How are you, Lucille? How is Randy?"

"Fine. We are all just fine." She looked at Bandido. "Oh my, I didn't even recognize your horse. I am such a foolish woman."

Callie put her arm around her as they walked into the house. "No you're not. You just wear your heart on your sleeve, like me."

Main Street, Columbus, New Mexico

Chapter 21

Lucille put two cups on the table. A pot of geraniums sat on the windowsill above the sink, a bright eruption of red in the well-scrubbed white kitchen. "I get so drowsy this time of day. It's so quiet in the house after being with those kids for six hours, and this heat. We'll both just have some fresh coffee."

Callie relaxed in the chair, admiring Lucille's ability to put people at ease. "Where is Randy?"

"Oh, I expect he's out gallivanting with his pals. They often go to the Camp and watch the soldiers."

"I was so anxious to see you I forgot about Camp Furlong. Is Lieutenant Castleman still there?"

Lucille set out a tray of cookies on the table. "I suspect you are awful hungry after that long journey." She smiled down at Callie, as if her own daughter had returned unexpectedly. "Lieutenant Castleman? Oh no, all of the younger boys went off to Europe. Things were very busy and prosperous for a while, but all that's changed, because of the war you see."

The coffee started bubbling its rich aroma into the air and Lucille poured the steamy brew into both cups, then pulled her chair right beside Callie. "You look wonderful, Callie. Tired, but wonderful. You are so dark from the sun, but it suits you." She brushed a strand of hair from Callie's eye. "Your hair's a sight though."

Callie smiled, ate a cookie, sipped the coffee, and had another cookie. "My goodness, but these are scrumptious," she mumbled, still chewing. "I feel wonderful. I swear, when I stepped off that train, I thought I had entered another universe. It is so unearthly quiet here."

"Well, I won't argue with you on that one. Drives some folks into a state of agitation, but I like it, after all the commotion in the classroom.

You must have been to such wondrous places. We got your postcards. Randy really liked the one of the pyramids. Look, I have it right here." She opened a drawer and produced the tinted postcard. "We neither of us could pronounce that name."

"Teo-ti-hua-can," Callie enunciated. "See that one? It's the

Pyramid of the Sun. I climbed it and there was no one up there but a cloud of beautiful butterflies. Oh Lucille, the view of the green valley was just grand. I didn't want to come down."

Lucille stared at the card and shook her head. "My oh my, that must have been a revelation. And you, all by yourself up there."

"Yes, by myself. That's why I'm here-to see you and Randy of course-but to be by myself again. I met some wonderful people in Mexico. It's such a strange and mysterious place, but I needed to get away. It started closing in on me. I've started to write about it. But a story, not an article. I wrote like a woman possessed, during the train ride. See?" She held up both hands and proudly displayed her ink-stained fingers.

Lucille tilted her head and regarded her fingers with a mix of curiosity and joy. "I remember some of those interesting newspaper articles you showed me before you left. I am so pleased." Lucille straightened up in her chair and took a long sip of coffee. "What about Casey?"

Callie's heart flinched, but she responded with a weak smile. "Well, he's in France, and I believe he's been training with the Lafayette Air Corps, so he's probably right in the thick of it." Lucille seemed to see right through Callie's composure and took her hand. "I'm glad he wrote you my dear and let you know he was all right."

"Oh yes, he's fine," she blurted. "He mentioned the Germans are closing in on Paris, and that their squadron flies several missions each day, and they're all great fellas. And I read somewhere that the life expectancy of the pilots is what, something like three months, but he would never write something like that." She slowly crumbled a cookie in her hands while she talked, then stood up suddenly and jarred the table, so that her cup tipped over and spilled the coffee. "Damn! What is wrong with me?"

She went to the sink for a washcloth, but just stared at the red geranium. Lucille came to her side and put a hand on her shoulder.

Callie bowed her head. "Oh, Lucille. I haven't treated him right." She started to shake with emotion and broke into sobs, twisted around and grabbed onto her friend, laying her head on her shoulder. Lucille stroked her tangled, wind-blown hair.

"After the expedition I craved more adventure. It felt...

empowering, but, I don't know- maybe it was just plain immoral."

The kitchen door swung open and Randy walked in, carrying his schoolbooks and a coyote skull. "Hey ma, look what I-"

He froze when he saw the two women embraced, Callie in tears.

"Look who's back, son. She's so happy to see us she's just cryin' her eyes out. I think she needs another hug."

Randy dropped his books and ran over to hug the woman who saved his life. "What in the world is that?" asked Callie, as Randy pressed the skull into her back.

"Oh, sorry. This here's a coyote skull we found out yonder behind the Camp. Ain't she a beauty, Callie?"

Callie took the skull in her hand, wiping her eyes. "It surely is a fine specimen, Randy."

He stared at her red, teary eyes. "You must *really* be happy to see us."

"Oh yes, very, very much."

"I was wondering why Bandido was tied up in front of the house. Want me to walk him back to the stables?"

"Would you, Randy? I hope he wasn't too much to take care of?"

"Oh no ma'am. Me and him are like this." He put two fingers together. "Once I learned his tricks I was fine. He only bucked me off a couple a times. And I sure do appreciate gettin' paid for it. Why, it's more fun than anything." He ran out the door and they heard him talking to the horse.

"I think I better go to the army headquarters," said Callie. "I already have a letter written and I'll wager they will get it to him faster than the regular mails. And I'll leave my name with your address, just in case Casey sends something here. If that's all right with you."

"Callie, you know you don't need to ask."

"Better neaten up a little first. After all, I was practically one of the troops under General Pershing." She went into the bedroom and reappeared in in a few minutes with brushed hair, a scent of rosewater, and a fresh blouse, free of ink stains.

She crossed the railroad tracks and entered Camp Furlong. It was practically deserted. Only a small group of horses stood in the corral, in pairs, front to back, tails swatting flies around their faces. She left

185

her letter and was assured it would get to France within the month. They advised her to put her name on a list of relatives and friends to receive letters from men overseas.

She also mailed one more letter-addressed to Chester Moon, at the *Biograph Motion Picture Company* in Hollywood, California. She was playing one of her aces and had high hopes riding on it.

She crossed the street. The hotel was fresh and bright, the sharp smell of its yellow pine boards still scenting the air.

Callie decided to retrace her steps from the night of Villa's attack. She had a weakness for revisiting places that held important memories. Walking out of the alley by the hotel, she stopped in front of the drugstore, where she cowered from the barrage of gunfire in the streets, and where she and Randy teamed up. She walked to the ditch they hid in, then across the field. There she stopped and looked to the west, where the makeshift airfield had been, where Casey had taken her up in the shaky old Jenny biplane for her very first flight. The weightless feeling, his white scarf, the achingly blue sky and tilting landscape below. She walked on, staring at the ground.

That evening Callie and Lucille sat at the kitchen table, enjoying after-dinner coffee.

"Aren't you concerned about not having a job, once you finally return to Houston?" asked Lucille.

"I won't be returning, Lucille. This will be a long journey."

"Well, how long?"

"My entire life, I suppose." She smiled and sipped her coffee.

"But honey, you just can't keep traveling and moving around like a . . . nomad. When will you settle down?"

"A nomad is just what I long to be. You know, I really like the sound of that word. That's what we all were once, following the game, moving with the seasons, before settlements, towns, and cities. The lives of our ancestors were probably comparatively short, but I imagine they lived them intensely. Think of what they saw-the glaciers come and go, saber-toothed tigers and mastodons, an untouched primeval landscape. My God, what I would give to have seen such things."

"What about comfort? A woman needs a domicile for herself and her husband. To cook and sew, raise children. A place of her own. A home."

"I admit that a stable home has its charms, although my experience wasn't particularly pleasant." She gazed out the window at Randy playing with his friend and thought of her adolescence, spent in her grandmother's house, sleeping in cramped rooms, sharing beds with cousins. "There's time enough for that. If I were to die in the next year, I would much prefer to leave this world on a journey of adventure, doing something that made me feel alive, than in a stuffy hospital room, surrounded by weepy relatives."

Lucille shook her head. "I have a notion that Casey shares your opinions. That's probably why you two got along so well."

"You know he mentioned that in one of his letters. That guy isn't ready to settle down by a long shot. He is very excited about continuing in aviation after the war, maybe up in Alaska, or down in South America. Can you imagine, Lucille? Those are still frontier lands. I could bask on a summer day where the sun never sets, see Mount McKinley rise up twenty-thousand feet into that big blue Arctic sky." Her eyes widened with excitement, just speaking of such possibilities.

"It sounds like a fairytale that you're describing."

Images were flooding Callie's brain now. She jumped out of her chair. "And imagine, Lucille, being perched on the edge of Tierra del Fuego, the very tip of South America, where Magellan and Drake navigated that treacherous passage. Those were my favorite parts of history lessons in school."

"But how will you pay for these elaborate trips? Have you considered that?"

Callie took her friend's hand. "If you put yourself in a place that inspires you, everything else will take care of itself. I really believe that."

"Darlin', that sounds so lovely, but it is such an insecure way to live, especially for a young woman."

"But isn't that just the problem, Lucille? We trade away everything that is meaningful-adventure, discovery, freedom- for the sake of security. Thoreau said he did not want to come to the end of his life and find out that he had forgotten to truly live. Well, neither do I." She slapped the table. "It's a terrible exchange! I can't imagine anything more terrible than laying on my deathbed, regretting all the crazy, wonderful things I *could* have done. I refuse to throw my life away like that. If that is how society expects us to live, then society is dead wrong." Her face flushed with emotion.

"Callie, I love you for your convictions, for your determination. But I feel responsible for you. I'm not sure why, but I do, like your own mother. You're just so impulsive that you forget to worry about your own safety, honey. It can be such a cruel world, especially for women who are on their own. I worry, that you might end up stranded somewhere, without a decent meal, proper clothes, or a place to stay."

"I know that, and I am grateful. But food and shelter simply enable us to exist. A well-lived life…that is what enables us to blossom. I have to accept the risks, Lucille, if I want the rewards."

Callie stood up, went to the sink and put her empty cup down, gazing out the window where she could see Bandido in the corral. A big smile spread over her face as she turned back to Lucille. The enthusiasm glittered in her eyes like sparks.

"I want to ride Bandido across the pampas, Lucille. I want to ride him under that midnight sun. I want to blossom!"

Lillian and Dorothy Gish, with DW Griffith

Chapter 22

Callie decided that she wanted a portrait of herself with Lucille and Randy. She borrowed a tripod from the local photographer and set the camera up in front of the hollyhocks. She didn't want a dressed up, formal picture, but simply how they looked on a normal day.

"Where do you want us to stand, Callie?" asked Lucille, not particularly comfortable with the whole idea. Callie guided her to a spot against the wall. "You here." She placed Randy next to her, with his rifle propped up on the ground in front of him, leaving a space for her in the middle, her arms draped around each of her friends.

"Am I 'sposed to frown, Callie, like everyone does, or can I smile?" Randy asked.

"I want both of you to smile, just as you always do. Be your sweet selves."

Lucille fussed with her hair. "I must look a mess in this wind."

"It's a picture of us on a Tuesday afternoon, that's all. This is how I want to remember us."

She looked at each of them. "Okay, are we ready?"

Just then, Bandido whinnied from his stall. "He must hear me talking," said Callie. "It's okay, amigo," she yelled, "I'll get a picture of you another time."

The horse snorted in reply, then whacked the side the side of the stall with his hoof."

"All right. I'll count to three," warned Callie. She had attached a long cable to the camera and held the bulb trigger in her hand. "One, two, three!" She squeezed and tripped the shutter, which elicited a sharp click, freezing the three of them, slightly windblown, holding on to each other, beaming their smiles into an unknown future.

Everything happened all at once. Chester sent a letter to Callie explaining that D.W. Griffith was about to begin a new film:

"It's called 'Hearts of the World', about the war in France. I have a feeling he could use your writing talents. But you need to get here soon. Lazlo and I would love to see you. Hollywood is a pretty little

place, lots of orchards and ranches. Very peaceful. I think you would like it here. And the rent is cheap."

Callie sat in the kitchen and reread the letter. Lucille and Randy were both at school. It was midafternoon. Columbus was quiet as a graveyard. The heat descended in undulating waves. The wind had given up and died.

A bead of sweat trickled down her forehead and landed on the letter, smearing the ink. She stared at the wilted geranium above the sink, looked past it at the forlorn little adobes outside, baking in the sun.

Callie folded the letter and went into the bedroom to pack her suitcase. She inquired at the railroad office about transporting Bandido on the train to California. An officer from Camp Furlong helped facilitate the arrangement.

She waited until Lucille and Randy arrived and said goodbye, once again. She couldn't wait until morning.

The train pulled out just as the sun flashed below the horizon and sprayed warm colors across the desert. She gazed at distant mesas in Mexico that glowed red in the deep heat, and, for a moment, wanted to rush back into that troubled land where she had felt so alive. But she was ready for something entirely new, in another place where nobody knew who she was, to try her luck in the movie world and see what might happen. She was still covering the revolution, but now it was her own.

Callie arrived in Los Angeles just as an erratic Pacific front slammed into the southern California coast. She telephoned Chester and asked if he could bring a trailer for Bandido. The driving rainstorm could not dampen her high spirits as she waited by the entrance. She saw palm trees swaying in the rain and graceful Spanish architecture. "It's not so very different than Mexico. And these scents- I don't know what they are, but they are delicious!"

"Callie!" The familiar dapper figure of Chester emerged from the car. He ran up to her and they embraced. "Oh Callie, it's so good to see you here. You made the right decision, you'll see."

"It already feels good, Chester. What about the trailer?"

Before he could respond, a loud honk came from a truck pulling up to the curb, with a trailer in tow. Lazlo jumped out, all smiles and ran over to give Callie another welcome hug. "Well, Miss Sharpshooter herself. How you like sunny California, eh?"

"This is so unusual, Callie," Chester interjected. "It never rains this time of year."

"Doesn't matter. I'm just excited to be here. Bandido's around back in the boxcar. He's probably wondering where he is."

Bandido's ears perked up when he saw the vehicles approach. Callie jumped out, as a worker put up a ramp for the horse, and ran up to untie the animal and lead him down to the trailer.

"Remember Chester and Lazlo, sweetie?" The two men stroked the horse, which shook his head in appreciation. "Good boy," said Chester. "A fine boy you are. Maybe we'll put you in a movie."

"Oh gosh," said Callie in mock amazement, "Did you hear that, Bandido?"

They drove down Sunset Boulevard, a dusty, winding road dotted with nurseries and small farms. Callie inhaled the strangely foreign scent of eucalyptus and peach blossoms that floated on the wet air and was fascinated with low-growing chaparral crawling down the mountainsides. She wanted to stop at the small fruit stands along the road and talk to the dark-skinned farmers in cowboy hats. "This is all so strange-it's not at all like Texas or New Mexico."

"Boy, you got that right, Callie. And you ain't seen nothing yet," said Chester.

They drove into a small canyon and negotiated some sharp curves. Callie looked back at the trailer to make sure Bandido was okay.

"Here we are, my dear. I think you'll like this little bungalow."

The rain had stopped and the sunshine sparkled on the rain-soaked oaks. A huge jacaranda tree, weighted with fragrant purple blossoms, stood in front of a small Spanish style cottage, complete with red tile roof and pots of geraniums on a flagstone patio.

Callie's eyes caught sight of bright yellow fruit from a small tree. "Oh my goodness, a lemon tree!" She walked over and plucked a perfect lemon, gazed at it with wonder and sniffed its citrusy scent. "I've never seen a lemon tree," she said, as if it were a shameful thing. Chester and Lazlo smiled at each other.

"This place belongs to a friend of mine at the studio, who hardly uses it," Chester explained. "You can stay here as long as you like. But you'll have plenty of time to settle in. Are you up for a visit to the studio? Mr. Griffith is anxious to meet you."

"Anxious to meet me?" Callie nearly choked on the words. "A famous director like that?" She stepped in front of a mirror. "Look at me. I'm a mess." She fussed with her hair and smoothed her dress.

"Believe me, you look fine, Callie. Mr. Griffith will be enchanted, just like the rest of us. Let's be off then!"

They rushed to the car, only to find Bandido confronting them with an impatient snort.

"Oops!" chuckled Callie.

"No problem, my dear, there's a nice little barn out back, with hay and fresh water," Chester assured them.

They unhooked the trailer and led the horse to the barn, where Callie was introduced to Antonio, a small mustachioed man in overalls and a straw hat.

"He does gardening and chores for my studio friend."

Callie extended her hand. "Hello. Habla español?"

"Uh, he's Italian, Callie."

"Oh, sorry. Buon giorno, signore," offering her hand again.

His face lit up and he took her hand with enthusiasm.

"Piacere, piacere, signorina."

"I am Callie," she said, patting her chest. She went over to the stall. "This, is *Bandido.*" She enunciated the word. *"Bandido."*

"Ah Sí, Bandido. Un bel cavallo!"

"He said Bandido is beautiful, I think," she said, turning to Chester. "Isn't that sweet?"

"Yes it is, my dear, but we really must be off."

As they hurried away, Callie turned around and waved, "Ciao, Antonio!"

They walked into the studio through a back door upon which a sign read: "Employees Only". Callie sensed a hushed intensity as soon as she entered. The smells of freshly cut lumber mingled with makeup and cigarettes. A small group of actors in a corner seemed to be rehearsing an argument. She passed a kitchen, a stable, and a bank in quick succession. There was a small group of people in deep discussion just ahead, the center figure, tall and distinguished, in a suit and large white hat, puffed on a cigarette.

Chester turned around, took Callie's arm and brought her right up to the tall gentleman, whose grave, gray eyes instantly latched on to Callie's.

"Mr. Griffith, may I present Callie Masterson, just arrived from New Mexico. Callie, Mr. D.W. Griffith."

She studied his face- regal, somewhat haughty, but presenting an undeniable Shakespearean integrity.

"Miss Masterson," he said, bowing slightly, "this is indeed a pleasure. Chester has related some of his adventures with you. You seem to be a woman to reckon with."

"Mr. Griffith, it is so good to meet you." She was only slightly intimidated, for here was a genuine artist who had created a thoroughly modern art form for the twentieth century. There was an instant rapport.

"Chester tells me you've written an account of the revolution from a reporter's point of view."

"Well, yes, actually I've been rewriting a narrative from my journal entries, mainly on long train journeys with crying babies and a few chickens." She paused with a smile, but Griffith remained unsmiling with arched eyebrows.

"But it's been coming along nicely, I think," Callie hastened to add.

"I would be interested in reading some of it. In the meantime, we could use someone to proof the scripts for errors. Does that interest you?"

"Very much so. I know no one in California, so it is much appreciated." Chester beamed like a proud father, just behind her.

"Allow me to introduce one of my actresses. This is Miss Lillian Gish."

Lillian Gish possessed a fragile elegance and was even more lovely than her cinema appearances would suggest. Callie suddenly remembered their supposed similarity in looks, but no one brought it up.

"Callie, welcome to our our little family. My goodness, what amazing adventures you've experienced."

"Thank you, Miss Gish. I haven't been able to see any movies lately, but I greatly admired your portrayal of Elsie in *Birth of a Nation.*

"Thank you, Callie. Come walk with me awhile."

Lillian took Callie's arm, and they strolled through the studio's cavernous sound stage.

"You know that Mr. Griffith's next film will be *Hearts of the World.*"

"Yes, Chester mentioned it in his letter, but I have no idea what it's all about."

"Well, it's about the war. It centers around some young people in a French village, which is invaded by the German army, bringing terrible destruction. But they resist, until the French retake the town."

Callie's heart fluttered at this fresh intrusion of the war. She strove to keep her emotions well-hidden. A piece of equipment fell with a sharp crash, close by. Callie jumped and grabbed Lillian, and then quickly released her.

"Oh, that's not like me at all. I'm sorry."

"It's perfectly all right, Callie. Is something else bothering you?"

Callie looked away. "Someone very close to me is in that war. He's a pilot. In France, I think."

"I see. Mr. Griffith will be leaving for England quite soon. The company will follow soon after. I thought we could use your reporting expertise...but perhaps that is not a good idea."

Callie's eyes narrowed with concentration as she considered the offer. "Maybe it is. Maybe it will give me a sense of control if I go over there. Maybe I could even..."

"See him? Your sweetheart, then?"

Callie nodded.

After Griffith read some of Callie's writing, he put her on the payroll as assistant writer and extra. They talked briefly between scenes outside on the back lot.

"I'd like you to think of this as a possible script. Your adventures as the lone woman in that band of ruffians has some possibilities. How in the blazes did you manage to keep your head during that night attack in Columbus?"

"Well, sir, I was alternately scared out of my wits and equally excited to be witnessing history. There wasn't much time to think about it."

"I see. By the way, Lillian told me about your beau in the war. Those boys were awfully brave to volunteer. I hope the French properly appreciate it. Callie, if there's a way we can find the boy I will do my best. We would love to have you along. I think you just may witness some more history."

"Then I accept. Thank you, sir." Griffith smiled, patted her hands and was about to go back to work. "His name is Casey Wilde," Callie added.

"Pardon?" he said.

"Casey Wilde. He's a Captain, in the First Aero squadron-at least that's what he flew here in the states. I think he's with a French group now. Casey Wilde is his name, Mr. Griffith." Her eyes were wide open and flashed with emotion that she no longer tried to suppress.

The stoic director looked as if he were grabbing his heart, but instead took out a small notepad from inside his coat and carefully wrote down the information, then turned around to resume the scene.

"Thank you," she whispered.

Zeppelin bomb damage in London, 1916

Chapter 23

Griffith left for London within the week. He would later tell Lillian that Prime Minister Lloyd George summoned him to 10 Downing Street and was blunt about his intentions: "I want you to go to work for France and England and make up America's mind to go to war with us." Griffith now had complete backing from both governments and would be able to film anywhere he chose.

Griffith arranged for Lillian and her mother to cross on the *St. Louis*, a camouflaged ship with a group of doctors and nurses. Dorothy Gish, actor Bobby Farron, Lazlo and Callie would sail some weeks later on the *Baltic*, a British ship.

She met with Dorothy, Lillian's extroverted sister, back at the studio. Dorothy was nervous about the journey. "There's somebody very notable on our ship. If the Germans find out, they're going to sink us for sure!"

Callie laughed. "Don't worry, Dorothy. I lead a charmed life. We'll be fine."

After a cross-country journey on the fastest train they could find, the group arrived at the docks at dawn in a cold drizzle. Callie walked up the steps with Lazlo, who gripped his camera as if it were his only child. The ship departed quickly, with no ceremony. Callie had hardly gotten settled in her tiny cabin when she noticed that they had come to a stop at the Ambrose Light. She peered out of her porthole. Tugs appeared out of the fog and she watched U.S. Army personnel climb aboard into the hold of the ship. The tugs were being tossed on the rough waves. Callie stared in terror as several boys were nearly crushed to death when they temporarily lost their footing.

After a few days out at sea Callie and Dorothy were walking along the deck, arm in arm, when they noticed a crowd of women abuzz with excitement. Dorothy leaned over to Callie. "Oh, this must be the mysterious celebrity."

They moved closer. A man in a suit was being accosted by a number of giddy women. She could only see his back, but Callie had a flash of recognition. "I think I know-"

He turned around. Callie's mouth fell open and she screamed. "General Pershing!"

Pershing's face lit up. "Callie!" All faces turned toward Callie and Dorothy, as the general rushed over and embraced his favorite reporter.

"I might have known you would follow the action, wherever it is," he said beaming. "How are you, my dear?"

"I'm fine, General. And don't you look dashing in that suit. It's a long way from the Chihuahuan desert, is it not?"

"Indeed it is." He glanced at Dorothy. "I know you. When we were on the Mexican border I saw one of your pictures. Now let's see, which sister are you?"

"I am Dorothy. Perhaps you were thinking of my sister, Lillian?"

"Oh no, it was you I saw in El Paso in, what was it, *Gretchen* something or other it was called."

"Gretchen the Greenhorn. I am so pleased you liked it."

"Tell me something about film making. These damn newsreels make me self-conscious. Callie can tell you."

"Well, we have a cameraman with us, and, if you like, we could practice shooting up on the deck."

"Yes, I'd like that."

There was entertainment in the evening, and Callie sat with General Pershing, while a pianist sang the sentimental *Keep the Home Fires Burning.*

"After we headed back to Texas I was never sure what became of you, Callie," said Pershing.

"I spent quite a few months traveling through Mexico and made some new friends," Callie replied. "It's a wonderful country, General, if only they could secure a stable government. Some of the ruins are just fascinating."

"So I've heard. Now, what became of Captain Wilde? You two were quite an item in the camp. I'm assuming he's somewhere in France."

199

"He was part of the volunteer group that joined up with the French air force to fight the Germans. That's one of the reasons I'm on this trip, apart from working for Mr. Griffith, of course."

"You're worried, of course."

"Yes sir, I am. I haven't heard from him for a long time now."

"That's not uncommon, my dear, in his situation you know-" He broke off when Callie gazed at him in sad resignation.

"Perhaps something can be done," he said quietly.

Dorothy rushed up to the table with a glass of champagne. "Callie, this is a lady's choice, so I must steal the general away from you."

Callie sipped her champagne. The sparkling wine and the warmth of the room made her a bit dizzy, so she wandered out to the deck. The fresh sea breeze immediately revived her. She leaned against the railing and watched the moving waves catch the moonlight in hypnotic sparkles that soothed her into a pleasing trance. A group of tipsy soldiers began singing somewhere above her.

The calamitous events she was heading toward were at odds with the enchanting night she found herself in. And, somewhere, hidden in some secret part of her mind was the stark reality of Casey's precarious situation, which she kept at bay with increasing difficulty as the ship neared Europe.

"Callie. What are you doing out here all by yourself?" Dorothy pranced over, champagne in hand and put her arm around her, somewhat unsteadily. "I just put mother to bed and all is well. See any German subs out there?"

"Everything is perfectly tranquil out here. The sea is like a dream. Do you always travel with your mother?"

"Oh yes. Mother and Lillian and I are a team. Always have been. Mr. Griffith likes that about us. It gives him a sense of family that's missing from his life."

"But, isn't he married?"

"They're separated. The cinema is his whole life. A man like that probably should never have married. The man's a genius. He truly is." She sipped and let out a long sigh. "General Pershing told me the most outrageous things about you in Mexico. Shooting those bandits when they charged you and Lazlo and Chester."

"I only did it to save other lives."

"My God, where did you learn such things? Women don't normally get caught up in revolutions."

"It was my job. I was a reporter. Anyway, my daddy taught me how to handle a gun and all us kids grew up on horses. Dorothy, don't you sometimes need to be on your own, away from your family?"

Dorothy looked at Callie as if she had said something unintelligible.

"Oh no, Callie. We three are all we have in this world. Our father abandoned us when we were children and it was only by sticking together that we have survived. Lillian and I have been actors since we were five. Mother took us on the road in touring companies and we've been a happy little trio ever since." She took out a cigarette from her purse and cupped it in her hands to light it in the wind.

"May I have one of those?" asked Callie.

"Oh sure. Say, what did you do when the expedition ended, and the army went back to Texas?"

"I stayed in Mexico. I wanted to explore farther south-Mexico City, the Aztec ruins, and the colonial villages."

"By yourself?"

"Of course, that's how I like to do it. Then I'm completely independent, can pack up and leave whenever I feel like it."

"But surely that is not a common thing. An American woman, unmarried and traveling in an uncivilized country like Mexico."

Callie bristled. "Uncivilized! Dorothy, do you even know the first thing about the country?"

"I've heard things."

"They have a glorious past-I climbed pyramids larger than the ones in Egypt; the most graceful architecture, fascinating cuisine. The people are the warmest and kindest I have ever met. I cannot believe you would pass judgment on a place that you have never seen."

"Don't get all riled. Here, have a sip of this, Miss Daniel Boone. But isn't it true," she whispered in Callie's ear, "that Latin men especially lust after American women, with our pale, sooft skin?"

Callie sputtered with laughter and downed the rest of the champagne.

"Hey, watch out! Now we have to get some refills and see if there are any interesting men still around."

"Lead on, Miss Gish."

The next day Dorothy put General Pershing before Lazlo's camera on the upper deck and tried some casual interviews. The sun shone down on the bright white deck and sleek brass railings and it all seemed like a pleasure cruise, with the General in a sport coat and Dorothy all made up, being her usual flirtatious self.

Callie watched from a distance, pleased that the General finally seemed at ease before the camera. But a feeling of dread mixed in with the excitement, and the conflicting emotions about Casey and her "Hollywood" job kept her off balance and vulnerable.

When they landed in Liverpool, a polished Welsh regiment greeted General Pershing with a spit-and-polish ceremony. Lillian waited at the dock, looking anxious and wan, and embraced her family with tears of relief. Callie started to move away but Lillian hugged her with great enthusiasm. "I am so glad to see you, Callie. Thank you for being such a good friend to Dorothy."

"You are most welcome, Lillian. We had a swell time."

After catching a train to London, they checked in at the Savoy, in rooms that overlooked the Thames. The staff was exceedingly attentive and devoted to making their illustrious guests feel at home in London.

On their first day, Griffith ordered the troupe to Victoria and Waterloo stations, where the soldiers departed for France. They watched the long goodbyes, the last waves, and the shattered look of those left behind. Mere boys, it seemed to Callie, in ill-fitting uniforms, were being sent to certain death, just as their lives were really beginning. In those scared faces, she felt the wrenching emotion, the collective shock of a nation suddenly forced to give up its youth to war.

The Gish sisters were aghast at the stream of casualties arriving from the front-mangled bodies, amputees, paraplegics. But Griffith was adamant: "You want to be actresses, but you've never lived. You don't know what life is all about. I hope you may never again have such an opportunity. But since it's here, I don't want you to miss it."

The actors stood in the shadows studying the dramas unfolding

202

around them, observing mannerisms and gestures that would serve them well.

The ladies were just finishing breakfast the next morning when a hotel manager informed them that anti-aircraft gun practice was to commence at eleven a.m. and not to be alarmed when they heard gunfire from the roof of the building next door. Just as he said this, the guns begin firing.

"That's odd," he said. "They've started early."

Griffith suddenly materialized at their table. "It's a German air raid!" He was beside himself with excitement. Everyone rushed to a large window in a corridor just as a formation of German Fokkers roared up over the Thames. The 75mm antiaircraft guns opened up on them and filled the sky with shell bursts and trailing tracers that illuminated their trajectory.

Instead of attacking the Houses of Parliament, the planes disappeared in the clouds, but bombing could be heard in the distance.

"They've hit somewhere," said Griffith. "Let's follow them."

He managed to bribe a taxi to Whitechapel. Callie had grabbed her notebook and piled into the taxi with everyone. She felt the same adrenaline rush that she had experienced in Mexico, but this was altogether of a different magnitude- a faceless war machine that came out of the darkness and obliterated whole blocks of houses.

They stopped at a large slum, which had taken a direct hit: a building in ruins, the smoke still rising from the rubble. People sobbing and desperate men trying to uncover buried victims. A tearful old man grabbed Lillian's hands and broke down. It was a school, the kindergarten. "They've murdered our little ones. The devils!"

Griffith had removed his hat and was in tears. "This is what war is. Not the parades and conference tables, but children killed, lives destroyed." He walked back to the cab, shaking his head.

Callie remained, unable to move, stared wide-eyed at the desperate men clawing the rubble for their children.

"Callie, we must get back to the hotel," called Griffith from the idling cab.

A few days later Callie sat in front of a mirror in her nightgown, brushing her hair, saddened that she no longer had her golden desert tan. London was blacked out and it was eerily quiet.

A terrible concussion sent shudders through the building and the lights went out. She rushed to the window. The Germans had bombed the Thames embankment, just below her. She could see everything in the moonlight and distinctly hear the cries of the injured. She grabbed a coat and went out into the hall. A woman from the room next door became hysterical and Callie led her downstairs to a safer area.

Everyone gathered in a large dining room where guests were still eating. Another bomb fell, not far away. Massive rumblings rolled under the hotel. Callie grabbed a glass of wine someone had left on a table and downed it. It was all too close to her harrowing night in Columbus, but worse, for death came out of the sky to find you.

The sisters found her huddled in a corner. Dorothy knelt down. "Callie, what's the matter?"

Callie stared straight ahead. "I hate this...I hate it! It's so awfully big, like a monster that no one can escape. It's much worse than the revolution. I had no idea it was this horrible."

That week Griffith accompanied them to the American Embassy to secure visas for the boat trip across the Channel. Because of mines, their ship was turned back three times before they were able to get through. The Gish sisters had bouts of seasickness, but Callie slept through the trip.

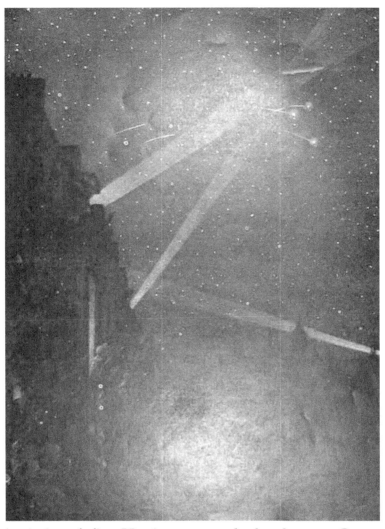

Anti-aircraft fire: Hoping to get a lucky shot at a German zeppelin over the night sky of Paris

Chapter 24

They arrived in Paris just after midnight. Callie wrote many pages in her journal about the next four hours:

June 8 1917.

It was one a.m. when we arrived at our hotel. The city was in complete blackout, except for the moon. Mother Gish was exhausted and went to bed, but we girls were much too giddy with excitement to sleep.

Mr. Griffith seized upon the moment and gathered us round him. "Now children, if you wish, I will show you what the most beautiful city in the world looks like with only the moon above it. You may never get another chance."

Our hotel was beside the lovely Jardin du Luxembourg and the four of us strolled under the perfectly-trimmed trees, past beds of daffodils, ghostly white in the moonlight. The fragrances of cherry blossoms intoxicated me quite easily, for between fatigue, hunger and exhilaration, I was in quite a state. Lillian and Dorothy began to chase each other across the lawn, giggling and horsing around, letting out all the stress of travel of the past few days. Mr. Griffith leaned against a tree, chuckling, puffing on one of his cigarettes. Even in a casual pose, the man is imposing.

We walked through the Latin Quarter, down Boulevard Saint Michel. The sound of distant cannon-fire followed us, but it was a good thing, for it signified that the French guns were between us and the Germans.

The war began to fade and the City of Light worked its magic. We three girls were all still young and hungry for excitement, and to stroll through the empty streets of Paris in darkness, lit only by moonlight as it was long ago, gave us the feeling of being in our own fairy tale. We peered into little pastry shops, elegant cafes, musty old bookstores. Every single thing looked enchanted.

"Where's my Prince?" Dorothy kept shouting. "I want my Prince!"

"Shhh," admonished Lillian.

Dorothy grabbed Lillian by the waist. "Lillian, dear sister, look around. Who's listening? No one else is awake. Paris belongs to us tonight."

My eyes were drawn to a figure across the street-a handsome young Frenchman, attired in a sleek tuxedo, holding a cigarette. A very real-looking mannequin in front of a boutique de vêtements.

"There's your prince!" I yelled to Dorothy,

She ran up and embraced him, planted a passionate kiss on his wooden lips, running her hand down his trousered leg.

"My God, Dorothy!" said Lillian, laughing in spite of herself.

This was all so far away from the blood and violence of a world war, or so it seemed that night.

We finally reached the Seine. All the bookstalls were locked up and no bateaus were to be seen plying its lazy waters. I walked in between Dorothy and Lillian, hand in hand, Mr. Griffith close behind. We were all three of us in white and must have appeared like three spirits softly blowing in the Parisian breeze, barely touching the ground.

A wave of melancholy for Casey came over me, but I kept myself in the present moment and walked on.

The magnificent bulk of Notre Dame reared up above the river, its massive facade and dramatic flying buttresses suddenly so reassuring in such mad times. We all stopped and just stared. "How many wars has that lovely church been witness to?" I wondered. "And yet, it is still here, in front of us."

I am exhausted, but I will never forget this night. To sleep.

After resting the remainder of the day Griffith brought his actors to the front lines to begin filming. His credentials from Great Britain gave him carte blanche to travel where nobody else could. They headed north in two cars-Griffith and Lazlo in one, the other with Bobby Farron dressed as a French private, Dorothy and Lillian with coats concealing their costumes, and Callie.

They passed the ruins of villages, empty trenches, and then huge swaths of forest and fields blackened by artillery. The sight of three beautiful American females brought incredulous looks, and a few whistles, from the soldiers, as they drove past the marching regiments.

The first scene was filmed at one of the bombed villages. Griffith directed his actors with his usual precision, but there was an anxious tension in his voice. The very ground shook with the concussion of battle.

After a quick lunch they moved closer to the front. It was a dangerous place to be, for they were now within range of the big German guns. Shells were falling uncomfortably close. The precariousness lent an authenticity to the actor's gestures they wouldn't have had otherwise.

Callie helped with script errors and costume problems, trying to keep her mind off the ominous rumbling. Otherwise, she sat and watched, fascinated with the acting craft and the lengths that Griffith would go to create his films. They were able to finish and return to Paris by nightfall.

Griffith would often leave the hotel alone and supervise scenes in which Lazlo filmed the actual warfare. They photographed graphic scenes of infantry combat, gravely wounded men, soldiers who died before their very eyes, the desperate conditions of trench warfare, with its mud, filth, rats, and the subsequent scourges of tetanus and typhus.

On their free days Callie would assist Griffith in sharpening the dialogue and tightening the narrative so that it flowed to its conclusion with greater force. His tendency toward melodrama was tempered by her hard nose objectivity as a reporter. She also presented him with more pages of her burgeoning novella, now titled, *Covering the Revolution*. She also wired Mr. Shaughnessy back at the *Chronicle* summaries of the war scenes and how the Parisians were holding up under the siege.

Callie was reading the *Times* in the lobby on a foggy evening when Griffith appeared beside her with a smile on his face. He crouched down in front of the chair. "My dear, I have some hopeful news. General Pershing sent me a telegram just an hour ago. He has located Captain Wilde's regiment and we are trying to arrange some sort of meeting between you two. There now, are you happy my child?"

Callie let the paper fall on the carper. She was thunderstruck. "I am astounded, sir. I wasn't even sure if it was possible. So many women, so many families would give anything to have the opportunity you are giving me. It isn't fair really, is it, in time of war, for me to be so privileged?"

"Callie, Callie, you mustn't feel that way. We hired you to come along, and if you have friends that can do this for you, there is nothing in the world wrong with that. After all, you risked your life to inform the American people of the Mexican conflict and you continue to do so with this war every day you are here. You have nothing to feel guilty about."

Callie nodded.

"You're a dreamer, like myself. We take things pretty hard. Why don't you and the girls go have some fun tomorrow? There's a café I've heard talk about, not far from here. The Flore, I think it's called. You might even meet some Americans there, some artists types I hear. Have some of that fancy French coffee. What do you say?"

"Sounds like a swell idea, sir."

"Wonderful. It will do you good. It's all settled then." He enfolded her hands in his for a moment, then turned and left.

The next morning the three young Americans walked down rue de la Sorbonne to the Musee de Cluny. They were impressed by the splendid *Lady and the Unicorn* tapestry and huddled close together like schoolgirls on a field trip. Callie whispered in Dorothy's ear. "Dorothy, this was woven over four hundred years ago."

"I can't imagine."

Back in the sunlight they continued their stroll.

"I feel like I've been in a time machine," said Callie.

"I'm hungry," said Lillian.

"I need a drink," said Dorothy.

Lillian bristled. "Dorothy, it's not even noon."

"Je veux un petit fours," Callie announced, somewhat smugly.

"Ah, moi aussi," agreed Lillian.

"Excuse me, but it isn't polite to speak French if someone else doesn't," Dorothy protested.

"There it is," yelled Callie, "the Café de Flore!" There it sat, on a corner of bustling Boulevard St. Germain, polished tables outside with cane back chairs, filled with all manner of bohemians, working Parisians, and military personnel, sipping espresso, absinthe or tea, and everyone with a cigarette, blithely ignoring the war that was bearing down on them, for it was a fine Spring morning, but still cool.

209

The tables were shaded by a white awning, under which the trio entered the cafe and plunged into a sea of boisterous patrons, white-shirted waiters and a pall of gray smoke, leavened with the aromas of rich pastries and strong coffee.

"Oh isn't this just the swellest place!" Dorothy exclaimed.

Callie pointed across the room. "There's an empty table by the window."

Once seated they couldn't stop gawking, imagining that secret liaisons were taking place at every table.

Dorothy leaned over and whispered in Callie's ear. "I'm certain that some of these people are German spies."

Callie ordered a cafe au lait, Lillian a hot chocolate and Dorothy a whiskey sour. She stirred her drink and leaned over to Callie. "That young man with the yellow tie-I think he's famous."

Callie casually turned to look at him. "Well, who do you think he is?"

"A writer, an artist, I'm not sure. But I'm sure I've seen that face. And he is so dashing, with that snazzy beret, don't you think?"

"Yes, he is rather good-looking. Why don't you go over there and accost him, Dorothy?" said Callie, with a mischievous twinkle in her eye

Lillian put down her chocolate. "Dorothy, don't you dare."

"Why not, Lillian? We're in Paris, for God's sake. We might all be dead in twenty minutes, blown to smithereens," she exclaimed, gesturing wildly with her arms.

"Well just how do you plan to communicate-sign language?"

"I was hoping you could be my translator, Lillian."

Callie snickered.

"Oh my gosh, he's looking right at me. I'm going over there."

"Dorothy Elizabeth Gish-you are only nineteen. That man might be a gigolo."

"Only one way to find out, sis." She got up and walked straight over to the man's table.

Lillian averted her eyes and stared out at the street. "What are they doing, Callie?"

"He stood up. They're talking, somehow. Now they're sitting. I think he just ordered her something."

Lillian sighed heavily.

"Calm down, Lillian. She's just having fun. She likes to flirt."

"I know. She doesn't have a serious bone in her body."

Callie looked distracted. "I'm sorry, what did you say?"

"Never mind. Mr. Griffith told me about your possible rendezvous with your beau. How are you feeling?"

"Oh, just like you'd expect-scared, worried, hopeful, anxious. But being here with you two takes my mind off it."

"Callie, did he actually propose to you, back in Mexico I mean?"

"No Lillian, he couldn't."

"Why not?"

"He was going off to war. He was going to fly rickety little airplanes and be shot at. He wanted both of us to have our freedom until he came back, if he comes back."

Lillian hesitated. "You have been with other men?"

"That's awfully personal."

"Forgive me. Why did I ask that?"

"I can't ignore my desires. I'm only twenty-five."

"Yes, a year older than me."

Callie stared at Lillian quizzically and was about to respond, but Dorothy came bounding back and nearly knocked over the table as she plopped down in her chair.

"Well Lillian, you were kind of right. After wooing me for fifteen minutes he admitted he was married, but was looking for a mistress, and he thought I would do fine. That is, if I understood his broken English correctly. He sure is cute though."

"But is he famous?" asked Callie.

"No, never heard of him. Claude something or other."

Callie ordered three petit fours-hers was pale yellow, Dorothy's pale pink and Lillian got pale blue.

Lillian stared at hers. "It's too pretty to eat."

Dorothy sighed as she took a large bite. "Oh dear Lord, it's as good as kissing a man."

Callie ate hers in tiny bites, to let the rich, creamy cake linger in her mouth, drifting along in the pleasantries of the moment. A Parisian café was a wonderful place to linger, especially during a war.

The Flyboys

Chapter 25

After numerous calls to various generals and commanders at the front, General Pershing located Casey-he was stationed in some barracks near Chaudun. Pershing contacted Griffith and warned him that the American pilots were on constant alert and were actually flying out of a secret airfield. It was not far from Paris, but it would be a risky trip, given the proximity of the Germans and possible surprise attacks from the air. He wanted to make sure Callie understood the hazards of the journey. He would send a French corporal and an American lieutenant to pick up Callie on a yet to be determined date.

That date soon came, with an urgent phone call from the area commander who informed Griffith that Callie must depart Sunday morning while there was a lull in artillery activity in that area. The two military escorts would arrive at the Grand Hotel at six a.m.

Griffith met with Callie on the eve of her departure in the hotel lobby. With the paucity of guests they practically had the lobby to themselves. A thunderstorm was brewing outside which made everyone nervous because it mimicked the sounds of bombs close by. They sat on a couch. Griffith was clearly uncomfortable.

"Callie. As you know, we're wrapping up the filming this week and there are some scenes I absolutely must finish, which means I shall be unable to accompany you on this trip."

"I didn't expect you to Mr. Griffith. The two gentlemen are coming for that purpose."

"Of course they are, but you have become one of my family these past weeks. I felt obligated to go and make sure you were properly looked after." He looked away, at a woman in a black dress standing in a corner. "It's a risky business traveling around here. Please do not take any unnecessary chances, do you hear?"

Callie smiled. "How can you say that sir, with all due respect, when you yourself have headed into the front lines to film scenes?"

"You have me there young lady. But that's just it-you are young, with a tremendous life all stretched out in front of you."

"I'm so close to him. I must at least try. He is young as well and risks his life daily, far more than I ever have. If something should happen to him I would regret it for the rest of my life if I chose not to go, simply because it was dangerous. I refuse to let fear control my life, Mr. Griffith."

"Of course. I was told not to see you off in the morning, so as not to attract any undue attention. The city is riddled with German spies. May God be with you my child." His serious face betrayed his own fears for Callie, as he rose and walked with bowed head toward the stairway.

Callie stood under the hotel's veranda and waited in the ashen dawn. She held only a small purse, with her notebook and some pens. A camouflaged military car pulled up and the young uniformed French driver hopped out, bowed and offered his hand.

"Mademoiselle Callie? I am Francois," he said in thickly accented English, "and I will drive you to your destination, I assure you."

Another young soldier exited the car and introduced himself. "Miss Masterson, I am Lieutenant Malcolm Straight and will accompany you to the airfield and back. We must leave immediately." Francois already had the back car door open and Callie was ushered in. She had no time to respond as they sped away. The Frenchman looked not even twenty, and the lieutenant not much older. Malcolm Straight-what a solid American name, she thought. He had beautiful blue eyes, but dark hair and skin. They both sat very erect up front.

"Where are you from, Malcolm?"

He didn't say anything at first, then finally, "Moab ma'am. Moab, Utah."

"Moab? Moab?" Her face lit up. "I do believe my grandfather mentioned it once-I think he was a miner up in that territory."

"There are a quite a few mines up there. It's rough, red rock country."

Callie looked out the window at a rural countryside, perfectly lush and seemingly untouched. "Is your father in that line of work?"

"No ma'am, he's a rancher."

"I'm curious Malcolm. People's ancestry fascinates me. Do have any Mediterranean blood?"

"It's my mom. She's part Ute. Miss Masterson, I need to tell you that our trip should take two or three hours, depending on the roads.

214

We will be passing through mostly safe areas, occupied by allied troops, but once we get close to your husband's airfield it could get pretty shaky. I just want you to know what we're in for."

"He isn't my husband."

"I apologize for that error, ma'am."

"No apology needed, Lieutenant. After all, you and Francois here are going to a lot of trouble for me. I don't feel quite right about the risks you are taking."

"No need to fret about that. Believe me, this is a big improvement. I'd probably be in the trenches right now if it weren't for you."

"Well, I think that makes me feel better."

Callie wrote a few paragraphs in her journal, describing the lieutenant and writing possible scenarios for a short story of his growing up in Utah with an Indian mother. She put down her pen and closed her eyes, for she had slept badly.

She napped for what she thought was only a few minutes, but the sound of a distant bomb roused her. When she opened her eyes the look of the countryside was a shock. The word "apocalyptic" came to mind, for it was all gray devastation. There were dead trees everywhere and not a farm or house in sight.

She leaned forward toward Francois. "What is this place?"

"The Ardennes. A very terrible battle here...when the war it began...many soldiers killed."

"The trees, so many destroyed."

"Yes, yes...used to be beautiful forest, tres, tres beau, many old trees, very big. But now...alle, how you say?"

"Gone, I think," said Callie, awestruck by the desolation.

The greenery returned as they drove through the hills of Picardy, but the ugly scars of bombs and cannon fire were everywhere. There was little traffic on the road other than military trucks. They stopped at a checkpoint just outside of Viller-Cotterets. Francois showed the guard a paper and was waved through. Callie gazed out at a pleasant looking village of red roofs along a slow moving river.

"Here Alexandre Dumas has been born!" announced Francois triumphantly."

"Ah, Dumas. *The Count of Monte Cristo,*" said Callie.

"*Les Trois Mousquetaires*-I like so much as little boy. I want to be

D'Artagnan, mon heros. How in English?"

"Same word," said the young Lieutenant. Both Francois and Callie looked at Malcolm. He hadn't spoken for quite a while. He turned around, half smiling at Callie. "I read that as a kid. That D'Artagnan fellow could really handle a sword. Haven't even thought about it until he just now brought it up."

"How old are you Malcolm?"

"Twenty."

"And Francois?"

"Eighteen, he claims. Probably mean he's sixteen."

Francois turned his head. "What? You talk about me?"

"Yeah," said Malcolm, punching him, "I told her that you're just a kid. Un enfant."

"Me? No, not true, not true."

Everyone laughed, which eased the tension for the moment. The car rounded a long curve and barely missed hitting an American truck, sitting upside down in the middle of the road. "Hold on, ma'am!" yelled Malcolm.

Francois swerved, just missing the truck and an army ambulance. They skidded into a field and lurched to a stop.

"Merde," muttered Francois, crossing himself.

The truck engine was still running. There was a large black jagged bomb crater nearby.

"Allons!" ordered Malcolm. "We are under orders not to stop. Francois!"

Francois restarted the engine, backed up on the road and drove away. Callie looked through the back window as the accident faded into the distance.

They stopped at an intersection. The lieutenant studied a map. He pointed left. "Gauche. Il est pres d'ici." He turned to Callie. "It's very close now."

"Oui, Je comprends."

The road turned into a trail with deep ruts. Planes flew in the distance. Callie stuffed her things back in the purse and put it on the floor. She began to lick her lips and fool with her hair. I must look awfully dusty and windblown, she worried.

An army truck drove up fast and blocked their way. Two armed soldiers jumped out and stared at the car, guns raised. Malcolm stuck his arm out, waving his orders.

One of the soldiers walked over to his side, bent down, and was taken aback by the sight of Callie in the backseat. "You must be them. By God, it's strange to see an American woman out here. Are you Miss Callie Masterson?" he asked, in a very familiar accent.

"Yes, I am. Are you from Texas, by any chance?"

"Why yes I am. San Antone."

"Well I grew up not too far from there."

"Well, son of a gun, ain't that-"

"Soldier! We don't have much time. I was told to deliver Miss Masterson straight to the airfield headquarters-to a Captain Pierce."

"Yes sir."

They followed the truck through a forest, which opened up into a large clearing, in the middle of which ran a long dirt airstrip. The "headquarters" was just a ramshackle structure made of wood, topped with a tin roof. Malcolm and Callie got out and were met by Captain Pierce, another twenty-something, but with that dash of bravado that all pilots seemed to possess.

"Welcome, Miss Masterson. General Pershing himself contacted us to make certain we were prepared for your visit. This is all highly unusual, but nonetheless a real pleasure."

"Thank you, Captain. Is Casey-"

"He's been supervising the fueling of his Sopwith Camel. Here he comes now. We heard rumors of a German squadron in the area, so you're gonna have to make it quick, I'm afraid."

Casey strode across the grassy field, half walking, half running. The stiff breeze blew his white scarf back behind him. Raw emotion overtook Callie, confronting him so suddenly, alive and smiling, and stared intently for any limp or difference in his gait. She ran up to meet him and stopped short. "I had to make sure it was really you."

"It's me all right." He embraced her so forcefully her feet came off the ground. Whistles and yells came from all around. "Let's go back here."

He led her behind the shack to a grassy knoll that overlooked a small valley. They stared at each other, gripping each other's hands tightly.

"God, it's so good to see you. Gosh, this is like some kind of dream."

"I hadn't heard from you," said Callie.

"The security is real tight. You look wonderful."

"And you are still your dashing self," she said, touching his lips, "but you have lost weight."

"Saves fuel."

She saw the lines in his face from fatigue, and some scars, but she laughed weakly and put her head against his chest.

He caressed her hair. "I can't believe you managed to pull this off, coming across the ocean like this, and finding me."

"Yeah, how many girls would do that for you, Captain?"

"You are a one in a million gal. You wouldn't believe how I've talked you up to my buddies." He looked uncomfortable to Callie. Maybe dealing with a woman was something he had forgotten how to do. He looked toward the planes.

She smelled the gas fumes. A plane backfired and made her jump. Somebody out there was pointing at the sky. She felt like they were on the edge of an abyss.

"Casey, I know we left it open back in Mexico...but, when you come back, do you want to keep going down that road we began in the Revolution?"

"You bet your bottom dollar, sweetheart. That's just what we're gonna do. I'm not so sure what this war is about anymore, but every time I go up there, I'm staying alive for you."

He smiled and was trying hard to reassure her, but Callie saw the consternation in his blue eyes. "Oh, I almost forgot." She quickly pulled a piece of paper out of her blouse. "It's a poem, by Walt Whitman."

"What happened to Shakespeare?"

"This reminds me more of us. It's about how you go through life. If you don't read anything else, read the last stanza."

He smelled the paper. "It's got your perfume scent. I don't have anything for you, but this." He cradled her face and kissed her.

A hideous wail shrieked from a siren atop a pole next to them. Callie slapped her hands over the ears, grimacing in pain. Then all became chaos.

"They're coming!" screamed the pilots.

Callie grabbed on to Casey. He kissed her passionately, struggled to break free from her embrace.

"Go! Get outta here. They found us." He waved the Whitman poem at her as he ran away, looking back. "I'm coming back, Callie! Don't give up on me."

She was frozen in place, infuriated by the interruption. "I wasn't finished!" she screamed at Casey's now faraway back. A hand grabbed her from behind.

"C'mon Miss, got to get away!" shouted Malcolm. She didn't move. He grabbed her from behind.

"Let me go! "She lashed out, swung at him, and clipped the side of his head, trying to see where Casey had gone. He had to drag her back to the car, half throwing her into the back seat, shaken by the fierce glare in her eyes.

Gotha twin-engine bombers suddenly loomed above like massive, ugly gray vultures.

Francois was revving the engine as she fell into the back seat. "Get us the hell out of here Francois! If we can get into the trees we'll be okay."

Callie hung out the window, craning her neck to watch the planes roar off in rapid succession. The car was approaching the forest when the first bomb hit and obliterated several planes.

Another bomb exploded just ahead, splintering tree, blocking the road into the woods. The windshield blew out and spit glass into their faces. Francois swerved left and raced across the field, hugging the edge of the forest.

Callie strained to see the planes ascending and thought she saw Casey's scarf blowing in the sunlight.

"Miss, keep your head inside!" Another bomb exploded fifty yards away, blowing out the windows. The concussion caused Francois to lose control.

The speeding car lurched and bounced wildly. Malcolm took the wheel, but Francois shook his head and regained control. "It's okay."

They both were bleeding. Malcolm turned around to check Callie. She lay on the back seat, limp, covered with dirt and glass, blood running down her face.

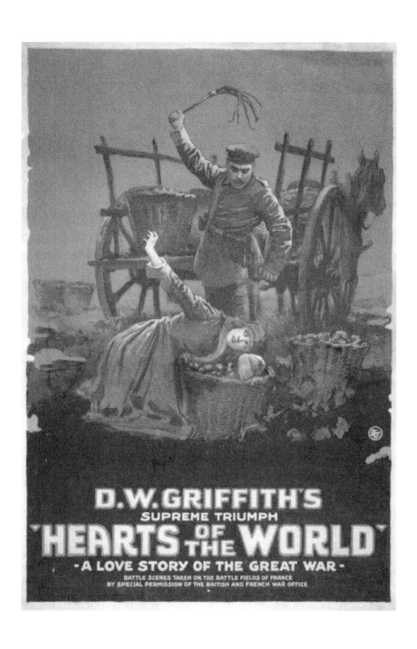

Chapter 26

They managed to find a local hospital where Callie was kept overnight for observation. The doctors treated their cuts and painstakingly removed each shard of glass. She was diagnosed with a mild concussion and released the next morning. The trip back to Paris was uneventful.

Griffith had completed European filming for *Hearts of the World*. This time the entire company departed for the states on the same boat, as summer came to an end.

Back in Los Angeles, Callie was haunted by her war experience. She was afflicted by nightmares, waking up suddenly in a sweat, trying to catch her breath as the bird-like bombers crossed the ocean and destroyed one American city after another, and then came for her. She watched Casey's plane go down in flames, in the daylight as well as the night, like some macabre movie that would not stop playing in her head. There was never any "enemy", only the growling planes and the huge black bombs that found her wherever she hid. She had never experienced such terrifying dreams and they exhausted her.

She spent more time tending the garden with Antonio at her cottage in Laurel Canyon. The daily chores of weeding, pruning and gathering the fresh produce helped to calm her anxiety. On some nights Antonio would hear her screams from his cabin, but he never mentioned it. He encouraged her to learn more about the garden plants and he began to notice that it was helping.

Callie took the trolley down to Santa Monica, to enjoy its wide sandy beach and brand new pleasure pier. The sound of the waves, the taste and smell of the salt water was therapeutic. She swam hard through the water until she had exhausted herself and collapsed on the sand and slept. The California sun quickly brought her Mexican tan back. She wrote for hours and tried to reconcile the guilt of what she considered her unfaithful behavior in Mexico-it seemed as if it was another woman who had done those things, not she, some other woman who was capable of such outlandish behavior. But in this carefree movie kingdom it wasn't so outlandish. Her Texas-bred, Methodist morals implanted by her grandmother would not go away so easily. She mirrored the Twentieth century's capricious growing pains, as society tried to find its way from a simpler, more circumscribed time to an ever more tumultuous future, that would experiment with new possibilities, tinker with both the dark and light aspects of the human psyche.

Back at the studio, Griffith began shooting the remaining scenes on the old *Intolerance* sets. The new art of cinema continued to fascinate Callie-she loved to watch Griffith, ensconced in his chair, immaculate white suit and white hat, riveted upon his actors, doing take after take until he saw perfection. She watched the Gish sisters blossom into fine actresses, especially Lillian.

Griffith wanted the film in theaters before the war ended, so he established a strenuous schedule of day and night shooting. Callie was told to report to the studio on Christmas Eve-they worked till midnight. In spite of it all spirits were high. They felt they were contributing to the war effort, and besides, the weather was unusually cold, which made it easier to be in a holiday spirit. And Callie was glad to be caught up in the whole frenetic scene. It kept her occupied.

Dorothy brought wine and snacks for the cast and crew on Christmas Eve. She also brought along her latest discovery, a young dark-haired dancer from Italy, Rudolpho di Valentina. He demonstrated the Argentine tango with several of the women, including Callie, who was taken with his gentlemanly Continental manners.

The next morning Griffith directed a scene with Lillian playing a French woman being manhandled by a German soldier. He kept egging them on to intensify the action, furiously puffing on a cigarette. Lillian gave it all she had. Callie's eyes kept switching between Griffith and Lillian, an invisible current of communication between them. During breaks she helped Lillian rearrange the protective padding under her clothes. "He's roughing you up pretty good. Are you all right?"

"Of course," she said, surprised at the question. "That's how we do it here, Callie. Mr. Griffith insists on reality." Callie thought the scene was too exaggerated, but said nothing.

 She spent more and more time refining her story into something that would make a suitable screenplay. While there was a chance that

Griffith might consider it possible cinematic material, the motivation was more materialistic-her funds were running low, as they only used her on a part-time basis at the studio. She was still waiting for a check from the *Chronicle* for the war articles she had sent to Mr. Shaughnessy.

Hearts of the World premiered at Clune's Theater in Los Angeles on March 18, 1918, then opened a few weeks later in New York. Callie continued to write long hours into the night, taking raw entries from her journal and fashioning them into readable prose that she hoped would hold the reader's attention.

The transition of spring into summer passes unnoticed in Southern California, but the longer days improved Callie's spirit. On her days off she rode Bandido through the wilder parts of Laurel Canyon, though she was disturbed to see that a trolley car now went to the summit of Lookout Mountain where a new hotel was perched.

One sunny afternoon Callie was feeling energized and let Bandido gallop down the canyon road faster than usual, for it was a sparsely settled community. They rounded a curve, and just ahead a small crew was laying drainage pipe directly in their path. Callie quickly looked for space to get around them, but the canyon walls were narrow at that spot and they were nearly on top of them.

"Cuidado!, she screamed, then switched to English. Watch out!"

They looked up and saw the charging horse and rider bearing down on them.

Bandido executed a magnificent leap that cleared their cowering heads by several feet and hit the ground at full speed, never breaking stride.

Callie let out a whoop and smiled back at their astonished faces. "Ha! Que divertido! Nice jump, Bandido."

She was always glad to get back to her little cottage in the canyon, for life in the studio could be claustrophobic. As the days warmed she would write all morning in a big wooden chair under the jacaranda tree.

A few days after the summer solstice, Callie presented Griffith with a rough copy of her story, tentatively titled, *Covering the Revolution.*

223

Antonio was harvesting lettuce on a cool morning, when he saw Callie ride into the yard after her daily jaunt up the canyon. She saw a letter sticking out of the mailbox and hopped off the horse to fetch it. Antonio watched her read it and then react as if someone had slapped her hard. She jumped back on Bandido and rode away at a furious pace.

"It's no good," he mumbled, "She suffer too much, too much."

She rode hard all the way up to top of Lookout Mountain. The horse's chest was heaving and he was foaming at the mouth. Her eyes were red and distraught. She looked over the fertile valley toward the San Gabriel mountains, still spotted with winter snows. The Los Angeles air was as clear as glass. She held up the letter and read it one more time.

Dear Callie,

I am writing you because Casey's plane has been shot down. The Germans sent a message to his airbase that two of our planes had crashed. One man was badly injured, the other, Casey, had died.

He had spoken so highly of you in his letters that I thought it only right to inform you of this terrible circumstance. He is our only son and we are heartbroken.

Thank you for being such a good friend to him.

Sincerely,

Gloria Wilde

She turned Bandido around, until her back was against the wind, lit a match and set the letter afire. She hurled it into the wind, watched it disintegrate, then whirled the horse around and galloped back down the mountain.

It was time to run again.

American Red Cross workers collecting victims of the 1918
Flu Epidemic

Chapter 27

On the train, rolling into the desert, yet another escape into the open space, the wild country which had become a refuge, a place to flee toward when the heartbreak began to close in. She was going to San Antonio to visit her past.

A headache pestered her and she was fatigued and restless at the same time. Not enough sleep, she decided. Those movie people keep crazy hours.

She paged through her sonnets, put the book down and lay back, with affectionate memories of the Breckenridge School for girls in San Antonio where she was required to learn many of Shakespeare's sonnets by heart. She never knew how her nomadic parents were able to afford the tuition, but the one year she spent there counted as one of the most important in her young life, her only academic training.

In 1904 San Antonio was a stop for the most famous actors, musicians and singers of the day. A seminal experience occurred when Callie's father took her to see Lily Langtry perform at the Empire Opera Theater. They walked to the railroads yard first to view Miss Langtry's private car, festooned with colorful decorations and a long red banner that read "Lily Langtry Grand Tour".

The theater was overflowing with boisterous Texans wearing big Stetson hats, all a twitter that this famous courtesan should grace them with a visit.

They procured a balcony seat. Callie gripped the gold railing and looked down at the excited crowd, restless in their seats. Everyone hushed when the ornate curtain whooshed open. Lily Langtry sat in a throne-like chair of red velvet; her head reclined against the chair back as if she were in a trance, a faraway look in her eyes.

She wore an elegant white gown which showed off her exquisite hourglass figure, and over that a kind of long black robe very tight about her arms and sequined, so that it sparkled under the strong lights. Callie's eyes fastened on a thin strand of pearls around her neck, then her piled-up hair, and the silver earrings, but most of all her mesmerizing eyes, which even from that distance seemed to be looking right at Callie, into her very heart.

The actress tilted her head upward as if looking at something hovering above the audience, then began to recite the lines of Titania from *Midsummer Night's Dream*, about fairies and jewels and airy spirits, in a beautifully clear British accent, enunciating each word, pausing at just right moment for dramatic effect.

Callie wavered between listening to her words and gazing at her demeanor. The majesty of the woman! How she could command the rapt attention of the huge audience with so little effort. A woman who represented an existence as far from her own paltry life as it was possible to be. And yet, she gave Callie hope: *She is so fine a lady, but more than that, she is an artist who can take our breath away. If only I could do such a thing.*

Titania's lines were whimsical, but it was Lily Langtry's voice that made her cry.

Callie slept in snatches as the train crossed the Painted Desert, into the vast Navajo reservation and through the still wild Apache country, then into New Mexico, far north of sleepy Columbus, in the shadow of Acoma, the Sky City, over the sagebrush range-land and into the immense spaces of West Texas, crossing the Comanche trail, then up on to the Balcones Escarpment

The conductor had to shake Callie awake. "San Antonio, ma'am."

She fumbled with her things, and retrieved her valise from the rack with difficulty, then made her way to the door where she had to concentrate on keeping her balance and hesitated on the edge of the steps, swaying, grabbing the support bar to steady herself, but her legs crumpled and she collapsed headlong into a pile of luggage below.

She lay there blinking, but there was no light, and the commotion of the station faded into blackness.

"A doctor, please! Hurry!" someone yelled.

An elderly man knelt down and put a hand on her forehead as he took her pulse. "She's hot as the blazes. I fear it's the influenza." The crowd gasped and backed away. "Porter-get an ambulance, and quick!"

The main hospital was already full of flu victims, overwhelmed by the sudden onslaught of the horrific epidemic. A smaller clinic was suggested-Santa Maria, housed in an old adobe Spanish hacienda on the outskirts of town. The ambulance, still idling, quickly drove off.

Nurse Agnes Scott watched as they brought Callie in on a stretcher. She took a quick look at the flushed young woman and shook her head. Her train ticket had been pinned on her dress, for name identification.

The nurse studied the young woman's ashen face. "Callie Masterson. I'm sorry, but we probably can't save you. Put her in Ward C. There's an empty bed in the far corner by the window. I doubt she'll be with us for long."

A few minutes later, Callie felt a cool hand on her fevered brow. There was a smiling face above her, with a calm, Buddhist like demeanor.

"How are you feeling, Callie?"

She could not answer. She wasn't even sure if he was real, for his image kept coming and going. Every part of her body ached, but it seemed to be someone else's body. The suffering was foreign to her. Was she dying? *Did I leave California? Or was that a dream? Where am I?*

Dr. Vincent Serena listened to the crackles of Callie's ravaged lungs coming through his stethoscope. He looked up at Nurse Scott. "The rales are pretty bad. It's odd how a healthy young woman could become this ill so quickly. It's as if this scourge is taking our most robust young people. We need to do a blood count, Miss Scott. And keep the cold packs coming."

"Do you think she has a chance?"

"Perhaps, if it doesn't worsen." He removed the thermometer from Callie's mouth. "Damn. One hundred and five." He wrote down a higher dosage of aspirin and handed it to the nurse, then rushed off to see his other patients.

If Callie had been conscious she would have appreciated the view through the big window-the rolling hills of Central Texas, the bright green oaks against the darker junipers. The air filled with the songs of mockingbirds and cardinals, bluebonnets carpeting the open fields and the great bowl of blue sky. The fresh breeze blew in and ruffled her hair, but she was oblivious. Her arm hung limp over the side of the bed. Miss Scott replaced the cold compress with a fresh one and stared at her patient's face. "I fear your pain will not be leaving soon, my dear. But I see something determined about you. Or am I just hoping?"

The room darkened and a small yellow light came on. Callie was wracked by convulsions of coughing fits. Late summer in the southwest is a time of sudden thunderstorms that extend into the night. The wind whipped rain against the glass and into the room. A nurse ran in to close the window. Lightning and thunder were simultaneous as the storm seemed to break right over the hospital.

Vicious chills attacked her and her moans were heard down the hall. The uncontrolled inflammation rolled through her body, causing terrific pain. Her moans became howls. She thrashed wildly. Dr. Serena could not give her a sedative, for her breathing was already labored.

Callie would break out of her stupor and see light one day, darkness another. When a face appeared she attempted to tell it what she wanted, but no words were forthcoming.

"She's babbling again," said Miss Scott when Dr. Serena walked in. "But I've gleaned a few names-Lillian, Dorothy, and especially Casey. Oh, and Bandido-who in the world could that be?"

"We still don't know much about her. Anyone working on that?"

"There's just no time sir. It's all we can do to tend to the patients."

"Of course. Her fever has been close to one hundred and five for four straight days. But she's tough. She's still with us, eh?"

"Poor thing."

The fever finally broke, but Callie's respiration symptoms worsened.

Another storm blew in late on a Friday night. Driving rain, then hail battered the roof, and lightning strikes exploded close by. The lights blinked on and off.

A young nurse came in. She let out a quick scream and dropped the tray she was carrying. Callie was crawling across the floor toward the window, coughing up blood-tinged froth, her eyes wide open but unseeing, drawn toward the intense flashes of lightning like a lost moth, braying with a hoarse, inhuman wail that sent the nurse fleeing for help.

A doctor on the night shift and two orderlies rushed in. They lifted

229

her back into the bed, which was stained with blood. "Get me a lamp over here, now!" ordered the doctor. A nurse held the light over her. "Dear Lord. She's cyanotic."

Callie's skin had transformed into a pale blue, there was so little oxygen in her blood. She was drowning.

"Get me one cc of epinephrine."

He dutifully administered the injection and ordered a nurse to remain at her bedside. "I can't imagine her lasting the night."

Miss Scott drove up the rutted dirt road to the hospital just before seven a.m. The torrential rains had made it nearly impassable. Workmen were arriving to repair the mess. The air was remarkably fresh and she inhaled the strong scent of juniper as she walked over the cobblestones that some Spanish nobleman had ordered laid out two centuries before.

She gazed toward the back entrance where a truck was carrying off more bodies for burial. Inside, the main hall was already bustling. She hurried down the hall to Callie's room with a premonition of doom. Dr. Serena huddled over the bed, assisted by a young intern.

"The pulse is terribly weak," he muttered to the intern.

"Doctor, how is Callie?" blurted Miss Scott.

He turned, surprised to see her so early. He slipped off his stethoscope. "She had a very bad night. I am surprised that she is still alive, Miss Scott. Our girl is a real fighter, stronger than I would have thought possible."

"Thank God."

He led her over to the window. "She still has a long way to go. It's a particularly virulent form of staphylococcal pneumonia, on top of the influenza. There's massive edema and her lungs are horribly inflamed."

"What about those canisters of oxygen?"

He shook his head. "We have no way to administer it. We really have no effective agent against this damnable plague."

The young intern tending to Callie turned to look at the two of them by the window. "Dr. Serena, I heard they tried injections of strychnine up in Boston with some success, especially in secondary infections like this."

"Strychnine? Indeed. Well, do we have some of the stuff here? If not, let's get it. We've nothing to lose."

"Yes sir, I'll see to it."

The hospital had confirmed Callie's address and age from the press credentials she carried. Cyanotic patients were invariably terminal, and as beds were at a premium, they readied a small obituary for the newspaper.

The attending nurse perused the paper that evening by Callie's bed. The Boston Red Sox, and their star slugger, Babe Ruth, seemed a sure bet for the World Series. Evangelist Billy Sunday held forth before thousands, insisting that they could "pray down" the spreading flu plague.

The nurse was going over the latest movies at the San Antonio theaters. She looked up and frowned, then put down the paper and stood over Callie. "Was that you, dearie?"

Callie's lips were moving, ever so slightly.

"Is she speaking, or just trying to breathe? Miss Scott should see this."

She left the room and in moments nurse Agnes Scott hurried in. "Callie! Keep talking child."

She knelt by the bed, leaned over and put her head on Callie's chest, cupping her ear, and grasped Callie's hand.

"What's that you said just now?"

Silence.

"Speak, Callie! Stay with me!"

Suddenly Callie seized the nurse's blouse and jerked her downward close to her face.

"Die..." Miss Scott thought she heard.

"No, no you will not. You will live. You must live. Lick this thing, Callie," she said, listening hard, her face contorted with the effort.

Callie's grip on Miss Scott loosened, and her hand went limp. The sounds trailed off to tiny, tenuous breaths, as the nurse struggled to hear.

"What did she say, Miss Scott?"

Miss Scott rose up as if she was in pain. "She wants to live. She's only twenty-five. She wants to live, that's all. Casey must be her beau.

Must be in the war, like all the young men. Isn't this world something? The war kills all our young men, and now this horrid pestilence is taking the rest, this lovely young woman, who had every reason to expect a full life ahead of her."

The young nurse was silent, but finally spoke. "She looks awful. The blue ones don't usually make it."

"Maybe not," said Miss Scott. She grabbed the nurse's shoulder, startling her. "but I could feel something inside of her. A fierce will to stay alive. I imagine she has big things to accomplish. And we must help her. We're going to try something. It's our ace." She looked down at Callie. "Put some more pillows under her head-every breath is a struggle."

"Yes ma'am."

Miss Scott went home to have dinner and a bath. She had been on duty for twelve hours, but she was reluctant to leave Callie. Feelings of guilt assailed her as she drove back to the hospital. She kept talking to herself. "As a nurse, I must treat all my patients equally, but none of us do. We have our favorites. It's only human."

Upon returning to Callie's ward she saw an orderly tying a tag on her foot. She let out a howl of rage and rushed up and nearly knocked him over with her shoulder. "What in the hell do you think you are doing?"

The young man stammered, "I was told-"

"She is still *alive!*"

"They made up a list of probable deaths...to, to speed up-"

Miss Scott broke the string and removed the tag, flinging it on the floor. "Tell them to scratch her off that damn list. It was premature. She is still alive. Now get out!"

He hightailed it out of the ward. She checked Callie's pulse. It was fast and thready. Her blood pressure was terribly low. Agnes Scott walked back to the nurse's station and phoned Dr. Serena.

"Doctor, Callie is worsening. What about that strychnine?"

"We've located some. I'll be there in an hour."

Miss Scott paced in front of the hospital entrance, eyes on the ground, smoking a cigarette, thinking out loud. "All the patients I've lost, many of them younger than Callie, my sister Mary, diphtheria

232

took her at twelve, had to become a nurse after that, I hate the helplessness. Now, this influenza. All of this science, but still helpless. Still helpless. Damn it all."

"Miss Scott, I have it." Dr. Serena was running toward her, holding up a small vial. He grabbed her arm and they both ran inside.

"It's a poison. How will you know the proper dosage?" asked Miss Scott as they rushed down the hall.

"We'll have to make our best guess."

They startled the nurse at Callie's bedside. "Doctor, she seems worse, I don't think-"

"That's all right. Stay here in case we need you."

He threw off his coat. Miss Scott handed him a fresh syringe. He withdrew a small amount from the vial, held it up to the light and nodded.

"All right, let's play our ace, Miss Scott."

Agnes Scott went to the opposite side of the bed, took Callie's hand and put her other hand on her forehead. She leaned down and whispered in her ear. "Callie, this will help you. Keep breathing. Be strong, girl. Be strong."

Dr. Serena rubbed her arm with a bit of alcohol. "This will be painful." He carefully injected the strychnine and immediately Callie stiffened and moaned. Miss Scott squeezed her hand and rubbed her forehead.

"Hold on my girl."

But Callie was far away, back in Comanche Springs, hiding from the pain, the feeling of being drowned. She was listening to her father tell her a story about how she had been dying from Scarlet Fever as a very young child. Her parents were desperate, when a Comanche medicine man, who had sold her father some ponies, appeared on the porch, braided hair with two eagle feathers, a vision of the past. He held a bundle of herbs wrapped in a beaded bag. He would make an infusion for the sick girl. He asked her mother to boil some water, which she did. He had Callie sip it during the entire night, chanting all the while, pagan cries so foreign to the whitewashed Methodist walls. It broke the fever and saved her life. It was the old man who threw her the little horse years later, come back to see her grown up and alive.

233

Callie cowered in a dark recess by the creek, waiting for the Indian to return, to help her again, for she felt so weak and lost that she feared she must be dying. She did not see him, but could hear him chanting close by, camped in the sagebrush, smelled the smoke of his fire and was comforted. In her hand, she fondled the tiny blue horse. She sensed the warm power of his healing that came from the earth, strong medicine that would destroy the demon that was killing her. But a long time went by.

Dr. Serena believed in fresh air. He thought it might stimulate the damaged lungs of influenza patients, so he ordered windows to remain open, weather permitting. One morning the cool breeze wafted into Callie's ward, and a confused sparrow came along with it and fluttered around the room, his sharp chirps echoing off the walls. The chirping pricked at her consciousness.

It was then that she crept out of hiding, from the dark place by the creek. It hurt so much to move, but she knew she must or she might never see Casey, or Lillian or Lucille, or anyone again. The light beckoned her.

The sparrow chirped louder as if it wanted her awake, until she blinked and focused on something for the first time in a long while. The petite creature sensed her weakness, and satisfied he was safe, remained perched at the foot of the bed, regarding her with little cocks of his head.

"Where am I?" She gazed past him, out the window. "That's the hill country" she rasped weakly..."know those trees...climbed those trees."

She coughed violently and the bird darted out the window, but instead of choking and gagging, she breathed, not perfectly, but sufficiently enough to fill her lungs and give her a blessed sense of relief. She felt alive again, as the life-giving oxygen coursed through her blood.

There was a partition of white sheets on either side of her bed. Everything was white, except the square of that green world she longed to return to. "I want to see my old house, the creek, mother's grave...wish Bandido was here."

And as if, until now, she had been mercifully granted temporary amnesia, a great sorrow broke over her. She flinched in pain. "Have to get out of here."

She attempted to sit up, and fell back. "God, I have no strength. Is anyone here?" But it only came out as a croaking whisper. She looked around. On the bedside table was a small white metal tray. She leaned over, picked it up and threw it with all her might across the room. It bounced a few times, making a racket.

The nurse, who had called her one of the "blue ones", came in and stopped in her tracks when she saw Callie staring at her with a confused look. She wheeled around and ran out yelling for Nurse Scott.

Miss Scott tentatively entered the room and peeked around the partition. Callie was propped up on her pillow, wan and grimacing. The nurse couldn't keep her lips from trembling, but she walked erect and calm over to her patient and took her hand. "Callie, you are back with us. I am so pleased." The intimacy in her eyes and voice unnerved Callie, for she had never seen this woman before.

"Who are you?" she uttered, in a barely audible whisper.

"I'm Miss Scott. You are a patient in Santa Maria hospital. Do you remember where you are?"

"You just told me.

"I mean what town you're in."

"Texas. I know that country out there, got off the train...when was that, a few days back? Can't remember. San Antonio!"

"Yes, exactly. You've been here quite a while, my dear. You were extremely ill, and to tell the truth, none of us was sure-" She squeezed Callie's hand and fought to control her emotions.

Callie looked down at their entwined hands. "I *do* know you. I heard you, talking to me, while I was hiding. Don't remember what you said...sound of your voice was comforting."

Miss Scott leaned closer to understand what she was whispering. "Hiding?"

"From the demon, whatever took hold of me."

"Influenza."

"Strange word. Don't like the sound of it," she whispered.

Miss Scott pulled up a chair and sat down. "I'm going to sit close, so I can hear you better. Your voice is very faint. Dr. Serena is your

235

attending physician. He and I fought a real battle to pull you from the clutches of death, my child."

"What is your first name?"

"Agnes."

"Thank you, Agnes."

"Oh, but you see, we did what we could do, but it was you that saved yourself. Sometimes you bit your lip so hard it bled. Because I just knew you had something important to live for. That you had people to live for. You even mentioned them in your delirium-Dorothy, Lillian, let's see, Bandido, and Casey, Casey the most. Is he your sweetheart?"

Callie's face darkened.

"Oh my dear, I didn't mean to-"

"I need to get out of here. Have a lot to do. How long *have* I been here, Agnes?"

"Nearly a month now."

Callie brought her hands to her face and gasped. "How can that be?"

"It doesn't matter. You're going to be all right. But you can't go anywhere just yet. You are still very weak."

Callie cleared her throat. "Could I try, and sit up?"

Agnes put her hand behind Callie's back and raised her to an erect position. She immediately began to swoon and collapsed backward. The cloth that had been around her head partially fell off.

Callie pulled at it. "What is this?" Her hands went up to fix her hair, but clutched a scalp that was nearly bald. She let out a howl that echoed down the hall.. "My *hair*-it's gone!" She wailed like a child. Miss Scott embraced her. "It was the terrible fever, and then the infection. Your body has been so through so much. Sometimes this happens. But it will grow back, Callie. I promise you."

Inconsolable, her voice cracking, she looked up at the nurse. "I had *beautiful* hair. Do I look awful, Agnes?"

"Nonsense, you are a lovely woman, a fine-looking woman. This is just temporary, you must believe me."

"Casey loved my hair. He told me...told me, many times."

"And he will love you just as much again when he comes back."

Miss Scott regretted the words as soon as she uttered them.

"Come back?" she said, suddenly calm, looking up at the nurse. "I don't think so, Agnes...from death? I don't know...is anyone really ever safe in this life? I don't think so anymore." She fell back, exhausted.

"What's wrong with me?" Miss Scott said. "You've worn yourself out, poor thing. You sleep now." She adjusted the pillows, but Callie was already gone, her soft regular breaths reassuring Miss Scott.

Central Texas prairie

Callie finally left Santa Maria Hospital on a September morning. Her hair did start to grow back, but slowly, and still wasn't much longer than a boy's, so she took to wearing a scarf or a hat, sometimes both. She rented a buggy and rode to Comanche Springs.

She was still weak, but determined to see her childhood home, if not on horseback, then from a buggy. After the letter about Casey, she just wanted to come back home.

The open country spread out in all directions. She was heading into the very heart of Texas and the horizons were a hundred miles distant. It wasn't long before the road intersected Indian Creek, so she followed it on little used dirt track that ran along the banks through open country. As she neared Comanche Springs a melancholy nostalgia enveloped her. Orchards and fields of cotton and alfalfa began to appear, but mostly it was open range-land.

There was the curve of the creek, where the water slowed to form a small pool, her swimming hole.

It was little changed. She climbed down from the buggy, slid down the bank shakily, and stood where she once played, with a few toys, a wooden doll and her own fantasies. Across the way she looked where the old Indian had surprised her. Had it happened twenty years earlier she might have been kidnapped and led a very different life. This was Comanche country, after all.

She pulled the small blue horse out of her pocket and walked over to about where she remembered it had landed, rewinding her past.

"He already knew who I was. He had saved my life and returned to check on me, to see his little patient." She gazed at the horse and fondled it in her hand, still smooth and glossy, still ready to take off and gallop.

The act of reaching across time made her a little giddy. It was easy-she was eight years old again, when a summer day might go on endlessly. Her long black curls blew in the wind.

I was different, with my black curls in a fair-haired clan. Granny teased me. "You're a changeling child."

She heard her mother call her in for lunch. "Callie, you come in now." She followed the sound, walking up a path her small feet had made, now barely visible

The little L-shaped log house sat all by itself behind the big oak tree, a quarter of a mile from the carriage road, forlorn and falling apart. Three rooms and a sleeping porch. The front door opened into the living room. There was only a small fireplace and Callie remembered how the chill of the north wind permeated the house through the numerous cracks and rattling windows.

She always went in through the kitchen door, and it seemed her mother was usually baking something, especially bread. She could yet smell the wonderful yeasty fragrance as she stood there in the high weeds and dry wind.

The row of china berry trees remained, stunted from drought. The garden stretched right below the kitchen window. Callie's eyes moistened, the image of the garden reappeared just as it was, the lettuce and beans were coming along well, a couple of bright red tomatoes hung inside a chicken wire cage, and over there, by the house, her mother's precious roses- pinks, reds, yellows, struggling in the desiccating wind. She could smell their sweet wine-like fragrance.

And there was her mother, Abigail, on the porch, still wearing her cooking-stained apron, wiping her brow and smiling at Callie, a smile tempered by the weariness of too much hard work. She barely remembered her mother, except for the feel of her arms around her and her sweet singing voice.

"How are you, mother? I've come to visit. A lot has happened to me, but I wanted...needed to come back..."

Callie wiped her eyes.

Her father was not there. He hardly ever was, always away on horse business, selling his small stock to army forts all over Texas. But sometimes he came back and stayed for awhile. They would ride together, check on the grazing ponies, go into town for a treat, and in the fall, go deer hunting. Sometimes he would take her on his horse buying trips.

Callie was a born rider and could handle herself so well that he considered entering her in the rodeo in Abilene. But then it would be time to leave.

After his wife died he lost his spirit and became a passive, broken man. That was when they went to live with her grandmother. Grandmother Masterson took her Christian duty seriously and was not one to shy from adversity, and Callie grew close to her. She read to the young girl, Shakespeare, Emerson, and the Bible, instead of fairy tales, and taught her to be independent and self-reliant. Callie held a vivid memory of her grandmother sitting in the Methodist church in a starched black dress singing, "Jesus is a rock in a weary land."

She walked around the house. It seemed much smaller now. "Well, let me go see how your resting place is faring,"and walked back to the creek and rode away, finding the dirt road that led to a cemetery.

As she stepped off the buggy, a dizzy spell came and went. Callie stood there, closed her eyes and took deep breaths. She walked to where a small grassy knoll looked out over the rolling landscape and fields of alfalfa. A white, rounded tombstone marked her mother's final resting place.

Abigail Masterson
1862-1898
Asleep in Jesus
blessed sleep
From which none
ever wake to weep

She stooped down to pull some weeds that partially obscured the last line. Nearby were some wild daisies, which she gathered and lay at the foot of the stone. She spread out a shawl and sat down, gathering her legs under her dress, sitting very erect, almost stoically. She cried softly, much quieter than the wind that hissed through the grass.

She wanted to get on with her life, wanted to make peace with Casey's death, and thought that by returning to her childhood she would find that sense of peace. She did for a moment, by the creek, but everything else left her troubled. She was lost in a sea of memories that she could not make sense of.

"Callie Masterson."

She jerked her head up. A lanky man of about thirty in a dusty black coat and brown pants stood ten yards away, hat in his hands.

241

"I sure didn't mean to scare you any."

She was in a perturbed state and felt uneasy by his sudden appearance. "Who are you? How can you know my name?"

"I knew Sam, your daddy. I used to help with his horses during summers, when I was out of school."

"I see. And did you just happen to ride by and see me here?"

"Not really. You see, the hospital in San Antone, when they thought you was gonna die, they got hold of Sam. He's been pretty sick, so he got hold of me. We sorta keep in touch. I telephoned that hospital and talked to a nurse by the name of Agnes Scott, and she said that you would be coming this way."

He fell silent, tugged at his hat, and seemed to be searching for words.

Callie stared at him. Her uneasiness had passed. The man had kindness in his eyes, something familiar in his voice. Perhaps she had some memory of him, after all. "You know my name, sir, but I do not know yours."

"Nathan. Nathan Dupree."

"Nathan. All right. I still don't understand why you have sought me out. It's true, I was very ill, but what is that to you? Do you have a message from my father?"

"You came back to see her?"

"That is rather personal, Nathan. I would like some time alone at my mother's grave, if you must know."

He came to where she was sitting and slowly knelt down on one knee. "Callie, if I may call you that, I am here to tell you that Abigail was not your real mother."

Callie's eyes flared. "What are you saying to me?"

Her angry eyes caused him to pause. He cleared his throat.

"Your daddy was on a business trip in San Antone, a few years before you were born. He met a woman there, Cristina Flores. She was nineteen and well known in the city for her singing and dancing at local theaters. She was also very beautiful, and he fell in love with her. He would see her whenever his business brought him down that way.

Sam dearly loved Abigail, Callie, but she was unable to have children. He got word that Cristina was with child. He made arrangements to be there for the birth. There were complications. She died, but the baby was fine. That baby was you."

Callie drew a sharp breath. Nathan pulled a flask out of his coat pocket and offered it to her. She shook her head.

"He brought you back home. They raised you as their own child."

Callie tried to collect herself. "But wait. My real mother. Who was she? Where did she come from? Mexico?"

"She was half Mexican."

Callie waited. "And the other half?"

Nathan wiped his mouth. "Comanche."

She recoiled from the force of the word. Every atom in her body focused on that word-"Comanche." Her heart raced and she felt light-headed.

Rising up, she began to walk in circles, crazy-like, muttering the word over and over. "Comanche."

Nathan stood there, anxious and uncertain. "I know folks in these parts are touchy about that sort of thing... people here lost dear ones in those terrible years, some of 'em still carry a hatred of anything Indian. Your daddy didn't know how you would take it."

She turned around. "You are telling me that I am Comanche?"

He could see that she wasn't angry, but he wasn't sure what that look in her eyes meant. "A good part of you is."

Callie put her hands over her face trying to grapple with the revelation, started to walk around the cemetery again, couldn't stop moving, shaking her head, touching her face.

Nathan followed a little ways behind her. "I could see it, soon as I saw you. The eyes, the hair. Well, not the curls, but the blackness, it's that pure black only they have. I can see her, I can see her in you. There's no denying that you are her daughter." He stopped and thought for a moment. "You should be happy that she is your mother. I would be. She was a very good person." He himself was overcome with emotion.

Callie stopped and looked back at her home. Everything had changed. Now certain things fell into place-uneasy looks from some of her friends, some of her relatives, the Indian kids treating her like one of their own. A changeling.

"And what about you, Nathan? Are we related?"

243

He smiled. "No ma'am. My mother was a good friend to Cristina. We are part Indian ourselves. I feel like we are related in a kind of way."

Callie smiled. "That is a sweet thing to say. What kind of Indian blood are you? Not Comanche?"

"Cherokee, as my mother tells it. Also French, Mexican, and white. Texas was a mess after it became a republic. There were all sorts coming here, by the thousands, because of the available land."

"And my father hired you?"

"Mostly to go with him on trips, help with the horses. I saw you a few times-you were a wild little kid-but I didn't stick around too long."

"How is he?"

"He's doin' all right. He had a touch of that flu that you got. Got arthritis pretty bad, but there's a maid who looks after him. He likes it in the city. Goes to the picture shows. I guess you two don't keep in touch much."

"No."

"He asked me to tell you that he'd be happy to see you anytime you wanted to stop by. Oh, one more thing." He drew an envelope out of his coat pocket. Your daddy sent this. It's a picture of her-Cristina, your mother. Well, I'll be goin' now. It was a pleasure meeting you, ma'am."

He put on his hat, walked a little ways and turned around. "It shouda been him that told you all this, but I guess it's too late for that now." He walked out of the cemetery and rode off.

Callie tore the envelope open and pulled out the photo. She held the sepia tone picture in the harsh light. Her mother looked directly at the camera, relaxed and smiling, sitting down at what seemed to be a picnic. There were other people in the background, but they were out of focus.

Her hair was long and a glossy black. She didn't look much older than Callie. *Your smile is so genuine. It must have been a good day to be alive.*

She brushed her finger across her mother's face. Dark eyes, but a little narrower than Callie's. *My father and you...how is it possible?*

Shaking her head, she put the picture back in the envelope and

244

walked back to Abigail's grave. She knelt down and touched the stone. "You didn't have to take me, but you did. I thank for that. You will always be a mother to me, Abigail."

The horse stomped his hooves in the dirt, as Callie eased herself up on the buggy and rode away.

Chapter 29

Callie took one more train ride to see the woman she considered to be her best friend. It was a ten-hour trip to New Mexico, and when the train left Callie on the platform she looked around once again at the familiar landscape.

Lucille had no telephone, but Callie had sent her a telegram, informing her of her plan to visit, and Casey's death. She gazed toward Mexico for a moment, then arranged for a boy to deliver her valise to Lucille's house.

She fooled with the scarf and hat upon her head in the reflection of the glass station window, and then slowly walked the half mile to Lucille's house.

Lucille ran over and embraced Callie before she had reached the kitchen door. "Oh, you are early! I would have met you at the station."

"It's all right, Lucille."

"Well, come on in, then."

Lucille beheld a different Callie. She moved slowly, as if exhausted. She had lost her golden skin color and become very pale, and was about as thin as Randy.

She took Callie's valise. "It is always wonderful to see you. Randy has been telling his school mates that you're a real movie star."

Callie smiled and sat down at the table. Lucille set about making some coffee.

"You look tired, Callie."

"I had a long battle with a demon, Lucille, but I won. With a lot of help from some good people. It's a wonder I don't scare folks the way I look. I think I scared you a little," she chuckled.

"You've been ill then, not with-"

"Influenza, yes."

"Dear God."

"I may as well get this over with," she said, removing the scarf and hat.

"Oh *darlin'*, your lovely hair," Lucille cried, as she gently ran her hand over Callie's head.

"It's growing back, but not real fast. You know, it does make life easier. I really fussed over that hair. I've got all sorts of extra time now," she said, trying to make light of it.

Callie related her long struggle at Santa Maria, and then fell silent. Lucille refilled her cup.

"I'm going to rent a room at the hotel, Lucille. I won't have to worry about cooking and I can concentrate on finishing my book, and getting stronger."

"It won't bother you, staying there?"

"That hotel burned down. It's a completely new building. No use clinging to the past." She struggled with her words. "After experiencing the war in France and England, what I went through here hardly counts. I was scared that night of Villa's raid, of course, but when I felt the very earth shake from those huge bombs in Europe, nothing felt safe anymore. I was terrified, Lucille. I tried not to let on, we all had a job to do, but Mr. Griffith brought us right to the brink of the front. I can tell you it gave the actors an authenticity they wouldn't have had otherwise." She paused, recalling the images in her mind. "I can't even describe the destruction, what the artillery and those bombs wrought upon that beautiful land, the cities, the countryside. It was fearful, truly fearful."

Callie obtained a room on the top floor of the new hotel, with a view looking north, framing a perfect picture of the nearby bulk of Tres Hermanas mountain. She pushed her desk so that it was right by the window, then set about refreshing her memory of her narrative and adding notes about things that had occurred to her since she left California.

She was not ready to share her experience at the cemetery with anyone. "There's only Lucille, anyway. Time enough for that."

But there was one thing she needed to do before she was satisfied-bring Bandido to New Mexico. Callie was certain that he thought she had abandoned him, and the thought of him abandoned pained her deeply. She contacted Chester and asked him to arrange for the horse to be transported to Columbus by train. Poor fella, she thought, I'm turning him into a traveling horse. She sent a check to cover the expenses.

248

Once Bandido arrived, Callie rode him every day in the mild New Mexico autumn. She began to regain her color and put on weight. The space and light slowly burned some of the pain and stiffness out of her body, and eased her sorrow a little. And, ever so slowly, her hair was growing back.

Sometimes Callie would take Bandido out for an evening ride, when the desert cooled down and there was a sky full of stars to ride under. Almost always, a meteor or two blazed across the firmament, at times erupting into a fireball that left a trail of pure white glitter hanging across the heavens. The sudden flash would excite Bandido into a hysteria, which took all of Callie's strength to control.

They were returning from one such ride when Callie decided to dismount and walk ahead of Bandido, who would linger a little ways behind to munch grass or inspect a cow skull. She reached the outskirts of Columbus and entered a narrow dirt lane that eventually ended up near the hotel.

"Hey! Whattya doin there?" A husky figure lurched out of the darkness and blocked her path. He swayed unsteadily, drunk and surly. "C'mon, you gimme a kiss. You're all alone, ain't you?" he slurred, moving toward her, stale scents of sweat and whiskey coming off his body.

"No, I am not all alone," warned Callie, and she let out a loud whistle.

He cackled. "Nobody's gonna hear that, sister." He was about to grab her, but she stepped aside and pushed him behind her, just as Bandido came charging down the road, snorting and shaking his head threateningly.

"Ohhh…" he moaned, temporarily paralyzed.

Callie raised her arms above her head and Bandido stopped and reared up, legs flailing the air.

The terrified drunk spun around and ran straight into a brick wall, bounced off and hit the ground. Callie peered down at him. He was out cold.

Bandido came forward, still excited. "Bastante, Bandido" she said, taking the reins. He calmed down.

"Que lastima. You wanted to play some more, didn't you?"

She gave him a light slap and darted back and forth like he was a big dog, but he was a thousand-pound horse who assumed knocking her over was part of the game.

She rolled in the dust, but was up in a flash.

"I'll get you!" and swatted him on the rear, which sent him running, Callie just able to leap up on the saddle as he tore down the road, setting off a chorus of barking dogs along the narrow street.

Randy would often accompany her on a Saturday or Sunday. They would ride up into the Tres Hermanas mountains in the morning, explore small canyons, surprising the grazing mule deer. Other days they would stay on the flat lands and watch herds of pronghorn grazing the desert forbs. Their white rumps were visible from a great distance, especially against the dark blue mountains.

"They say only a cheetah is faster than them antelope," commented Randy.

"I wonder why," Callie wondered. "What predator would pose a threat to them?"

"Well, I know lions can get 'em, if they get close enough and have some cover to hide behind. But it's pretty rare, I think. We went on a field trip to a museum in El Paso once, and the man there claimed that they was designed to outrun animals that aren't around anymore. We used to have our own cheetahs, right here in New Mexico. Now that sure is somethin'."

"Well now, that makes sense. You seem to have a real interest in animals. You think you might like to study it in college?"

Randy snorted. "Shucks, I don't see me going much further than high school, Callie. Oh, it's interesting all right, that scientific stuff, but I'd like to try something' more exciting, that don't take no schooling. I sure would like to learn how to fly an aeroplane. I watched them boys when they were here for the Villa expedition and I was picturing myself up in of those Jennies."

Callie looked away and clinched the reins. *Randy's forgotten about Casey. Why shouldn't he? I can't have people tiptoeing around my feelings, scared to say this or that. He is forever a part of me, but he's dead and gone and I must accept that.* She patted Bandido and gazed at the distant antelope. "You're awfully young, Randy. See what comes along, talk to people before you make your mind. There will be all sorts of wonderful things for you to do in the coming years."

"I guess. You've done an awful lot Callie, for a woman I mean."

"I suppose I have. And, why not? It's the Twentieth Century for God's sake, Randy! Doesn't that just have the most wonderful sound-the Twentieth Century! It sounds so... revolutionary!" she chuckled.

We can fly, actually loose ourselves from the earth-who could have imagined such a thing? And moving pictures-why it's miraculous. You should see how they do it. Mr. Griffith, the man I worked for in California, is such a visionary. He creates these wonderful stories with light, that inspire people to rise up and make the world a better place. I'm beginning to see changes. It's only a matter of time before we get to vote, and it's a great injustice that it's taken this long.

"Yes ma'am, I agree. It's not right. Ma always gets upset when neighbors say Mexicans and Indians should never be citizens."

"I believe most white people feel threatened by those who choose to live a different way. I remember seeing small groups of Comanche travel through our county in Texas when I was little. They'd camp out in their teepees and we could hear them singing during the night. They were able to live right off the land. I thought that was the most wonderful thing-to be that independent, pick up and go whenever you wanted. And the way they dressed was so colorful. We white folks looked drab beside them. I admire those people." Callie had temporarily forgotten that she was now one of "those people."

"Ain't nobody can ride better than a Comanch. Full speed and drawing a bead on a buffalo at the same time."

"That's why they were so feared, by Indians and Whites alike, not to mention the Mexicans. My old home was in their southern territory and we heard all sorts of stories about them. One of our neighbors actually rode with Colonel Mackenzie in his pursuit of the Comanche."

"They do any raiding around your place? They were terrible raiders."

"They were all on the reservation in Oklahoma by time I was born. The hunters slaughtered their buffalo, so they had nothing left. But once my daddy took me with him on a horse buying trip up there, to Fort Sill, and I got to see Quanah Parker, the most famous chief of all,

251

the very last one to surrender. As young as I was, I'll never forget that man's face." She closed her eyes, conjuring up the image. "Long black hair, parted in the middle, with braids and feathers, high cheekbones. Fierce eyes, that could see right through you. Very stern, somewhat sad, but the noblest face I have ever seen."

"Wait-wasn't he the half-white Comanche chief?"

"His mother was white. Captured by a raiding party at Fort Parker. Cynthia Ann Parker. All of us school kids knew the story. It was very sad. They eventually rescued her, but not until twenty-five years later. She was a true Comanche by then, but they wouldn't let her go back to her people. She died of a broken heart."

They said nothing for a while. The wind moaned across the grass in undulating waves

"Okay, young fella, let's see if you can ride like a Comanche." She gave Bandido a little kick, let out a yelp and bolted away. Randy gave chase and soon caught up, flashing Callie a big smile.

They might as well have been the same age, for Callie smiled back, laughing like the twelve year old girl she still was whenever she rode that horse.

They gradually slowed down to a trot, and then stopped. "What's all that noise," asked Callie. They were still some miles away from town but could hear yelling, and what sounded like banging pots.

"Hey, now they're firing guns," said Randy. All at once the church bell sent long wavering peals into the desert air.

Callie looked at Randy-"Oh, you don't suppose-"

Randy frowned, then his eyes got big. "You mean?"

"The *war,* Randy...it must be over."

They both hightailed it into town and nearly plowed into crowds of town folk pouring into the street, waving flags and shooting guns in the air. Bandido reared up in fright.

"Easy boy." Callie quickly dismounted and led the horse around to the back of the hotel with Randy and then ran into the lobby.

"Is it really true?" she asked, running up to the desk clerk.

"Yes ma'am, it is. According to the wire, they signed the armistice on the eleventh hour of the eleventh day of the eleventh month. Isn't that something?"

"Yes, yes. It's wonderful." She hugged Randy. Tears rolled down her face. They walked to the window and watched the pandemonium in the dusty street. She could not stop crying.

Callie typed out page 295 of her story. Nearly finished, but the conclusion eluded her. She would let it rest for awhile.

There was a tap on the door. "Telephone call, ma'am."

"For me?"

"Yes, ma'am."

"I'll be right down."

Phone calls were strange intrusions she had never gotten used to. She embraced the isolation of Columbus, a place where it would be difficult to find her while she worked on both her imaginary and real life. Only a handful of people knew her whereabouts.

She hurried down the stairs and the desk clerk pointed to the phone booth in the corner. She went in and pulled the door closed.

"Hello?"

"Callie, this is Agnes Scott. How are you getting along?"

"Agnes, what a surprise. You got my letter?"

"Yes, and I am glad to hear you are nearly your old self again and back with friends."

"I've gained most of my weight back, I'm not nearly so pale, but my hair, well, it's taking its time."

"That's normal. It will grow back. Someone called about you, a friend of your father's. Did he get in touch with you?"

"Yes, thank you, Agnes."

Well, I'm going to visit my family in Arizona and thought I might see you while the train stops in Columbus. It will be this Friday."

"This Friday? Why, that's Christmas Eve."

"Yes it is."

"Well of course, I would love to see you, Agnes."

"I want to see how my patient is getting along. We'll only have about ten minutes, so be there on time. The train arrives at 4:45p.m."

"The station is only a short walk from the hotel. I'll be there."

"Wonderful. See you on Friday, then."

Callie hung up the phone. What a surprise, she thought. She had pictured Agnes as all alone in the world, a middle-aged woman

253

comfortable and resigned to her life as a nurse in a small rural hospital. "It will be so nice to see her-she practically brought me back from the dead."

She rode Bandido up into the mountains that evening. As they gazed across the silent desert a familiar sound made her heart jump. A lone biplane appeared, a tiny, toy-like thing in the blue firmament. She put her hands over her ears until the noise went away.

Callie walked toward the train station under strings of colored lights that sagged like clotheslines across the main street of Columbus. She was not feeling too Christmasy, but was determined to put on a good face for Agnes. The El Paso train would be full of Christmas-shopping townspeople, coming and going, along with visiting relatives come to share the holiday with loved ones.

She walked out on the platform and breathed in the pleasant smell of tortillas that floated over from Palomas. She heard the corralled horses at Camp Furlong, restless, whinnying as evening approached.

The sun had not been down very long, but whatever heat the ground had absorbed, rapidly radiated up into the clear atmosphere.

She wore a short blue jacket and a black Spanish style hat, with a neck strap. A chilly wind blew across the tracks causing her to pull the brim down tighter and button up the jacket.

The little station invariably evoked emotions from all the arrivals and departures she had experienced here, like some crucial crossroad in her young life. She smiled at an elderly Mexican man in a sombrero and poncho, sitting on the ground against a wall, waiting for the "show" to begin.

The yellow light of the locomotive was visible some distance away, finally easing up to the platform, hissing and moaning like a temperamental old lion.

"Now how do I know which coach Agnes is in?" She stood in the midst of the temporary clamor of passengers disembarking, looking here and there, until everyone had gotten off, but no Agnes. She stopped a conductor. "I'm looking for an Agnes Scott-is she on this train?"

He looked at a list and shook his head. "No one by that name, ma'am," and walked away.

She stared at the empty coach.

What was happening? She was tired, tired of waiting, tired of sadness.

A hand on her shoulder.

"No, no," she moaned. "Who's tricking me?"

"Shall we stick by each other as long as we live?"

Callie spun around.

He stood there, faded uniform, leaning on a cane, black patch over one eye. His exquisite smile.

"Callie, my dear... sweet... Callie."

She gently embraced him, nestled her head under his chin. They held on to each other for a long time.

The train lumbered out of the station, leaving them on the deserted platform as the first stars came out of hiding.

"Casey?"

"Yes?"

"How did we get this second chance?"

"I don't know," he said, shaking his head, "I don't know."

The old Mexican smiled broadly and nodded his head in approval. A group of Mexican children carrying candles through the street sang *Noche de Paz.*

They walked down the festive Main Street of Columbus, towards Lucille's house, holding on fast to each other.

Epilogue

July 19, 1948

It is a sad day. General Pershing lies in state in the rotunda of the U.S. Capitol. They say three hundred thousand people witnessed the funeral cortege, led by President Truman himself. I was one. It was indeed a typical July day here in Washington. Hot and humid, with nary a breeze to relieve the heat.

A team of handsome white horses pulled the caisson which held the coffin, the rider-less horse being led close behind, a pair of empty boots facing backwards in the stirrups. That pretty black horse was perhaps the most melancholy sight of the entire day, and I shed some tears upon this page just recalling it.

I arrived there only three days ago, after a hurried arrangement for a train from San Antonio, which I nearly missed, due to a torrential downpour. The monsoon season has already begun in Texas.

I was able to pay the general a visit in his room at Bethesda Naval Hospital. There were reporters milling about. I talked to a few-one of them had almost taken a job with the Chronicle down in Houston, but had decided against it when he was told about the torrid summers. I laughed, and teased him that I, a "delicate" woman, had spent three years there, long before air-conditioning was invented. I think I was stalling, dreading going into the room and seeing my old friend so gravely ill.

But I went in, and his face brightened, just as it always did when we saw each other. He was my second father, and I so cherish our time together.

I tried not to cry, but it was no use. A stroke had left one side of his face paralyzed and I could tell he was suffering. "Callie," he whispered, reaching out with his hand. I sat right beside the bed, holding his hand. He couldn't say much, so I did the talking. Recounted the old days down in Mexico, teased him about how handsome and proper he looked that day in Fort Bliss where we first met. He liked that. He sort of smiled. He mentioned Bandido. I told him that my sweet horse had lived another seventeen years after the Expedition. Then he squeezed my hand and said, "Captain Wilde?"

I related that Casey was lost in a flight over the Peruvian Andes a

256

few years ago, doing what he loved, flying and exploring, and that he may yet be out there somewhere. I haven't given up. After all, he surprised me before. The General nodded sadly at this news.

He was awfully thin and frail. Well, my gosh, the man was eighty-seven. He had fought battles with the Apache, the Sioux, the Spanish-American War, Villa, World War 1. I guess he had a right to be worn out. He was just a man, after all, but a just man. I will say that to anyone who dares question his integrity. It was he who was happy to command the Buffalo Soldiers at a time when Negroes were still treated terribly. "They're fine soldiers," he once told me. I found out he learned some Apache while on that campaign in Arizona, was fascinated with their customs and ceremonies and greatly admired the Indian people.

It was not until much later, after the Mexican Expedition, when I learned of his personal tragedy. While at Fort Bliss, his wife and three daughters all perished in a fire at their home in the Presidio in San Francisco, just before they were to join him in Texas. He returned to California to bury them, and then resumed his post in Texas. I can only imagine how devastated he must have been.

This happened about a year before I met him.

I told him I was staying at a hotel not far away and would come back and see him again, maybe see if I could find some biscochitos, like the ones we had in camp. That made him smile for sure.

I gave him a hug and a kiss, and left.

He passed away in his sleep the following day.

His last request was that his grave be marked with the same white government regulation tombstone that marked his men.

Bien viaje, amigo.

Callie put the journal down on her lap. The powerful diesel train had left the lush eastern forests far behind and was coming into the dry open country of Texas. As the hill country came into view, Callie leaned against the window, squinted her eyes and thought she saw a young woman on horseback, braided hair flying in the wind, wearing a buckskin skirt, her big smile catching the sunlight, urging on her handsome pony, decorated with ribbons and bangles in his mane and tail, flying across the prairie, outrunning the mustangs, the antelope, even the roaring train. For as everyone knows, there is nothing in this wide world faster than a Comanche racing across the land on her favorite pony.

Made in the USA
Las Vegas, NV
29 November 2022

60599084R00152